SHAKESPEARE'S SECRETS

A Caulfield, Sheridan Mystery

D1636410

BONNIE HOOVER BRAENDLIN

The Ardent Writer Press
Brownsboro, Alabama

*Visit Bonnie Hoover Braendlin's Author Page
at
www.ArdentWriterPress.com*

The Ardent Writer Press
Brownsboro, Alabama

For general information about publishing with The
Ardent Writer Press contact *steve@ardentwriterpress.com*
or forward mail to:
The Ardent Writer Press, Box 25, Brownsboro, Alabama
35741.

Cover art and composition the work of The Ardent Writer Press using Photoshop techniques. Central image of fireplace poker and Shakespeare books/plays by Wolfgang E. Adolph. Composition and cover are covered by the same grant for noncommercial use noted above.

Library of Congress Cataloging-in-Publication Data

Shakespeare's Secrets: A Caulfield, Sheridan Mystery, by Bonnie Hoover Braendlin

p. cm. - (Ardent Writer Press-2020) ISBN 978-1-64066-098-4 (pbk.); 978-1-64066-099-1 (eBook mobi)

Library of Congress Control Number 2020940351

Library of Congress Subject Headings
- Mystery & Detective - Women Sleuths.
- Mystery.
- Mystery and detective stories.

BISAC Subject Headings

- FIC022040   FICTION / Mystery & Detective / Women Sleuths
- FIC022100   FICTION / Mystery & Detective / Amateur Sleuth
- FIC022000   FICTION / Mystery & Detective / General

First Edition (Copyright Bonnie Hoover Braendlin © 2019)

Acknowledgments

Many thanks to Wolfgang Adolph for his excellent photography and his helpful computer assistance.

As always, heartfelt thanks and gratitude to Jeanne Ruppert for her expert reading and judicious editing and for her continued personal support and friendship.

Thanks also to Steve Gierhart and Doyle Duke at The Ardent Writer Press for their sound and helpful advice and their dedication to the book from cover to cover.

I, of course, accept responsibility for any errors in the text.

Dedication

... for Nikki and Andrea and Hans, as always
And in memory of JoAnne Butler, who loved mysteries

1

"...O wondrous thing!
How easily murder is discovered!"
Titus Andronicus

BRIGHT JAGGED flares of lightning, accompanied by
thunderous roars, hushed the chattering crowd and drew
all eyes to the stage as the last stragglers found their seats
and the drama began. Outside the theater a late summer
storm, a "gully washer" or "toad strangler" in the North
Florida lingo, echoed the theatrical gale, but subsided as
The Tempest progressed through its five acts, culminating
in Prospero's epilogue speech.

Rain was still falling as professors Ariadne Caulfield
and Judith Sheridan left the theater and dashed to Ariadne's
silver Beetle. On their way to a party at a friend's house,
Ariadne carefully steered through Tallahassee's flooded
intersections.

At the Raines' house they were welcomed by Robert, an
old friend of Ariadne's husband, Ándre, who had drowned
some years earlier in a boating accident in the Adriatic Sea,
"It's wonderful to see you again," he said as he enveloped
her in a warm hug. "And you too, Judith," he continued,
hugging her also.

Robert led them inside, where they found several
other friends, who asked them about their experiences in
Venice, Italy, over the summer, when Ariadne had taught
at the American International College there, and Judith
had worked for a women's shelter. "What we really want to
know is how you came to be in that gondola with that guy
who was shot." Brandon Fleming, who, like Ariadne, was

a full professor in the history department at Rutherford College in Coowahchobee, seldom minced words.

"You've asked her that before, Brandon, so you know she doesn't like to revisit that scene," Judith interjected, pushing her glasses up on her nose as she glared at him.

Pat Raines, always a solicitous hostess, came to the rescue. "So how was the play tonight? Tallahassee's Little Theatre usually does fine Shakespearean productions."

Ariadne smiled. "It was excellent. I especially liked Prospero's performance. The actor was a very convincing magus." Brandon, uninterested in theater, gave the women a slight bow and went off to hunt up another margarita.

"When I first read the play in high school," Judith said, "I was a typical teenager, more interested in the love story than anything else. I wanted to be just like Miranda, who found her true love in Ferdinand. Later, in college, having realized I preferred women to men as love interests, I was still infuriated by Prospero's domination of his daughter."

Ariadne nodded. "I suppose all parents have to contend with the urge to control, but I think we gave David plenty of freedom to make his own choices."

"It's such fun to recognize him on TV." Pat smiled. "Robert and I saw him in another commercial last night."

As Ariadne and Pat discussed her son David's life in Los Angeles, Sally Stephens, who taught in the Rutherford English department with Judith, brought over a small plate of hors d'oeuvres. "Try the spiced mushrooms; they'll knock your socks off." As Judith obliged, Sally asked where Judith's new partner, Suzanne Hanks, was. Suzanne had been warmly welcomed when she had recently joined their social sciences department.

"She stayed home to catch up on her reading. She's teaching the beginning sociology course and a poli sci seminar that was already scheduled before she arrived here."

"And how is that new women's literature course you two are team-teaching this fall?"

"Just great!" Judith replied as Ariadne nodded agreement. "We chose novels from the early twentieth century and are now reading *The Awakening*. We'll follow it with *The Yellow Wallpaper*, *My Ántonia*, and *The Age of Innocence*."

Ariadne and Judith continued to discuss classes with Sally and then circled the room, chatting about the play, which a couple of others had seen, and about the fall semester courses at their colleges, including Southwestern Georgia State where André had taught. After an hour or so, already well past midnight, they excused themselves to make the hour-long drive back to Coowahchobee. Outside, they discovered that the rain had slackened to a drizzle and the thunder was only a faint rumble on the far horizon.

An hour later the women reached Coowahchobee and turned into Ariadne's driveway on Tupelo Court, where Judith's white Escort was parked beside the two-story white colonial house. The streetlight barely illuminated the cul-de-sac and heavy clouds eclipsed the moon.

Peering out the windshield at her house and reaching for the car door handle, Ariadne said, "Something's wrong. The porch light is out …and the side door's wide open. I have to see if Cassandra's all right."

As she scrambled out of the car and ran toward the house, Judith, fumbling for the cell phone in her shoulder bag, called out, "Ariadne! Don't go in there—" In her haste she dropped the phone on the car floor, struggled to retrieve it, and then punched in 911.

Ariadne dashed up several steps to the wide veranda, ducking a shower of raindrops from the drenched overhanging branches of a live oak tree. Barely noticing the broken window on the open side door, she stepped inside, flinching as her sandals crunched on shards of broken glass. Hearing nothing else but the whoosh of the air conditioner going full blast, she continued down the hall. "Cassandra, where are you?" Her voice quavered but steadied as she heard faint mournful wails. Following the sound, she entered her study and flicked on the overhead light.

"What—" The question stuck in her throat as she surveyed the room. Most of the books from the floor-to-ceiling bookshelves lining the room lay scattered like fallen dominoes on the hardwood floor, many spread-eagled with crumpled pages, as if a child had played too roughly with them. "Cassie?" The words were hardly out of her mouth before thirteen pounds of fluffy black Persian knocked her back against the wall as Cassandra leaped down from her perch on the bookshelves. Ariadne staggered as she caught the cat in her arms.

"Oh …my …god!" Ariadne shivered as she looked across the room toward her large oak desk, its drawers open, their contents spilling out onto the floor. A man's body lay sprawled across a small oriental rug near the desk. Clutching Cassandra and stepping over and around the books, Ariadne felt compelled to inch across the room for a closer look. Dark blood pooled around the man's curly blond hair and his half-closed eyes peered blankly toward the ceiling. A wave of nausea swept over her as her mind flashed back to Venice, the gondola swaying as the shot rang out and then sticky blood staining her hands and her green cocktail dress.

"Holy shit—Randall Medina." Judith's voice behind her was barely a whisper. She glanced around the room. "What on earth happened here?" Suddenly aware of Ariadne's distress and the possibility of potential danger, she drew her friend and Cassandra into her arms. "Let's get out of here. Now."

Opening her eyes and still clutching Cassandra, who was hiding her head under her mistress's arm, Ariadne whispered back, "Call 911."

"Done. Come on. Let's go."

In tandem the two women backed away from the body, turned and left the study through the side hallway, where Ariadne retrieved Cassandra's travel cage from a closet and stuffed the plump cat into it. The women crossed the veranda just as an official green and white car, lights flashing, squealed to a stop in the cul-de-sac. When a sheriff's deputy jumped out and waved them toward him, they splashed through water puddles toward the street.

The deputy spoke quickly. "Is that your house, ladies?"

"It's mine," Ariadne told him, trying to steady her voice. "And there's a dead man in my study." She felt slightly ridiculous saying words that seemed to belong to a mystery novel or TV crime show rather than the reality of life in sleepy Coowahchobee.

"Stay here," the deputy commanded as he approached the house, his gun drawn. Ariadne and Judith stood close together intently watching his retreating figure while absently batting at the humming mosquitoes and silent moths that swarmed under the street light in the warm night air. High up in the live oaks cicadas released a chorus of insect arias and then fell silent.

"I almost panicked in there," Ariadne confessed. "It felt like I was back in the gondola, trying to stop the blood."

Judith gave her a hug. "That murder will haunt you for quite a while and so will this one!" With shaking hands she fished in her bag for her cigarettes and lit one, demonstrating her own distress.

Red and blue flashing lights announced the arrival of a green and white car marked "County Sheriff" and two law enforcement officers came toward them. Sheriff Beaufort Hammell walked straight and tall in his dark green uniform. At sixty-two he was still physically fit and fully engaged in his work, though retirement sometimes tempted him, especially during fishing season. Police Sergeant Ellen Nolle, a short African-American woman just turned forty, dressed in regulation black with several pounds of equipment—a gun, flashlight, nightstick, and radio—hanging on her belt, tried to keep up with his longer stride. The officers knew both women by sight and they were familiar with accounts, carried in the local newspaper, of how the husband of Ariadne Caulfield, history professor at Rutherford College, had some years earlier drowned in a boating accident in Venice, Italy, and how Ariadne and Judith Sheridan, her colleague in English, had helped the police capture a killer while teaching at the American International College there last summer.

"Professor Caulfield?" The sheriff nodded at Ariadne and then at Judith. "Professor Sheridan?"

"Yes, yes," they chorused.

A stickler for detail the sheriff sized up the two women as his partner began her questioning. Ariadne Caulfield, a tall woman, about five foot eight, in her mid-fifties, he thought, slim with good posture, although her shoulders slumped a bit now, bobbed honey-blonde hair that shone in the streetlight glow and hazel eyes that were now misty with distress. And Judith Sheridan, maybe a few years younger, at least two inches shorter and a good bit skinnier, with unruly dark brown hair curling over her shoulders, escaping the silver clips behind her ears. Her blue-green eyes peered myopically from behind rimless glasses. A former smoker himself, he understood why she would need a cigarette under these circumstances.

Sergeant Nolle pulled out her notebook to begin the questioning, but an always impetuous Judith interrupted. "I know the dead guy. He's an adjunct in our English department."

"How well did you know him?" Sheriff Hammell asked.

"Not very well, actually," Judith said. "He teaches two composition classes …I mean, he did teach them. But they only met afternoons on Tuesdays and Thursdays. And he didn't spend much time other than that in the department."

"What else do you know about him?"

Judith spoke slowly, thinking. "Randall Medina is … was a graduate student at Southwestern Georgia State. And he was one of several adjuncts the English Department hires every semester because we don't have enough professors to cover all our classes. I think his family lives in Blountstown but I'm not sure."

Sergeant Nolle continued the questioning. "Can you tell us what happened from the time you arrived?" She glanced at her notepad. "Not long ago?"

"Yes, about three o'clock," Judith said. "That's when I called for help."

Ariadne felt the calming effects of the sergeant's professional manner and tone of voice. "We'd just returned from Tallahassee. I knew something was wrong when I saw the side door open and the porch light out so I ran inside," she said, looking apologetic. "I know I shouldn't have but I had to rescue my cat. I didn't see or hear anyone, thank goodness, until I heard Cassie's meow from the study. I was taken aback when I went in and found it in shambles, the furniture out of place and books lying everywhere. But the most shocking thing was that bloody body on the floor beside my desk. At first I thought it was a manikin but then I realized it was a dead man." Her voice trembled and trailed off.

Sheriff Hammell spoke gently to her, "We understand, ma'am. You've had quite a shock. Take a deep breath. It'll calm you down."

Ariadne doubted that but she dutifully breathed in the warm, humid air and continued, "Judith came in, too, after calling 911, but we left the house as soon as we realized that someone could still be in there." She shook her head as she glanced toward her house. "Who could have done this?"

The sheriff stopped writing in his notebook and looked at her for a moment before he changed the subject. "What exactly did you do in Tallahassee earlier tonight?" he asked and waited patiently for her response.

"We attended a play, Shakespeare's *The Tempest*, in the local theater," Ariadne replied. "Then we went to a party at our friends' house."

Sergeant Nolle looked up from her notebook to ask, "What's their name and address? Phone number too, please."

Ariadne stared at her. "Why do you want to know that?" Her eyes widened. "Surely you don't think we had anything to do with this?" She looked over at Judith, who began twisting a strand of her long curly hair around her finger while frowning at the officers.

"Just a routine question, ma'am," the sergeant replied.

After Ariadne had given the information requested, along with the names of others at the party, the officers excused themselves and walked back up the driveway to speak with a deputy standing on the porch, hands on his hips, protecting the entrance.

"Like Cerberus at the gates of hell," Judith scoffed as she lit another cigarette.

Ariadne shivered despite the oppressively warm night air. "I need one of those, too," she said, reaching for the pack with a shaky hand.

"Hey, you don't smoke anymore."

Ariadne raised an eyebrow and held out two fingers, ready to receive a cigarette. Judith shrugged as she handed her one and lit it. One deep drag and Ariadne felt dizzy but calmer. She took another puff before dropping the cigarette down the storm drain. "Can you believe it? They think we might have killed that man."

"And trashed your study to make it look like a burglary? Preposterous." Judith shook her head and waved her cigarette in an arc that sent sparks flying. "Still, I suppose we're the most likely suspects. But we won't be after they check up on where we were in Tallahassee." She smoked in silence for a minute and then said, "Doesn't the sheriff look a lot like that actor who played Prospero? Tall, lean, rugged, dark graying hair."

"Sorry, I didn't really notice." Ariadne was still picturing the bloody dead man in her study.

Sergeant Nolle returned to say, "We've secured the house, ma'am, so we can begin our investigation. We can't let you return home until we're finished, which will take a day or two."

"We had nothing to do with this, Sergeant," Ariadne blurted out, her tone of voice tinged with resentment. "We barely knew Medina and had nothing against him."

The sergeant's face remained impassive. "We'll check with your Tallahassee friends as soon as we can. Just part of our routine investigation. Do you have a place to stay?"

"She's coming with me. There's an extra bedroom in our condo," Judith said.

"Good." The sergeant turned to Ariadne. "You'll be well looked after, I think. You need to rest because you've had a tremendous shock." She paused, assessing Ariadne's demeanor, which seemed to become calmer as Judith put her arm around her shoulders protectively. "We'd like you to come back here tomorrow to check the house for any missing valuables. Will late morning be all right? We'll send an officer to accompany you. And right now you'll probably need to pack an overnight bag. We'll know tomorrow how long you'll have to stay away."

After reluctantly agreeing to revisit the grisly scene the next day, Ariadne followed the sergeant into the house and down the hall past the study, where flashes of light indicated the photographing of the crime scene, then upstairs to the master bedroom, where she quickly packed a few necessities. When she returned outside, the local TV van was parked in the street and a couple of reporters started toward her. Judith intervened, flapping her arms at the reporters like a protective mother bird as she guided Ariadne to her Escort, where a forlorn Cassandra waited in her carrier on the back seat. Judith then drove off down Tupelo Court as several neighbors watched them from their porches. This crime, like the one in Venice, would be the major topic of news and gossip for a long time to come, not just in small Coowahchobee but for miles around. Ariadne dreaded the notoriety.

2

"The gentleman is not in your books."
Much Ado about Nothing

ON SUNDAY MORNING, as the sky on the east side of County Courthouse Square began to redden, Tilda Kent locked the doors of her newspaper office and headed for the adjacent parking lot, accompanied by Josh Posey, her editorial assistant. Tilda normally refused his offer to see her to her car, remaining outwardly polite but inwardly resentful at what she considered ageism. Now in her seventies (she refused to reveal the exact year), she was still mentally and physically fit, in need of no assistance. But this morning she was fearful because of the murder at Ariadne Caulfield's house and the possibility that the killer could still be in the vicinity.

Earlier that morning, at the crime scene, Sheriff Beau Hammell, always cooperative with the press, had given her as many details as he could, knowing her desire not to be scooped by larger newspapers in the nearby cities of Tallahassee and Elliottville, Georgia. She and her staff had quickly written the story and then rearranged the front page of the *Courier's* Sunday edition, bumping the lead article on alleged corruption in the county council to below the fold and inserting a two-column photo of Ariadne's house and yard. Because they couldn't question Ariadne, they fleshed out the sparse details about the break-in and the murder by adding some information about her from earlier front-page stories, when her husband had drowned in the Adriatic Sea off the Venetian Lido and more recently when she had been with a murder victim in a Grand Canal gondola.

Now Tilda sat in her '88 Honda Civic, doors locked, watching the sun rise over Elkins' Hardware and the Gallinule Drug Store, two small shops on the square still surviving stiff competition from the new large chain store just west of town. Glassy-eyed she stared at the county courthouse in the middle of the square, an imposing three-story white stone building crowned by a cupola and shaded by several ancient magnolia trees on a wide green lawn and bordered by azalea bushes that in early Spring exploded with pink, red and white blossoms. She turned her head to view rows of two-story buildings housing various shops, the community center, an art gallery, and an old movie theater that struggled to stay alive by showing second-run films at reduced ticket prices.

Trying to calm her nerves she drove off down Blue Butterwort Street, a U.S. highway dividing Coowahchobee into two main sections. The northern, hilly, predominantly white area was dominated by Rutherford College, surrounded by large brick and clapboard houses, many, like Ariadne's, built in traditional Southern styles, with columned verandas and long shuttered windows. These spacious homes stood on manicured lawns under massive live oaks festooned with clumps of gray Spanish moss. The southern part of town, filled with small, run-down clapboard and cinder block houses, sprawled on the flat plain south of the highway. Everyone still called this area Cottonville, though few could remember the old cotton mill that had burned down there in the 1920s. As is the case in most small Southern towns, integrated only since the 1960s, a large portion of the black community still resided within this segregated area. Many people had relocated after Hurricane Michael had swept through the area, slashing tall pines that fell, crushing houses. Most of the debris had been hauled away but broken trunks and stumps still dotted the yards of semi-repaired and abandoned houses alike.

IN JUDITH'S CONDO Ariadne woke with a start after several hours of restless sleep as Cassandra jumped onto the bed and began to claw the sheet. She smoothed the cat's ruffled fur. "Poor Cassie, all that excitement at home. You must be a nervous wreck." Like I am, she thought, pushing aside the fragments that remained in her head of her nightmares. She slid out of the guest bed, wrapped a green-and-purple-flowered cotton robe over her nightgown and went downstairs to the kitchen. Cassandra followed after her, sashaying down the hall and stairs as if running were unseemly for an elegantly plump Persian princess. Waving her fluffy tail overhead, she stopped short before an empty dish on the floor beside the refrigerator and reproached Ariadne with a plaintive meow.

"Always hungry, aren't you? Lucky for you Judith has stocked tuna in her pantry."

As the cat gulped down the pungent fish, Ariadne started brewing coffee and plopped a piece of whole-wheat bread into the toaster, mundane activities that temporarily deflected her thoughts from the ghastly image of the dead man lying in her ransacked study. She shuddered as she felt a hand on her shoulder. "Wha—?"

"Sorry. Didn't mean to spook you." Judith, dressed in faded denim shorts and a ragged tee shirt embossed with a faded "Sisterhood is Powerful" slogan, gave Ariadne a hug. "Thinking dark thoughts about last night?" She reached in the refrigerator and pulled out a jar of jam. "Me, too. A crime like that in Coowahchobee, where we don't even lock our doors half the time, is frigging unbelievable. What were they looking for, pulling all those books down? A wall safe? And what happened to turn thieves into murderers?" The questions tumbled out as she reached for the coffee pot.

"Ariadne, you poor thing!" Suzanne entered the kitchen, looking sleek as an otter in black satin pajamas, her tousled red hair glowing in the sunlight, her dark green eyes filled with sympathy. She hugged Ariadne as she asked, "Does anyone think a professor at a small college like Rutherford would have a fortune hidden in a wall safe?" Her only impression of such a crime came from the occasional heist movies she watched on late-night television, where thieves scaled high-rise city buildings to raid luxury apartments or adroitly contorted their lithe bodies through multiple red or blue laser beams to steal museum treasures. "I'm sorry I didn't go to the play with you last night, especially to support you afterward. But I'm glad Judith was there."

Judith returned Suzanne's warm smile and then began arranging three woven orange and yellow striped placemats and napkins on the smooth butcher-block table along with plates, whole wheat bread, jam, honey, blueberries, and granola with yogurt.

"Who knows what the community really thinks of us academics or what students believe about professors' lives?" Suzanne mused as she poured coffee into yellow mugs festooned with clusters of purple grapes hanging on green vines. "Most of them probably can't imagine us having a life outside the campus."

"I know. Students even look shocked to see me in the grocery store, as if we live off the air like the Spanish moss," Ariadne replied, sipping coffee as she watched a brilliant red cardinal picking at a fallen pine cone on the back deck railing. Cassandra emitted soft chattering sounds and pawed the blue and orange plaid window-seat cushions, her whiskers twitching as she eyed the tempting prey. "It galls me that we're considered suspects."

Judith added milk and sugar to her coffee. "I guess they could envision us bashing Randall's head in if we caught him ransacking your place. But as soon as they check with Pat and Robert in Tallahassee, we're off the hook."

Suzanne hugged Judith. "No one could think you were capable of killing anyone! Or you either, Ariadne."

"Ha!" Judith retorted. "You haven't met that formidable sheriff-sergeant crime team!" She reached out and squeezed Ariadne's hand. "Look, Ari, I know that returning to your house isn't going to be easy. Why don't we go with you?"

"No, no, I'll be all right." Ariadne tried to refocus her thoughts. "I want to help those officers, though I dread seeing that chaos in the study again."

Judith studied her for a moment. "Just remember," she said, "you're a teacher, not a detective."

After they had finished breakfast Judith and Suzanne went upstairs to dress, while Ariadne remained seated, smiling at Cassandra who became even more agitated at the sight of a female cardinal joining her mate on the deck. The bright morning sunlight streaming into the kitchen made the dead body in her study seem unreal. Her thoughts turned to the consequences for the community. A murder would be disturbing in this idyllic town tucked away in the middle of North Florida, where criminal activity consisted mainly of minor burglaries, domestic violence, and some drug buying. She couldn't remember any recent crimes of this magnitude, except the man who in a jealous rage had shot his wife in the parking lot of Roger's Roadhouse. In a press conference at that time Sheriff Hammell had reassured the public that however tragic this incident was, there was no danger to the community. But this time was different, more sinister, with a killer at large, someone who might still be around town, even someone who lived here. She shivered. I've got to calm down if I'm to be any help to the police, she thought. A glance at the wall clock told her she didn't have time to call David in Los Angeles. She'd do that first thing when she returned. As she climbed the stairs to the guest room, she steeled herself for the ordeal ahead.

📖

AN HOUR LATER a young policeman drove Ariadne to her house. The reality of her situation struck her when she saw the garish yellow and black crime-scene tape stretching from one pillar to another around her veranda. Sheriff Hammell opened the side door to let her in. "The intruders gained entry by breaking a pane of glass in this door window and then reached in and turned the lock to open the door," he said, showing her the cardboard square now mounted over the hole. Feeling like a visitor, Ariadne laid her tan straw hat and sunglasses on the hall table and followed the sheriff into the study.

Once again she was shocked by the nearly empty bookshelves lining the walls and the hundreds of books strewn over the floor. Cautiously stepping around and over them, she edged toward two beige and white striped armchairs and ottomans flanking a small white brick fireplace. The green wrought-iron coffee table still stood between them, but the matching floor lamp lay toppled across one chair, its metal shade askew. Like a robot without a battery, she thought. She peered at the green marbled mantelpiece where several family members smiled out from photographs in pewter and wooden frames, somehow untouched by the violence that had shattered the rest of the room. A set of ornate iron fireplace tools, a souvenir of a family trip to Spain years before, lay scattered across the hearthstones.

Sheriff Hammell led Ariadne to the other end of the room, where Sergeant Nolle introduced Silas Henley from the combined municipal-county Criminal Investigation Division. He explained that they needed to take her fingerprints to eliminate them from their search. This done, Ariadne resumed her survey of the room.

"What are you doing with my books?"

Realizing that Ariadne's sharp intonation expressed anxiety, not rudeness, Sergeant Nolle spoke softly to her. "We're examining them for evidence. Blood, maybe fingerprints, hair, or fibers we can use to identify the intruders. Don't worry, we won't damage them."

Ariadne tried to focus on the sergeant's words, but her attention was drawn to the dark brown bloodstain remaining on her treasured olive-green oriental rug, a present from André on a wedding anniversary years ago. All she knew about police procedures came from old *films noir* on television or her mother's frequent commentary on her favorite classic mystery novels. "Where's the white silhouette?" she asked.

The sheriff suppressed a smile. "We don't use the tape anymore. We photograph and videotape the body before removing it for autopsy."

"What do you think he was looking for?"

"We suspect that Medina and whoever killed him, probably his accomplice, were after cash since they apparently didn't steal anything they would have to fence, like your computer or the TV in your living room. We checked your jewelry case in your bedroom but need you to tell us if anything is missing. We can have you look there later."

She looked directly into his eyes, bright blue in his tanned face. "Then you no longer think Judith and I had anything to do with this?"

"The coroner says Medina was dead at least an hour by the time you phoned in. I sent a deputy over to Tallahassee this morning to talk to your friends. If you were with them at the time, you'll be cleared of any suspicion."

Ariadne turned away, her attention drawn again to the fireplace tools. "The poker is missing. Was that the murder weapon?"

The sheriff hesitated, but realizing that she'd already jumped to the apparently correct conclusion, decided to trust her. "Medina was killed by a blow to the head and the poker appears to be the weapon. We're not releasing this information so please don't repeat it to anyone."

As Ariadne continued to survey the room she fought the urge to pick up the scattered books, to reshelve the French versions of *David Copperfield* and *The Last of the Mohicans*, two of André's favorite boyhood novels (they'd named their son after Copperfield), and to smooth the bent pages in the women's history books she kept within reach on her desk. Oversized tomes of *The Complete Works of Shakespeare* lay piled atop one another under the side windows. She cherished those books with their soft maroon leather covers and thick creamy-white gilt-edged pages. Not that she had read all the plays, only the ones in the Shakespeare course she'd taken to fulfill her undergraduate literature minor at UCLA. *Hamlet*, of course, and *Macbeth* and *A Midsummer Night's Dream*; those she had liked. But not *Julius Caesar* with its boring speeches. As she knelt down and absentmindedly picked up *As You Like It,* a crisp bright yellow maple leaf slipped out and swirled onto the floor.

Sheriff Hammell crouched down next to her and squinted at it. Sergeant Nolle joined them, bending over for a closer look.

"That leaf has been in this book for years," Ariadne told them. "When my son David was young, he collected and pressed leaves and flowers for his school projects. I guess he overlooked this one." She stared at the heavy volume in her hands, then murmured, "Oh, let my books be then the eloquence—" She closed her eyes for a second, as if searching for another word.

The officers looked bemused.

"Sorry." She shook her head. "I don't know where that came from. I mean, it's from some poem but I don't remember which one. And I don't know why I thought of it just now."

"Maybe the shock of seeing your books like this," Sheriff Hammell said, making a mental note to ask more later on when she'd had time to think about it.

They all stood up and Ariadne replaced the Shakespeare volume on the pile. She looked around her. "I have the feeling something is out of place or missing, but I don't know what. And I still can't understand why they vandalized my books."

"Probably looking for a wall safe," Sergeant Nolle said.

"A graduate student like Medina might think that a professor who lives in an imposing house like this one would have one." Sheriff Hammell regretted his comment when he noticed Ariadne's frown.

"Students often have an inflated notion of professors' material wealth, Sheriff."

He quickly changed the subject. "About Medina. You said you didn't know him?"

"I've seen him around campus so I should have recognized him last night. But I couldn't look very closely at him."

After another tour around the study and other rooms, the sheriff thanked Ariadne for her help and offered to drive her back to Judith's condo, but she said she wanted to walk. She needed to get away from the bloodstains and chaos, out into the normality of her neighborhood. She collected her belongings from the side hall table and then walked across the house to the front door to avoid having to see the cardboard-covered window on the side porch again.

"It's pretty hot out there now, ma'am," Sheriff Hammell said, following her out. "You don't want to risk sunstroke on top of shock."

When he smiled at her, she suddenly became aware of how good-looking he was, his angular sun-tanned face enhanced by tiny laugh wrinkles around his blue eyes and a small cleft in his chin. She had always been susceptible to an overbite like his, subtle but sexy when his smile widened. She realized she was gripping his extended hand and for a crazy moment she half expected him to bend over and kiss hers. I must still be in shock, she thought as she pulled away, but slowly so as not to offend him.

"Are you sure you're all right, Professor? I'd be happy to drive you." The sheriff wanted to touch her hand again, to say something to make her smile. Although he had dated off and on since his divorce years ago, he hadn't been very interested in any of the women he'd met. Now his sudden forceful attraction to this woman took him by surprise.

Ariadne shook her head, as much to clear it as to indicate a negative response. "I'll be fine. I always use sunscreen." After adjusting her wide hat brim over her hazel eyes, she put on her sunglasses and stepped out onto the veranda. But when she noticed the crowd of people and the TV van at the other end of the street, held back by a patrolman, she turned back to him. "Sheriff, I think I'd like that ride after all."

They cruised past the neighbors on the sidewalk along Tupelo Court and the crowd at the intersection. The sheriff saluted Tilda Kent, notebook in hand, talking to the officer on duty at the corner. He knew she'd come by later to extract from him whatever new details he would give her. Not many in this case. Better to keep as much information as possible out of the press.

Ariadne waved briefly at those she knew and then slumped down in the seat, her hands twisted together on her lap. It could have been so much worse, she thought. What if I'd been in the house? But you weren't, she told herself. Luckily, Cassie and I are alive and unharmed.

When the sheriff glanced over at her, he recognized signs of distress he'd seen in both victims and witnesses to violence. "Are you feeling all right?" he asked.

"I …I'm fine, Sheriff." Ariadne said, struggling for control.

He didn't believe her but had to be content with her answer as they arrived at Judith's condo and she seemed anxious to get out of the car. He walked her to the door and told her to call him or Sergeant Nolle if she needed any help and not to discuss the details of the crime scene with anyone. As he spoke, Judith opened the door and rather unceremoniously pulled Ariadne inside with a curt good-bye to him.

Back in his car the sheriff sat for a few minutes, feeling foolish but realizing he didn't want to leave Ariadne just yet. Then his radio crackled out a report from the deputy in Tallahassee and he returned to the condo.

"Yes?" Judith opened the door just a crack, her voice suggesting her irritation at seeing him there again.

Ariadne joined her. "What is it, Sheriff?"

"We've checked with your friends in Tallahassee. They confirm your presence at their party until after two o'clock." He smiled. "So you are no longer suspects."

Judith nodded abruptly and went back inside, but Ariadne stepped out onto the porch and held out her hand. "Thanks for telling us this, Sheriff. It's a relief."

As he said good-bye and turned to leave, she suddenly blurted out, "Oh, learn to read— " She hesitated, trying to remember the rest.

Sheriff Hammell stared at her. ("As if I'd gone completely mad," she told Judith later.)

She held up her hands in a helpless gesture. "I'm sorry, Sheriff. You must think I'm crazy, spouting phrases like that. I still can't remember the poem they're from."

Looking at her sparkling hazel eyes, her shining honey-blonde hair and her open, honest face, he thought it didn't matter what she said or didn't say. "I'm not much of a poetry reader, ma'am, so I can't help you there. But call me if you come up with it." He waved as he left.

"What was that about?" Suzanne asked Ariadne as she reentered the condo.

"When I saw my poor books tossed around the study, I started remembering snatches of what I think is a poem. 'Oh, learn to read.' Where does that phrase come from? Or this one, 'Oh, let my books be then the eloquence.'"

"The eloquence? Sounds Renaissance," Judith fiddled with a springy lock of dark hair as she often did while thinking. "Just those few words aren't a lot to go on. Can you remember anything more?"

"Just something about an actor and the stage. Maybe it's not from a poem but from some part David had when he was in theater school. I used to help him with his lines. Or if it is a poem, maybe it's something André once read to me. You know how much he loved poetry."

"Have you called David yet?" Judith asked. "He'll be upset if he hears about the murder from someone else or on the news."

"I should have called first thing but I didn't want to wake him. I doubt that the national news or L.A. outlets will carry the story, but you never know what one might find on the Internet." Ariadne dug her cell phone out of her handbag as she headed for the back deck. "I'll be back in a minute."

Her son was shocked when she told him the news. "Mom, are you all right? It's a good thing you weren't home at the time. You might have been killed." Having heard the anxiety in her voice, he refrained from mentioning the frightening gondola episode of the previous summer.

Hearing his calming voice reminded her of how much she missed him now that he was an aspiring actor in Los Angeles and she saw him only a few times a year . "You don't need to come home, David," she assured him when he asked. "Judith and Suzanne are looking out for me." Although she would have liked to have him near her now, she did not want to take him away from his life, which for him was a constant struggle to get film or television roles.

When Ariadne walked back into the kitchen, Judith said, "Hey, let's Google the parts of the poem you remember. I do that often when I can't find a quote I need for a journal article."

"Right now we need some lunch," Suzanne said, entering the room. "I have everything ready on the patio."

"Did the sheriff tell you they're interviewing faculty and students this afternoon?" Judith asked Ariadne as the three women sat eating sandwiches and drinking lemonade while Cassandra gulped down more tuna. "His office phoned to ask if I could be at the conference room in J. D. Hall around two o'clock. Said they were calling in everyone they could find who knew Randall Medina. Our office staff is helping them locate people. I gave them some names."

Ariadne looked surprised. "He didn't say anything about that to me. But I wouldn't be included since I didn't know Medina at all."

"Just as well. You need to rest. We've hardly had any sleep and you look beat." Judith pulled out another cigarette but shoved it back into the pack when she saw Suzanne's frown. "I wonder how the police will deal with students who might have been involved with Medina, considering that one of them might have murdered him."

"It's more likely he was involved with graduate students at Southwestern or others he met somewhere else," Ariadne said, fingering her half-eaten sandwich.

"I certainly hope so," said Judith, without conviction.

3

"...distill'd
Almost to jelly with the act of fear ...."
Hamlet

BY LUNCHTIME on that Sunday small groups of people had congregated on Courthouse Square carrying copies of the *Courier*, its glaring headline, "MURDER MOST FOUL," fueling their fear. Many carried babies or clutched the hands of small children, while warning older ones to stay close to them. The mid-day merging of sun and humidity felt like a sauna.

"Hey, ya'll. Hot enough fer ya?" Some of the men tried to act as if nothing had happened, while here and there women hugged one another, seeking solace.

Several paper mill workers and their wives crowded into The Blue Cat Café, lured there today by the refuge it offered in bringing people together. Protective parents tried without much success to keep their children uninformed as they talked in hushed tones about the crime. Swiveling on padded counter stools covered with cracked and peeling red plastic, men in jeans and tee shirts feigned bravado as they offered whatever explanations they could conjure up from the meager details in the newspaper story.

"Says here the victim was an instructor at Rutherford."

"Yeah, but he was also a student at Southwestern." The loyal Rutherford supporters—always defensive of the small college and derisive of Southwestern Georgia State University, just over the border in Elliottville—frowned and shook their heads.

"Bludgeoned to death, it says. Means he was beaten."

"What was he doin' there? Stealin'?"

"Doesn't say. Do ya think Miz Caulfield surprised him and kilt him?"

"Na. She's a nice lady. Wouldn't do nothin' like that. He was probably part of a gang."

Several women pulled tables and chairs together in the center of the small café, where ceiling fans stirred the stale air that two air-conditioning units struggled to cool. Small children crawled onto their mothers' laps or scrunched together, two or three to a chair, as the women cut up and doled out grilled cheese sandwiches. Two intrepid eight-year-olds wheedled quarters for the gum machine from mothers willing to send them out of earshot. Taking deep breaths to alleviate their anxiety, the women scrutinized the newspaper photo of Ariadne's large white frame house. Square white pillars supported the veranda's gray shingled roof, above which rose the second story, lined with tall windows matching those on the first level, all complete with narrow green shutters. Above the upper story, a single round attic window, set in a triangle formed by the pointed roof, peered at them like the eye of a Cyclops.

"That is some beautiful house, all right. Not as fancy as the old mansions on Mimosa Drive but still lovely."

"Pretentious. That's what it is. One of them old homes built in the twenties and thirties by rich folk. Those professors must have bought it in the seventies when they came here and such houses were still affordable." Susan Monty, who lived in a modest brick house around the corner from Tupelo Court, considered herself an authority on the neighborhood.

"Never was a crime like that around here that I know of. Who do y'all think done it?"

"College kids, most likely. Murders and robberies goin' on all the time around them big schools in Tallahassee and Elliottville. Dens of iniquity, Preacher calls 'em. Was only a matter of time 'fore it happened here."

"Poor Professor Caulfield. She was so upset after her husband drowned and now this. Imagine havin' your house trashed like that!"

"Well, she can afford to have Zora Eppersley clean it for her."

Sharon Bly looked up from reading the newspaper account. "Lord, her carpet's sure to be ruined and maybe the hardwood floor will need refinishing, if the blood soaked through. And that'll cost a pretty penny."

"Anyone who owns a house like that can afford it."

The women stopped talking abruptly as the front door opened and Sergeant Nolle entered, looking stern and preoccupied. She nodded toward the women and children as she made her way to the counter, where the men turned to look at her, but no one spoke.

"Two coffees to go, Mavis," the sergeant said to the young woman who was wiping off the counter top with a limp rag. Mavis stood staring at the uniformed sergeant as if she'd never seen her before although she was a frequent lunch-and-coffee-break customer. "Please," Sergeant Nolle prompted. "We're in a hurry."

All eyes swiveled to the large plate glass window framing Sheriff Hammell in his white and green car and then back to the sergeant. They watched as she paid Mavis, picked up the two coffees and headed for the door, which Frank Cropp opened for her.

"Have a nice day," he blurted out before he realized that this day was not a nice one for any of them.

Sipping their coffees Sergeant Nolle and Sheriff Hammell proceeded to Rutherford College to interview the faculty and students they had managed to contact on short notice. This would be a small group because most students had gone home or to the beach for the weekend. The officers entered the campus through a gray stone archway, donated by grateful alumni, and followed a wide paved road to the administration building, Jefferson Davis Hall, a four-story brick structure with tall round tapering white pillars evenly spaced along a wide concrete veranda. Behind the hall a quad stretched over the hill, lined with red brick and white clapboard buildings, more thrown together over the years than carefully planned. The various academic departments were housed in several of these, which clustered around a general classroom building, a library, a gymnasium, and two dormitories, one for men and the other for women. In a slight valley beyond them lay the football stadium, the track, and the baseball field.

Several students were clustered around the larger-than-life bronze statue of the college's founder, Oliver B. Rutherford, shielding his eyes with one hand, as if searching for something. Perhaps a long-lost love, students said in a favorite campus guessing game, or maybe he was just trying to keep pigeon droppings off his aquiline nose. They liked to hang out there, hashing over the latest campus gossip. But today the students were somber, quiet, some clinging to each other, others sitting or standing alone, not looking at anyone else. They feared that Medina's killer might still be in the area, though they didn't want to believe it could be anyone at Rutherford. In a small college filled with familiar faces, the idea that a murderer might reside among them seemed remote but still scary. One student stood distinctly apart from the group, his hair streaked pink and purple, his eyebrows, ears, and lower lip pierced with silver rings, his black tee shirt emblazoned with an intricate, multicolored dragon entwined around the word ANARCHY. Three young women, students in Medina's first-year composition classes, sobbed openly.

All heads swiveled toward the white and green car rolling past them and stopping in front of J. D. Hall. The sheriff went inside while the sergeant approached the students. "Thanks for coming out to talk with us. Your information could be crucial to our investigation." She spoke gently, sensing their unease. "Please come inside with me." For a minute no one moved as they stared at her or at the ground. Then the freshman comp students, wiping their eyes and holding hands, joined her. The others trailed along into the building and up the stairs to a hallway on the second floor. Several faculty members were already waiting outside a small conference room next to the president's office. Julian Baldwin, an untenured assistant professor of music, and Chris Bannerman, a tenured associate professor in art history, stood together in a corner, pretending not to notice that the coeds who usually flirted with them were indifferent to anything but their own anxiety. Judith Sheridan paced up and down, impatiently twisting a strand of her unruly hair.

The sergeant announced that the faculty would be called into the room individually and questioned first, followed by the students. Sheriff Hammell let the sergeant conduct the interviews as she was more comfortable with this role than he. Seated at the end of the long conference table, he could observe the faculty and students, positioned opposite her in the middle, as she spoke to them.

When her turn came, Judith reiterated her earlier comments on the night of the murder, adding that the faculty had been friendly to Medina but his responses were always perfunctory. Her English Department colleagues added only that he seemed to be a popular teacher though he was a "tough grader." No one knew of any reason why someone would want to kill him.

Julian Baldwin leaned forward and clasped his hands together in his lap. "Randall sang in our chorus, which I direct. A responsible young man, always on time and enthusiastic in his singing, but he rarely talked with anyone and never stayed to chat with us after rehearsals. I had the impression he was a loner, uneasy in a crowd, and maybe even secretive." He paused, not wishing to malign the deceased, then added that he had occasionally spoken to Randall on campus but about nothing other than the chorus's practice schedule or music selections. When asked where he'd been the night before, Julian obligingly recalled in some detail the evening he and his wife Elizabeth had enjoyed in Tallahassee, eating at the Bahn Thai restaurant and watching an award-winning Chinese film at the All Saints' Theater. "Mary Matthews babysat for us so I can vouch for her whereabouts. I drove her back to the dorm just after midnight and then returned home." He said he had no idea who might want to kill Randall or why.

Chris Bannerman winked at him as they passed each other on the way in and out of the room. Julian, who liked Chris but didn't trust him, responded with a half-hearted smile. Inside the interrogation room Chris, in crisp tennis whites, sat back in his chair, crossing and uncrossing his tanned muscular legs and occasionally pushing a lock of sandy hair back into place over his forehead. When he grinned at Sergeant Nolle, his teeth gleamed white in his bronzed face. He talked about playing pool on one occasion with Randall, who had become unusually upset when he lost. "In fact, he stalked away without a word, slamming his pool cue into the rack as he bolted out the door. Mean temper, seems to me. But that's probably not reason enough for anyone to off him." Chris had decided not to talk about his contacts with Randall up at Southwestern, where they had both dated coeds. Worse than that was the fight he'd had with Randall's friend after some stupid argument at a party. He thought it best not to reveal anything about having met Randall socially or about his own personal life. On the way out he shook hands with the officers, still smiling broadly.

Sergeant Nolle asked the same questions of the other faculty but garnered no relevant responses. After all had been dismissed with a number to call if they thought of anything else, the sheriff stood up, stretched his long limbs, and said to the sergeant, "Now let's talk to the students."

4

"...guiltiness will speak,
Though tongues were out of use ."
Othello

ALLISON McENVOY sat on the edge of her chair, crossing her legs at the ankles while self-consciously tugging down her pink cotton mini skirt. Her blonde hair, fluffy from the humidity, blazed in the shafts of sunlight slanting through the venetian blinds. She hunched over, as if trying to appear as inconspicuous as possible. She'd never been in a situation like this before, but she knew she wasn't the only nervous one. None of her friends, waiting outside, had done this before either. She looked timidly over at Sergeant Nolle, who asked her where her home was.

"Atlanta, ma'am. Well, actually a suburb. Marietta."

"Have you lived there long?"

"All my life ma'am. Except the last three years when I've been at Rutherford."

"How well did you know Randall Medina?"

"I saw him sometimes when a group of us went somewhere and he came along with Jason—Jason Overstreet." Allison blushed and looked down at the shoulder strap of a small pink purse she was twisting in her hands.

"Is Jason a special friend of yours?"

"Yes, ma'am." She felt awkward talking about Jason with these officers. What difference did it make who her boyfriend was?

"What was Medina like? How did he act when he was with you?"

"He didn't pay any attention to us girls. Last semester Cindy Donaldson had a crush on him and kept trying to get him to notice her, but he just smiled and one time even patted her on the head like she was some sort of puppy dog!" Seeing the small involuntary smiles on her interrogators' faces, Allison blushed again and freed her fingers from the tangled purse strap. Gosh, I sound stupid, she thought. Why did I have to say that about Cindy? "Once when Mr. Medina and Jason were playing pool in the student lounge, I joined them. They let me have a turn now and then, but I wasn't very good at it and Mr. Medina got impatient. Jason told me that he had a temper and that I should be careful not to make him mad, so I didn't hang around too long."

"Where were you last night and early this morning?"

Allison was prepared for this question because this was a routine procedure in police interrogations she'd seen in the movies and on TV. "I was going to go swimming with my friends but I didn't feel well, so I stayed in the dorm and went to bed early."

"We may want to speak to you again," the sergeant said, handing her a card. "Here's our number if you think of anything else to tell us."

Out in the hall Allison brushed past Jason, who was being summoned into the room, and Mary Matthews, who tried to get her attention, and headed outside, back to the statue, where they had all agreed to meet later. She sat at its base, her head in her hands, worrying about her answers. Why didn't I tell them that I went out for a walk when I couldn't sleep? What if they find that out later and arrest me for lying? She slumped down in the shadow of Oliver B. Rutherford, wiping away sweat and tears from her face.

Inside the room, Jason took the assigned seat opposite the sergeant and flexed his muscles as he gripped the chair arms, first spreading apart his long legs, clad in baggy cotton shorts and then bringing them together as he straightened up and sat erect.

Sergeant Nolle tapped her finger on her notebook. "Jason, did you know Randall Medina in Blountstown before you came to Rutherford?"

"Yes, ma'am. We both lived there but he was older than me. He came to town when he was in high school, I think. At least I never saw him before that. He was on the varsity basketball team, and sometimes us middle-school guys used to hang around when they practiced, hoping they'd let us shoot baskets with them afterwards. Sometimes they did. Mr. Medina sorta liked to give us pointers, like a coach and all."

"Did you know any of his friends?"

"No, ma'am, not really. I mean, they were older guys who didn't want to have much to do with us."

"Did you ever see him around town, other than on the basketball court?"

Jason squirmed a bit in his chair. "Sometimes we saw him hanging around with others outside the high school or at the movies. Not much to do in our town, so on weekend nights they'd usually drive off in their cars, probably going over to Tallahassee or up to Elliottville. Me and my friends were too young to drive so we had to stay put."

"Did you see him often after you came to college here?" the sergeant asked.

"I saw him at chorus rehearsals but he didn't pay much attention to any of us. When we hung around afterward to talk and drink sodas, he didn't stay. I guess he had to get back to Southwestern or grade papers or something." Jason thought for a moment. "And I saw him sometimes in the Merriman Building, where I took a class last semester. Great Literary Masterpieces. It's a required course. Otherwise, you know, I probably wouldn't have taken it. I'm not a great reader. Math is my strong point."

"I liked math, too." Sergeant Nolle said, trying to relieve his nervousness. "Where else did you see Medina?"

"He sometimes played touch football with us and a couple of times we shot pool together and with others."

"Yes, Allison McEnvoy mentioned that. She told us that you warned her about his temper."

"He got angry sometimes. Especially when he wasn't winning. He liked to win." Jason felt a trickle of sweat run down his neck and he slid down a bit in his chair to catch it on his tee shirt. Why was it so hot in here?

"Did he ever fight with any of the guys? With you, maybe? When he didn't win?"

"Oh no, ma'am. But sometimes he yelled at us."

"Yelled at you? What did he yell?"

"I mean he just swore or like that. He didn't hit us or anything."

"Where were you last night and early this morning?" Sergeant Nolle hoped to catch him off guard but his quick response told her he'd been anticipating this question.

"I was swimming at Cyprus Sink with my friends. After we swam we laid around on blankets and most of us fell asleep." The officers exchanged glances. They were well acquainted with sinkhole parties that involved underage drinking and drugs. But those offenses were not their concern just now.

After Jason left, Lyman Litchgate, III, clumped into the room in his black Doc Martens and collapsed into the designated chair as if he couldn't stand up another minute. When Sergeant Nolle pointed to her own ears in order to draw his attention to his, he pulled out his ear buds and stuffed his iPod into the cargo pocket of his flaring black canvas pants leg.

She tried not to stare at his streaked hair, spiked leather bands, piercings, and ANARCHY tee shirt. Wasn't there a college dress code?. She'd seen similar garb often enough on a few Coowahchobee teens and many more at the malls in Tallahassee and Elliottville, but it still fascinated her.

"How well did you know Randall Medina?"

"Didn't."

"You didn't know him well or not at all?"

"Didn't know him."

"Were any of your friends in his classes?"

"No."

"Do you have any idea why he was in Professor Caulfield's house last night?"

"No." Lyman was clearly a man of few words.

"Where were you last night?"

"Tallahassee."

"Where exactly in Tallahassee?" Sergeant Nolle's tone indicated she was losing patience.

"Club Onyx."

"Listening to punk rock?" Sergeant Nolle knew the club.

Lyman nodded.

"Who was playing?"

"Second Class Losers."

The sheriff coughed to suppress a laugh.

"What time did you return to Coowahchobee last night?"

"Didn't."

"Didn't what?"

"Didn't come back until this morning."

"How early this morning?"

"About seven."

"How did you get here? Do you have a car?"

"No. Hitched."

"Hitched a ride? With a friend?" Sergeant Nolle felt like part of a comic routine, though none of this was funny.

"No. Just a guy."

"Someone you met at the Onyx?"

"No. Just a guy in a red truck. He picked me up on the highway."

Lyman shifted in his chair, extending his legs out under the table, then pulling them back again, as if trying to find a comfortable position. He glanced quickly at the sheriff then focused his attention on the sergeant. What was she looking for? What did she want from him?

"Lyman, you grew up in Blountstown, didn't you?"

"Yes."

"Then didn't you know Medina when you were a boy? He was a bit older than you but you must have seen him around town. Small place like that, everybody knows everybody else, right?"

Lyman looked down at his hands. "Not really."

"Not really?" The sergeant's voice remained calm but her tone had an edge to it.

No one ever really knows anyone, Lyman thought as he took a deep breath and for the first time spoke in complete sentences and in a rush, as if to tell them everything he could and then get out of there. "I saw him sometimes around the high school and the drug store downtown. He was with his friends but I don't remember who they were. They didn't like us younger kids hangin' around them." He slumped back into his chair, as if the effort to speak that much had exhausted him.

"Jason said he sometimes played basketball with the older boys, including Medina. Did you do that too?"

"No."

"Why not?"

"Don't like it."

"Basketball?"

Lyman nodded.

"What about here at Rutherford? We know he played some sports with students and pool games in the student lounge."

"I don't."

"Don't what?"

"Play sports. Or games."

Deciding that more questions would elicit only more nonresponsive replies, Sergeant Nolle dismissed Lyman with her usual comment about contacting him if they needed more information and gave him the number to call if he thought of anything helpful.

Back in the conference room the next student entered, stooping slightly as if his large oval head were too heavy for his long, thin body. His skin was pale and dry, slightly scaly around his elbows and the nape of his neck. Unlike the other students, who opted for shorts, tees, and flip-flops in hot weather, he wore pressed blue chinos, a short-sleeved white polo shirt, and leather loafers without socks. Pushing back a lock of stringy brown hair with bony fingers, he glanced around the room, then moved directly

to the sheriff and stuck out his hand. "Good morning, sir .
I'm Jonathan Kennedy, a junior from Boston."

Moving to the middle of the table, Jonathan bowed in
Sergeant Nolle's direction. "Good morning, ma'am." He
again held out his hand and when the sergeant reluctantly
extended hers, he grasped it and bent over as if to draw it
to his lips. She tried not to flinch as she extricated her hand
and pointed to the chair behind him. He bowed again and,
with a sly grin, slid into it.

"How well did you know Randall Medina?"

"He and I were fast friends and I'm devastated by his
demise. Why such a wonderful person should come to
such an untimely end is beyond my comprehension."

Jonathan's reply brought his listeners to attention. Here
at last was someone who knew Medina well. Maybe now
they would acquire some useful information.

"What can you tell us about him that would help to
explain why he was burglarizing Professor Caulfield's
house?" the sergeant asked.

"I refuse to believe that Randall was in any way
responsible for his behavior last night," Jonathan replied. "It
occurs to me that he must have been coerced by someone
else, a Dr. Caligari with a tendentious drive to succeed in
that iniquitous activity the law terms 'burglary' and with
the willpower to mesmerize Randall into assisting him. Or
her, since of course his murderer might well have been a
female, given the power and authority of women in our
present society." He bowed slightly as if to pay the sergeant
a backhanded compliment.

She refused the bait. "You said you knew Medina very
well. Were you with him the night of the murder?"

Jonathan's pale gray hooded eyes widened a little as he
hesitated before straightening his curving spine. "Oh, no,
ma'am. Perhaps I've conveyed an erroneous impression by
intimating a close alliance with the man. Actually, I knew
him only slightly but we appeared to share an appreciative
regard for higher learning."

Sheriff Hammell's sharp retort startled the student. "Which is it, Jonathan? You knew him well or you didn't?"

Jonathan swiveled his chair in the sheriff's direction and inclined his large head slightly. "Sir, I apologize profusely if I offered delusive information by suggesting that he and I were in any way closely associated. Occasionally, we encountered each other in the library while researching materials for our diverse studies. Once I inquired about the most expeditious procedure for acquiring information about a literary text I was explicating, and he graciously introduced me to various computer databases affording access to special collections in a multitude of universities. I was grateful for his solicitude and recommendations."

Sergeant Nolle frowned. "Are you now telling us that you weren't close friends with Medina? That you hardly knew him?"

Jonathan entwined his narrow fingers and locked them between his knees, hunched his shoulders, and hung his head.

After a minute of silence, when it was apparent that Jonathan had become unresponsive, the sergeant tried a different tack. "Where were you last night?"

Lifting his head Jonathan spoke more confidently again. "I was in my room reading *The Awakening*, one of the novels Professor Caulfield and Professor Sheridan have assigned for their course this semester. I like to be prepared, especially since this class promises to be a challenging one."

"Did anyone else see you there?"

"I doubt it. Very few students stay here on weekends and most of those go out partying. Frankly, there aren't many students who are as serious as I am about the pursuit of knowledge."

Sergeant Nolle had seen and heard enough. She dismissed him with her usual requests for additional information and then turned to the sheriff. "I'm sorry, I should have asked him more pointed questions, but I just couldn't stand his pretentiousness a minute longer."

She next ushered in Mary Matthews, the last student to be interviewed that day. Neither shy nor afraid, Mary bounced her five-foot-one-inch chubby body into the room. The sergeant was struck by the resemblance of the young woman's curly red hair, bright dark eyes, and wide smile to the embroidered features of a Raggedy Ann doll. A frivolous image crossed her mind. Maybe underneath that white frilly blouse was a red candy heart with "I Love You" written on it.

Mary plopped into the leather chair offered to her, caressing its polished wooden arms with her plump fingers. She stared across the table. "Wow, ma'am, you really, like, have a load to carry. What all is on that belt? A gun, I can see that. And a flashlight. But what are those other black things?"

Sergeant Nolle, taken off guard, pulled her chair closer to the table, concealing her lower body. "I'll be glad to talk to you about police equipment when we have more time. But right now we need to focus on the murder. How well did you know Randall Medina?"

Mary wasn't chastened by this dismissal of her interests or disconcerted by the question. "I took one of his writing classes last year when he taught advanced comp. I wanted to, like, know him better because he was so cute, but he never really paid any attention to us girls. You know what I mean? We were friendly and all, but he wasn't." She paused for a breath. "Allison told me she played pool with him and Jason sometimes, but they never asked *me* to come along and I'm, like, Allison's best friend, so we usually do things together. You know what I mean?"

"We got the impression that Jonathan Kennedy knew Medina quite well."

Mary snorted. "Jonathan's a creep. He's a name dropper. He'll tell you anything you want to hear. I don't think he knew Mr. Medina at all. At least I never, like, saw them together."

"Where were you last night and early this morning?"

"I babysat for Professor Baldwin and his wife until midnight." A slight frown appeared between Mary's eyebrows, just below her short curly red bangs. "They have these three *impossible* children. Very intelligent, like all professors' kids are. But they are, like, a handful, if you know what I mean. After Professor Baldwin drove me back to the dorm, I went right to sleep. I'm always *exhausted* after taking care of those kids."

"Did you see anyone in the dorm or did anyone see you?"

"I saw a couple of girls in the bathroom down the hall. Karen Stuart and Rita Gill. They were just coming in from dates."

"Any others? Allison McEnvoy, for instance?"

Mary's eyes widened. "You don't suspect her, do you? Heavens, Allison wouldn't hurt a fly! You know what I mean? She's the best, always friendly and helpful to everyone. We're, like, best friends, so I know she couldn't possibly kill anyone."

Sergeant Nolle sensed that Mary's defensive attitude would keep her from revealing any pertinent information, if she had any, and that she might soon be off on a tangent. "Thank you, Mary, that's all very helpful. You may go now and we'll get back to you if we need anything else."

Mary clutched the armrests and furrowed her brow. Had she really been all that helpful or was the sergeant just saying that? Well, at least she hadn't told them how mad she'd really been at Allison the times she'd left her behind when she'd gone off with Jason to play pool. Of course she didn't expect to go on dates with Allison and Jason, gosh no, but—. Her train of thought was interrupted by the officers, who stood up and began to gather their papers together. "Okay, that's fine. I'll be glad to tell you anything else I know. And I do want to talk about your equipment." She gestured toward the sergeant's belt. "I've been thinking about getting a degree in, like, criminology and becoming a policewoman."

"And I'm sure you'd be a good one, too." Sergeant Nolle camouflaged her annoyance. She ushered Mary out the door before closing it with a firm push. She grimaced. "That was, like, excruciating. You know what I mean?"

The sheriff laughed as he stood up. "I'd like to ask Professor Caulfield to join us for supper at Ott's, if that's okay with you. She can fill in background information about the faculty and students we interview. They're in their own little world over here at Rutherford and she's part of it. She understands them better than we can."

Sergeant Nolle raised an eyebrow but decided to say nothing.

The sheriff knew he was right about the professor's ability to help them decipher the faculty and student responses, but he admitted to himself that his real reason was more emotional than logical. A visceral attraction to her that defied logic.

He saw that the sergeant was scrutinizing him. "What?" He grinned sheepishly.

She smiled. Maybe it was time for him to become interested in a woman again. Whether it was or not, she saw that Ariadne Caulfield had attracted his attention. They'd make a nice couple, she thought, both attractive, kind, intelligent people. But what did he know about college life or she about police work? Well, it wasn't any of her business.

"I think it's a great idea," she lied as she followed him out the door.

5

"O, beware, my lord, of jealousy!
It is the green-eyed monster which doth mock
The meat it feeds on…"
Othello

AFTER THE FACULTY INTERVIEWS were over, Judith headed for the parking lot, annoyed to find Chris Bannerman keeping pace with her. "Man, that Allison McEnvoy is some stunning broad!" he smirked.

"Shouldn't you focus on students' brains rather than their beauty?" she snapped back.

"Well, sorry. Didn't mean to offend Rutherford's resident feminist."

Judith bit her tongue, but as she followed his blue Miata out under the alumni arch, she obsessed over his ignorance and male chauvinism. How had he been hired here when it was obvious to everyone that he had no sociopolitical insight or capability for critical thinking? He was simply self-interested, always complaining about their low salaries even though he wore expensive clothes and drove a flashy car. What really irked her was his insolent attitude toward women in general, except as sex objects. Of course she was a feminist and she deeply resented his pejorative use of the term, though she saw his ignorance for what it was.

A few minutes later she came to a screeching halt in her condo parking lot as she remembered something else about Chris. Last summer he had been caught brawling with a Southwestern graduate student at a party in Elliottville, an incident that became fodder for campus gossip at Rutherford. Judith had acquired most of the story from a friend on the Southwestern faculty, who had heard it from her students. "Shit." Judith spoke aloud. Could Randall Medina have been that graduate student? Could Chris have beaten him to death this time? Careful with these wild speculations, she admonished herself. There's no evidence to support such a deduction. She hesitated, and then pulled a cigarette out of her pack. Her sixth today? Seventh? Wasn't she supposed to be quitting? Oh, what the hell, she needed something to assuage her annoyance with that idiot.

Meanwhile, driving to the tennis courts, Chris was obsessing about the same incident at Southwestern with that arrogant asshole graduate student that Medina had brought to the party, a know-it-all jerk who had talked all evening about some stupid experiment he was conducting for his thesis in psychology. Based on some cock-eyed theory about the effect of brain chemistry on male dating behavior. Brain farts, Chris had called them, riling the student right away. The guy's date, a sexy, slim, buxom blonde, had laughed, and then flirted with Chris, annoying the jerk even more. That volatile dick wad deserved what he got, Chris thought, remembering the blow he had delivered after one too many insults. But he'd been rewarded by the blonde, who had been a very fine lay. If Judith, that self-righteous puritanical feminazi had learned about that escapade, she would have seen the fight with a student over a woman as a heinous crime. But she wouldn't have reported him because the college rules governing faculty conduct didn't cover off-campus activities. Unless they fell under the category of 'moral turpitude,' a ridiculous catchall phrase he ridiculed as 'moral turpentine'.

After word got around about that skirmish, his colleagues had continued to smile and offer a friendly face-to-face greeting, but Chris was often omitted from someone's dinner party list or snubbed by a faculty spouse in the grocery store. Most of the time he curbed his annoyance and continued to court students with his easy camaraderie and even easier multiple-choice exams. "Mooks," he called them as well as most of his colleagues. But he didn't care if his art history students couldn't tell an expressionist from an impressionist, as long as they continued to give him high marks on their annual evaluations. Still, having little ambition and less interest in the scholarship necessary to move to a university, he counted his blessings that Rutherford was more invested in teaching than publishing. Teaching was a breeze, leaving him plenty of time for tennis, golf, and pursuing women, who were easily seduced by his good looks and suave manner. As he parked his Miata at the end of the lot beside the city tennis courts, where there was little danger of another car denting it, he waved to the attractive redhead waiting for him under a cluster of tall pine trees. Now to enjoy a Sunday as it was meant to be enjoyed.

📖

AS SOON AS THE LAST STUDENTS had finished their interviews, a group of them had piled into Ted Clark's old pickup truck and headed south across the Panhandle toward the Gulf. Mary and Allison were squeezed into the front seat with Ted and his girlfriend Suzette Buie, their sweaty bodies sticking to the torn plastic seats. Jason and a couple of other guys rode in the truck bed, grateful for the breeze that swept over them as Ted broke the speed limit down the back roads in the Apalachicola National Forest. The early evening sun blazed through the tall pines and the squat palmettos spread like fans underneath. After cruising through the small towns of Sopchoppy and Panacea, they stopped at a convenience store near the Ochlocknee Bay Bridge to buy sodas, chips, and packaged sandwiches.

At the end of a stretch of road lined with small cottages, they came to Mashes Sands, a strip of beach facing Ochlocknee Bay and the Gulf of Mexico beyond. Already in their swimsuits, the students headed for the shallow water, which was tranquil, almost stagnant, and warm as a bathtub. But after their ordeal and hot drive, they found the tepid water refreshing and for a long time they swam about, splashing one another and shouting to relieve their tension. When they'd had enough, they toweled off and wolfed down their food. Then, laughing and joking, they strolled along the beach and around a huge uprooted, weather-beaten tree to a more secluded area near the marshlands, where a couple of snowy egrets and a great blue heron waded in slow motion, looking for fish. Here the students rubbed on insect repellent, sprawled on their towels and an old blanket, and fell asleep. In the row of long leaf and pond pines behind them a cicada chorus rose and fell and mosquitoes hovered around their recumbent bodies as the sun sank farther down toward the smooth sheet of pale blue seawater.

Sometime later six pelicans flying in V-formation glided in and landed together on a sandy peninsula several feet away, followed by a cloud of shrill sea gulls, waking the students with their shrieking demands for a handout. Jason sat up with a start, feeling Allison's eyes upon him. "Wha? What's the matter?"

"I'm scared." She moved into the circle of his arm and whispered so the others wouldn't hear. "I know why those officers would want to talk to everyone at Rutherford, but I just can't imagine one of us breaking into someone's house to steal something. Or killing Mr. Medina."

"Whoever did that probably needed money. Even decent people can be driven to steal if they're desperate," Jason said, pulling her closer.

"Maybe they needed drug money." Nobody in their own group used drugs but she knew plenty of students who smoked pot and some who tried party drugs on weekends. "But the newspaper story said nothing was stolen. Why didn't they take her TV or computer?"

"Too hard to trade for cash? Or they were going to but got into a fight? I suppose after someone hit Randall the others just fled the scene." Jason held Allison away from him and looked at her closely. "What did you tell the officers?"

"Nothing much. Just that I was in the dorm all night." She couldn't quite bring herself to mention the trip to the drugstore. Not that she didn't trust him—of course she did—but he might scold her for not telling them that.

Jason brushed her hair away from her face and traced his finger down her cheek. When she held his hand against her lips, he took her face in his hands and kissed her. "They said you told them about Randall's temper."

"His temper? I don't think I did."

"You told them I warned you about his temper when he got impatient with your pool playing. Why'd you do that?"

Allison put her arms around his neck. "What was wrong with that? Maybe his temper got him killed."

A sleepy head rose up from the adjoining towel. "What are you two whispering about?" Mary Matthews sat up, rubbing her shoe-button eyes and fluffing out her red curls.

"About the murder, what else?" Allison's tone of voice was sharper than she meant it to be. Lately she was getting tired of Mary, especially when she begged to go along with her and Jason when they wanted to be alone.

Mary dragged her towel over and plopped down beside them. "Hey, wasn't it, like, weird being questioned by the police? That sergeant was good at it, though. I'd like to be just like her someday. Wearing a uniform and questioning suspects. I'd have to, like, change my major, I guess, and transfer to a university to study law enforcement. But my dad would have a fit if I switched from accounting. You know what I mean? He's decided I should be a CPA like him and now that my sister dropped out of school to get married, he has, like, all his hopes pinned on me."

Jason grimaced. Why did Mary always have to tag along with them? She was so annoying with her constant chatter and always about herself. "What did you say in there?"

"Nothing. Not a thing." Mary, as usual, felt defensive in Jason's presence. What did Allison see in him anyway? Controlling jerk. "What did you say to them? You were, like, his friend, weren't you? I know you both came from Blountstown." Mary spat out that name as if it were a circle in hell. Coming from Orlando, she viewed the small North Florida town as Hicksville personified. She resented the fact that her parents didn't have the funds to send her to the University of Miami, where two of her best friends had gone, and that she hadn't had the grades to earn a scholarship there. She'd had to settle for second-rate Rutherford in podunk Coowahchobee, where her parents' friend on the Board of Trustees had pulled strings to get her admitted.

"Just because Blountstown's not a city doesn't make it a bad place to grow up in. Randall and I both liked the town and he was always good to me." Jason jumped up and ran into the water.

"Did you have to say that?" Allison glared at Mary.

"Say what? All I did was mention Blountstown. How would I know that it would, like, set him off?"

"You know him well enough and probably said it deliberately to annoy him. You're always trying to get at him in one way or another. Why don't you like him? Jealous?"

"Me jealous? That's, like, crazy. If you really want to know, he's just too good to be true. I don't trust him. You know what I mean?"

"You don't trust him without a reason? That's dumb. I think you *are* jealous."

Mary shrugged, hurt. "He and Lyman are from Blountstown and they, like, knew Mr. Medina. Isn't that why the sergeant was asking about where we all come from? She must think whoever killed him is, like, from around here."

Allison reached for a bottle of water from their cooler. "Did you know that icky Jonathan grew up in Bristol?"

"He did?" Mary's black eyes sparkled. "How do you know?"

"Jason told me. He said Jonathan shouldn't act so superior because he was born in Bristol and only moved to Boston to live with his grandparents when his parents divorced."

"Wow, why didn't he, like, live with one of his parents?"

"I don't know. Who cares?" Allison pulled her long hair up off her neck and into a clip. "I don't think the killer was one of us anyway."

"Me neither." Mary's tone suggested she wasn't too sure but didn't want to annoy Allison by pursuing the topic. "What did you tell those officers?"

"Nothing." Allison frowned and began to chew her lip. "Well, I guess I did a dumb thing. I told them that Cindy Donaldson had a crush on Mr. Medina and that he didn't give her the time of day. I hope that doesn't get her into trouble. She'd never forgive me."

"Cindy's a flake. But my mom says it's normal for girls our age to have crushes on an older man. Like Professor Baldwin and Professor Bannerman." Mary thought the latter was a jerk but she knew Allison admired both men.

Allison thought better about saying how Professor Baldwin's graceful waving hands made her heart flutter when he directed the chorus.

"What do you think those geeks told the policewoman?"

Allison brushed sand off her long slim legs before slathering on more suntan lotion. Even this late in the day the sun was brutal. "Lyman's a dopey loner, but pain-in-the-butt Jonathan knows everything that goes on around campus. I don't trust him."

Mary shook her carroty curls. "But he says he's rich so why would he steal? If he did."

"He lies about having money. But why did Mr. Medina steal? He had a job."

"Does anybody ever have, like, enough money? Everybody wants more. You know what I mean?"

Allison readily concurred. After her father's death last fall, her mother had continued to send her monthly checks, but they never were enough to meet her needs. As soon as the lawyers got her father's will straightened out, she'd inherit a lot of money. But they were still looking for her older half-sister, who had left home when Allison was just a baby. She didn't want to share with someone she didn't even know, but there wasn't any help for it. Unless they never found her sister. Allison hoped she'd vanished for good. She shifted her attention back to Mary. "Where did you tell them you were last night?"

"Babysitting. Until midnight, then I came back to the dorm and went straight to bed. A couple of the other girls saw me in the bathroom, so I have, like, an alibi, as they say on TV." She turned to look directly at Allison. "And where were you?"

"I went to bed early."

"How come you didn't go with Jason and the others to the sinkhole?" Mary's sharp tone revealed her annoyance that they hadn't asked her to join them.

"I just didn't feel like it."

"Then why weren't you there when I looked in after I got back?" Mary straightened up as if she were rehearsing to be a police officer. "Do you have an alibi?"

"Are you accusing me?" Allison sat up. "Well, shit, so much for friendship."

"Hey, no, I didn't mean anything. I just, like, wondered where you were." Mary, afraid she'd crossed a line that might alienate the only real friend she had, reached over and touched Allison lightly on the shoulder. "Hey, I'm sorry. Of course you had nothing to do with that terrible crime. You, like, couldn't have. You're too good."

When their friends joined them , Allison gave Mary a forgiveness hug and picked up her towel just as Jason doused her with a full water bottle. She chased him back into the shallow water, where they splashed each other until Jason pulled her to him and they began kissing. Mary turned away and began picking up their empty bottles, plastic sandwich wrappers, and potato chip bags. Of course Allison hadn't killed Mr. Medina, what was she thinking? Just like she'd told the officers, Allison was an angel. And her best friend.

As darkness set in, the group made their way to the small cinder-block restrooms near the parking lot to change from bathing suits into shorts and tees for the trip back to Coowahchobee. This time Allison and Mary traveled in the truck bed with Jason, Allison close to him, his arm tightly around her, with Mary on her other side, absorbed in identifying star formations in the vast black sky. Before they reached Sopchoppy, both Allison and Jason fell asleep, leaving Mary to her stargazing.

📖

BACK IN COOWAHCHOBEE Lyman was also looking up at the heavens, stretched out on a blanket on a hill behind his apartment house, where he'd gone to escape the oppressive heat in his room. Damn bastard landlord was so stingy with the air conditioning that the room was like an oven, even with the fan he'd brought from home. If his even stingier dad would give him a bigger allowance, he could afford a better place. As he watched the red and green wing lights of a small plane overhead, he thought about Allison, who, as usual, had snubbed him in the hallway as they waited to be called in for questioning. What a bitch. Who did she think she was, parading around like a queen? Just another dumb blonde 'ho' who thought she owned the world. He grasped the blanket folds and gave them a shake as if she were in his hands, and then sat up, his anger suddenly dissolving into a dark despair. His blanket dragged on the ground behind him as he trudged back to his claustrophobic room.

In the Rutherford men's dorm, Jonathan tried to read *The Awakening* but every mention of Edna Pontellier conjured up images of Allison's seraphic face and glorious golden hair, the perfect beauty he adored from a vast distance. Fearful of rejection (as had happened with other girls), he avoided contact with her. Not that he would want to associate with her group of friends, heaven forbid. Imbeciles, most of them, not a genuine intellectual among them. What did she see in that inarticulate boyfriend? As far as he could tell from classes they'd had together, Jason's intellect was less than stellar. What a shame, all that beauty wasted on that beast. Of course, as he had garnered from his reading, beauty was no guarantee of faithfulness. Eve, Guinevere, Madame Bovary, and a legion of other legendary pulchritudinous heroines were ultimately exposed as perfidious temptresses, epitomes of unfaithfulness and treachery. Better to steer clear of a femme fatale like Allison, but even as he thought it, Jonathan realized that his conclusion was really just sour grapes.

6

AFTER BREAKFAST on Labor Day, two days after Medina's murder and three weeks into the fall semester, Ariadne, Suzanne, and Judith sat together at the small butcher-block table in Judith's kitchen, finishing their coffee. Cassandra sprang onto the window seat to spy on a minuscule hummingbird hovering in midair, sipping nectar from the orange blossoms on a trumpet vine. When it darted away, the plump fur ball stretched out and began to lick her paws. Ariadne laughed. "She's pretending she caught and ate that delectable morsel. Not that she's ever tasted hummingbird. Or any other bird as far as I know. But I suppose the jungle instinct survives in house cats fed on canned food."

"In a cat's eyes, all things belong to cats," Judith said, adding, "English proverb." She reached for another cigarette, looked at it, then at Ariadne, and put it back.

"I'm off for a run." Suzanne said. "I'll leave you two to your essay grading.,"

After wishing Suzanne a good run, Judith spun her cigarette pack around on the smooth wooden tabletop. "Are you okay? I worry about your state of mind."

Ariadne gave her a wan smile. "It's hard teaching our students while wondering if one or more of them could have been involved."

"And we can't rule out our colleagues," Judith said. "Chris Bannerman, for one. That jerk is capable of anything, possibly even murder."

Ariadne shook her head. "Whoever killed Medina could be someone else entirely. Maybe one of his fellow graduate students or a gang member who talked him into participating in the burglary."

"I wonder what the investigators will discover after they interview others this week. And will they tell you anything more?"

"I doubt it. They seemed very reluctant to share any information." Ariadne hesitated. "What do you know about the sheriff as a person?"

"You mean as an eligible male?" Judith asked with a straight face. "I'm pretty sure he's divorced, but you can ask one of your gossiping neighbors." She knew Ariadne would never do that, but she was glad to see that her friend seemed interested in a man more responsible than that womanizing lawyer Miles Duvall, who had been after her ever since her husband's death. "Look, you can ask about his marital status if you want, but I don't think you should continue to inquire about the crime. It might be risky for you to know more than you should. It might even be dangerous for you to associate with those two officers."

"The intruders are probably far away from here by now. Wouldn't you be if you'd killed someone?"

"Just be careful."

A half hour later, Judith was upstairs doing some computer research while Ariadne remained at the table, staring at ungraded papers and thinking about their friendship. She had mentored Judith from the beginning and over the years they had developed team-taught interdisciplinary courses in literature and history. During their frequent theoretical discussions Judith loved to expound on theories like "deterritorialization," while Ariadne focused on the "new western history" that demythologized traditional views of America's Old West.

"Ari, can you come up here?" Judith called down to her. "I want to show you something."

Ariadne went upstairs to a small study, where the walls were covered with framed photographs of Judith's family, beginning with her ancestors, stiff and proper in dark suits and dresses with puffed leghorn sleeves, and continuing through three generations. Several new photos lay on a side table, ready to be framed. On one wall hung a sampler with a proverb cross-stitched by Judith's great-grandmother: "Never put off till tomorrow what may be done today." Next to it, pinned to the peeling rosebud-sprigged wallpaper, were several sample strips of new paper Judith had been contemplating for months, trying to decide which one would replace the old. Now she sat at an old wooden desk near the front windows, peering at her computer screen. "I found the poem you're trying to remember, Ari," she said, pushing her glasses up on her nose. "Turns out I was right. It is Renaissance, Shakespeare specifically. Sonnet 23. Here, I printed off a copy for you."

"A Shakespearean sonnet? How would I have remembered lines from that? In college we never memorized anything except the usual familiar quotations. 'To be or not to be,' 'Out, out, damned spot.' That sort of thing."

Judith shook her head. "I don't know. Read it and see if it triggers any memories."

"Look, here's the phrase 'actor on the stage' that I remembered." Ariadne began to read aloud:

"*As an unperfect actor on the stage*
Who with his fear is put beside his part—"
Or some fierce thing replete with too much rage
Whose strength's abundance weakens his own heart ...."

Judith interrupted. "'Fear,' 'fierce thing,' 'rage.' Sounds like murder and mayhem to me."

Ariadne read silently for a moment. "Yes, but just metaphorical mayhem here. The next part seems to be about a stymied lover.

"*So I, for fear of trust, forget to say*
The perfect ceremony of love's rite,

And in mine own love's strength seem to decay,
O'er charged with burden of mine own love's might."

Judith broke into a spirited imitation of Tina Turner, "What's love got to do with it?"

Ariadne laughed. "Exactly. And here's the 'books' part."

"O, let my books be then the eloquence
And dumb presagers of my speaking breast,
Who plead for love and look for recompense
More than that tongue that more hath more express'd."

"More and more and more," Judith echoed.

Ariadne read on. "Here's the couplet."

"O, learn to read what silent love hath writ:
To hear with eyes belongs to love's fine wit."

"'To hear with eyes' is a good example of synesthesia." Judith's voice was professorial. "One sense does the work of another. I think your mind is telling you to listen with your eyes."

"Great. Wonderful. That might make poetic sense, but it doesn't really help me. My eyes didn't hear a thing at the house."

"Stop thinking about that now," Judith said. "You don't need more stress. And neither do I. Let's forget about crime and classes for awhile and watch one of those movies I rented last week."

Just then Ariadne's cell phone rang. "Hello, Professor. Beau Hammell here. Just checking to see how you're doing."

She stepped out into the hall. "Teaching two classs and grading papers hasn't left me much time to think about what happened or how I feel about it."

"Good idea to focus on something else at this point. Helps to calm your nerves." He hesitated, as if calming his own. "I was hoping that you could join Sergeant Nolle and me for supper tomorrow night at Ott's barbeque place over on the highway. We'd like to get your input on the faculty and students we interviewed today."

Ariadne took a deep breath. Much as she wanted to learn more about the investigation, she didn't think she should discuss her colleagues or the students. But she knew that she certainly wanted to see the sheriff again. "I'm not sure I can be of much help but I'll be happy to join you," she said.

"Great. Seven o'clock then." The relief in his voice was audible.

"Oh, I almost forgot," Ariadne added. "Judith found that poem I was trying to remember. 'O, let my books be then the eloquence.' Remember how I was trying to figure out what those phrases meant?"

"Yes, and did you?"

"No, I can't decide what the poem's telling me. If anything," she finished lamely, hoping he didn't think her crazy.

He tried to think of an appropriate response that would not offend her. "It'll probably come to you sooner or later. See you tomorrow at seven."

Ariadne hung up and stood for a moment, with his deep vibrant voice echoing in her head. So much had happened in these two days that she'd had no time to think about her unusual personal response to the sheriff. During the past three years, since André's death, she'd had no romantic interest in another man. Miles Duvall, her lawyer, clearly wanted to be more than a friend. But while she enjoyed being with him, laughing at his jokes (at least the less outrageous ones), seeing and discussing films with him, and exploring new restaurants in the neighboring towns, she didn't take Miles seriously A more involved relationship couldn't lead to anything except a short-term affair, the kind of fling he engaged in with other women. Not that she wanted any serious commitment and certainly not with Miles. But she was surprised to find herself responding to the sheriff's attention and interest, not to mention his intelligent blue eyes and intriguing overbite. Definitely a distraction from her work and the murder investigation. She suppressed a laugh. Mind over matter, ha. What did the philosophers know about women's desires? She glanced into the hall mirror. But what did she know about her own?

IN HIS OFFICE at Rutherford College that afternoon, Julian Baldwin sat contemplating his upcoming promotion and tenure process. Having been reassured by the music department's chairperson, Andrew Holrood, that he was on a solid track for promotion, Julian was feeling hopeful but somehow uneasy and not as happy as he thought he'd be at this stage of his career. He swiveled around in his gray tweed desk chair, surveying his small office, gloomier on a cloudy day than on days when sunlight streamed in through the venetian blinds in the east window. The desk and chair were all right but he hated the old brown Naugahyde couch scrunched between two file cabinets, a relic from his graduate school days, which he hoped to replace when he could afford it. The best he could do now was to partially cover it with a blue afghan, crocheted by Elizabeth in one of her rare domestic moods and then moved to his office, since it clashed with the green leather sofa they had bought for their living room with wedding-gift money.

His thoughts drifted back to their Boston wedding, a huge affair in her parents' Episcopal church. His family, from a working-class Presbyterian background, had been overawed by the opulence but captivated by the friendliness and courtesy extended them by Elizabeth's CEO father and socialite mother. Their wedding had been the crowning moment of their golden days of courtship after they had met as students at Amherst, Julian in grad school and Elizabeth about to graduate with a B.A. in Classics. They had been the perfect couple in those days, physically attractive—her glossy black hair, marble-white skin, and brown eyes complementing his Greek-god profile and piercing azure eyes—and intellectually aware and articulate. They were sought after by a circle of friends for discussions after visiting lecturers, scintillating conversations at intimate dinner parties, or just laughter and fun at occasional dances. Together they enjoyed going to movies, especially French films or documentaries, and afterwards sipping a good Cabernet and talking late into the night, infatuated with each other's ideas about art, politics, and music.

Julian shifted about in his chair. Where had it all gone wrong? What had happened to them over the years? After graduation and their marriage, Elizabeth had postponed graduate school in order to get a job in a bank to help him finish his doctorate. He had promised to reciprocate once he had the Ph.D., but at that point he realized it would be better if he went on the academic job market. College and university teaching positions, he had explained to her, are easier to get when one is fresh out of grad school, while professors still remember you and will write good recommendation letters. And administrators searching for the best investment want young hires, those they can exploit for several decades with low wages and poor fringe benefits. He had smiled when he said this and they had both laughed as they often did when they imitated their professors' complaints, though they secretly hoped those were exaggerated.

Julian's expectations of landing a position at a prestigious research university had not materialized; he thought his credentials were impeccable and his musical talent impressive, but no major university had responded to his applications. He was invited only twice to smaller college campus interviews, the first one in Montana, where the temperature in April had not risen above forty degrees and snow flurries greeted both his arrival and departure. When Rutherford College had recruited him, both Julian and Elizabeth had decided that torrid was preferable to frigid, so they headed to Florida.

The years in Coowahchobee had been rough on Elizabeth, who felt alienated from the conservative southern townspeople and both bored and harried as a stay-at-home mother forced to relinquish her dream of graduate school. Julian, on the other hand, had grown to appreciate the area. The tall pine forests resembled those in his native Pennsylvania, without the mountains, of course, and Coowahchobee was not unlike Galeton, his hometown. For the most part he liked his Rutherford colleagues and spent much of his free time, of which there was precious little, talking with them in the halls between classes or in the cafeteria during lunch and coffee breaks. And he thrived on his musical endeavors, his classroom teaching, private voice lessons, and the college chorus. Directing the chorus made him feel accomplished because he was able to elicit the best singing possible from those young and previously untrained voices.

Then why wasn't he happy? Why this constriction in his chest? He stood up and paced around the office. Glancing out the window, he noticed dark clouds gathering in the west. A vigorous wind began to sway the upper branches of the stout live oaks and push the slender pines to and fro. He looked at his watch. Almost noon. He should be heading home but he continued to stand at the window, fascinated by a two-inch-long brown and yellow striped banana spider just outside. With its six long legs pressed together in twos, two stretched up and four hanging down, it resembled a tiny trapeze artist clinging to its elaborate, violently swinging web. Below him in the quad two coeds struggled to hold down their miniskirts in the blustery wind. He clutched the venetian blind pulls in one hand and pried apart two slats with the other, then released them quickly as he realized he was trying for a better look at their exposed bodies. Fuck. What was he doing? Ogling coeds again. He was no better than Chris in that respect, except that he didn't date them. Couldn't, of course, being a married man.

He sat down on the sofa, sinking back into the fuzzy afghan, which he grasped with his long, slim, now sweaty fingers. Was it sex he was craving? He always avoided analyzing his salacious urges, regarding them as innate impulses, voyeuristic desires he struggled to keep in check and hidden from Elizabeth, who often chastised him for his responses to young women's infatuated smiles.

For a time after he had met, dated, and wooed Elizabeth, he had easily curbed his impulses, but after the children were born and her interest in sex had waned—. He couldn't blame her, though. He suspected that his attraction to and desire for attention from nubile young women was also fueled by his growing awareness of the aging process. He ran his fingers through his thinning hair. Still handsome, he knew that, but no longer young. And no longer free to pursue his desires.

He sat upright with the full recognition of his condition—that he was trapped. Not only in a deteriorating marriage, but also in his professional situation. But how ridiculous that was. He shook his head. How ludicrous to think of himself this way when he was about to be secured in a job he was lucky to have and one he loved. Promotion and tenure just around the corner. A goal he'd dreamed about and worked for, now about to be realized. He sighed. But a finale too. From now on into old age, he would be stuck in a small school with people he would have to work with every day and in a small town where cultural opportunities were pathetic compared to those in a city. And encumbered with an unhappy, overly censorious wife, who longed to be elsewhere, probably with someone more successful. His children were the only bright spot in his life now, he realized, and they would grow up and leave home to explore wider and more promising possibilities for their own futures.

The jangling phone jolted him out of his reverie. Damn, that would be Elizabeth wondering where he was and reminding him he'd promised to stop for groceries at Piggly Wiggly before coming home. He grabbed his briefcase and headed out the door.

7

"…a dish fit for the gods, …"
Julius Caesar

ON TUESDAY EVENING, after a strenuous day of teaching classes, made more exhausting by having to discuss the murder with friends and students, Ariadne joined Sheriff Hammell and Sergeant Nolle at Ott's BBQ. Tiny Ott, whose beefy two-hundred-pound frame belied his nickname, greeted them as they entered the long, low, rustic building and led them to a back room he reserved for small community meetings, hoping to curry favor with the town's V.I.P.s, the sheriff among them. From the corner jukebox Willie Nelson wailed his regrets at having nothing left to lose as the restaurant staff and patrons hushed their conversations to ogle the four newcomers. The officers smiled at those who greeted them but didn't stop to chat. When the door to the back room closed, the cacophony of rattling dishes, country music, and chatter resumed as hungry diners returned to plates heaped with pork ribs, beer-battered fries, and Ott's famous pickle-relish coleslaw.

"We're always of interest to Ott's customers," the sergeant said, trying to reassure Ariadne, who seemed disconcerted by the attention paid to them. "Especially now when they want to ask about the murder. But it's the best place to eat in peace while we're working. Tiny makes sure we're not disturbed."

The corpulent restaurateur smiled and nodded as he handed Ariadne a menu. He assumed the other two would order their favorites, pulled pork sandwiches smothered in tangy barbecue sauce with a side of slaw and glasses of sweetened iced tea, a year-round Southern staple. Ariadne scanned Tiny's variations on the barbeque theme, opting finally for a tossed salad with grilled chicken strips. "And may I please have the dressing on the side?" She hoped that her low-cal request would not offend Tiny, who merely shrugged to suggest that she was missing the best meal of her life by passing up the pulled pork.

The sheriff grinned. "You've probably made the healthiest selection. The weight-conscious among us like to refer to this place as the 'fat-e-cue,' but we can't resist the food."

After Mabel Hazelschmidt, the most experienced of a half-dozen waitresses Tiny paid well to keep happy, brought them their drinks and handed out straws pulled from her apron pocket, the sheriff stirred the ice cubes around in his tall olive green plastic glass and looked over at the women. "I think it's time for us all to be on a first-name basis, don't you?"

Ariadne smiled, a bit self-consciously. "Yes, please call me 'Ariadne.'"

"I'm 'Ellen,'" the sergeant said.

"I prefer 'Beau' to 'Beaufort.' It's a whole lot easier to say." The sheriff smiled at Ariadne. "Let's talk over the interviews while we wait for our food. We want to hear your take on the faculty and students."

She pleated and then smoothed out her paper straw wrapper as she spoke. "I'm not sure it's a good idea for me to discuss my colleagues. Some of them are very particular about privacy."

Beau smiled at her. "Those who have nothing to hide should have nothing to fear."

"It really upsets me to think that someone I know could have burglarized my house and killed a man. Most of the faculty are my friends, ones I've known for a long time. I just can't believe it was one of them."

Ellen tried to reassure her. "I know it's pretty upsetting, but at this point we have to consider almost everyone as suspects."

Beau opened his notebook. "I was surprised that no one could tell us much about Randall Medina. They don't seem to have known him well."

"Judith says that she rarely saw him even though he taught in the same department," Ariadne said. "Apparently, he came in, taught his classes, and left without paying much attention to anyone. Unusual for someone teaching in a small college. We're a pretty congenial group on the whole." Except when we're at each other's throats in a faculty meeting, she thought.

"What do you think about Julian Baldwin?"

Ariadne stiffened. Commenting on her colleagues was going to be even more difficult than she had imagined. "Julian's been with us for several years. He's a good teacher and well-liked by everyone." She paused. "He's under a lot of stress right now because he's being evaluated for promotion to associate professor and for tenure. That will mean more money for him and job security."

"Job security?" Ellen's question reflected non-academics' frequent unfamiliarity with academic procedures.

"Tenured faculty can be dismissed only for egregious violations of academic standards."

"Or violations of the law?" Beau asked.

"Certainly. Especially felonies. But I really can't see Julian jeopardizing his career by participating in a burglary. He's worked hard to get where he is and he has a family to support. Besides, he's a gentle person, not at all violent as far as I know."

Ellen consulted her notebook. "Chris Bannerman seemed to know Medina, at least he'd experienced his temper. I wonder if he was holding something back."

"That bothered me too," Beau said. "What do you think of him, Ariadne?"

"If he's hiding something, it's most likely about dating students, something the college tolerates as long as he doesn't date those enrolled in his classes." Ariadne thought for a moment. "Did he mention the fight he had last summer with a Southwestern graduate student in Elliottville?"

"No, he didn't, but we discovered it when we checked his background," Beau replied. "If Medina had a temper, then he could have provoked almost anyone who was with him at your house into violence. Especially someone like Bannerman who can be goaded into fighting."

Ariadne shook her head. "I can't imagine Chris involved with burglars or killing anyone either, even if provoked."

When Mabel angled the door open with her ample hips and carried in a tray with their dinners, the hungry trio suspended their conversation to concentrate on the food. Beau slathered more barbecue sauce onto his pork sandwich, while Ellen doused her French fries with catsup. Ariadne, who usually dipped pieces of lettuce into the dressing that accompanied her salads, poured the honey mustard directly into the bowl and began to eat as if famished.

After they had finished and had assured Mabel and Tiny how delicious the food was, but that they couldn't possibly manage any dessert, Beau handed Ariadne a sheet of paper. "Here's a list of students we interviewed. What can you tell us about them?"

She studied the list. "I haven't taught any of these particular ones so I don't know them very well. Judith and I have Jonathan Kennedy in class this semester. She's taught him before and says he's a bright student although self-serving and conceited." She refrained from repeating Judith's favorite word for him, "toady," and Judith's explanation of that word, "a contraction of toadeater, in the sixteenth century a charlatan's attendant who ate supposedly poisonous toads so the quack doctor could pretend to save him."

After learning that Jonathan claimed to be in the library Saturday night, Ariadne continued, "He's an extremely conscientious student, so he probably was there.."

"He's a slick one." Ellen continued to sip her tea. "Every word he uttered seemed insincere."

Ariadne decided not to repeat Judith's occasional references to him as "Uriah Heep."

"What did you think of the anarchist, Lyman Litchgate?" Beau asked.

Ariadne smiled. "That's a pretty strong word to describe Lyman. He and a few others are often referred to as 'punks' by the faculty and 'Goths' or 'grunges' by their fellow students. Their styles are calculated to shock and annoy Rutherford's administration, which is quite conservative overall. They flout the dress code every chance they get, but I've never heard any of my colleagues fault them for cutting classes or causing disturbances. Lyman is pretty uncommunicative, as you undoubtedly noticed."

"He certainly didn't give us much to go on, but we're checking on his whereabouts that Saturday night. Any thoughts about Jason Overstreet? He seemed nervous."

"That might have been just fear of the police. Students are jittery as mice around cats when talking to authority figures."

Mabel brought the check to the table. "Sure you don't want dessert, Sheriff?"

Beau assured her he couldn't eat another bite, not even of Tiny's scrumptious key lime pie. After Mabel refilled their tea glasses and left, Ellen continued, "One of the young women we interviewed could have been with Medina that night. What do you think about them?"

Ariadne studied the list. "Mary Matthews is quite high-strung, volatile, and chatty, while Allison McEnvoy is a quiet type. She was in one of Judith's classes last spring when her father died. Judith said she was distressed the whole semester, but that's not unusual in the case of a family death." She thought for a moment. "Of course, if whoever killed Medina was a partner in the burglary, then any of our students could have been with him. Or none of them. It could have been one of his fellow graduate students at Southwestern, for instance." She sat back in her chair. "Oh dear, I don't think my impressions are very helpful and may even be misleading. I suspect you want to warn me not to speculate without evidence."

"We often talk about possible suspects, only we call it 'theorizing,' not 'speculating.'" Ellen smiled. "Not so different from what professors do?"

"Yes, I guess so," Ariadne said. "Except that our theorizing is usually confined to ideas garnered from texts or lab samples rather than people. I don't envy you your job, which is certainly more dangerous than ours, and your misinterpretations have more serious consequences than ours." She blushed. "I don't mean to imply that you misinterpret..." She trailed off, not knowing how to extricate herself from a potentially embarrassing situation with people she hardly knew.

Ellen came to her rescue. "Of course we misinterpret, but the more we can learn from concerned people like you, who cooperate with the law rather than just criticizing it, the less mistakes we're likely to make."

Fewer, Ariadne thought, *fewer* mistakes. It was a grammar error that always made Judith cringe but she never corrected anyone except students.

Beau picked up the check, laid several bills on the tray, and then glanced at the wall clock. "Eight-thirty already." He stood up. "Sorry, but we have to get back on duty. Thanks for your invaluable input, Ariadne."

Ariadne thought he was offering a polite exaggeration. "I only hope my comments won't be misleading."

When the three wound their way past the salad bar to the cash register, Willie Nelson's lament over the last thing he needed the first thing this morning blared from the jukebox and the noisy crowd paused again to watch them leave. They threaded their way to the wide wooden porch, where those waiting to eat sat in high-backed wooden rockers or lounged around the steps, smoking and talking.

Ariadne almost bumped into a tall figure silhouetted against the slanted rays of the setting sun. "Miles, is that you? I thought you were in New York." She shaded her eyes to peer up into his.

Miles hugged her close. "Hello, Beautiful!" he said in his deep, sexy voice. "I've been back awhile, but have been so busy I haven't had time to call you. Sorry.. You must feel violated. A couple of my clients over the years have been robbed and it's no picnic." He drew back and looked Ariadne in the eyes. "And finding a dead man in your home was most certainly even more traumatic."

Beau cleared his throat as he and Ellen stepped around the couple.

"Oh, I'm sorry, how rude of me," Ariadne said. "Miles, do you know these officers?"

"Sure. We meet quite often at the courthouse." He flashed a practiced smile at them as he continued, "Let me introduce my new legal secretary, Diana Macomb." He stood aside to reveal a tall, slim woman with sculpted muscles, a pale complexion, steely blue eyes, and glossy black hair caught up in a chignon. Her sleek black A-line sundress piped in white along the décolletage made Ariadne feel dowdy, although to anyone else's eyes her green, yellow, and white striped skirt and white scooped-neck blouse would appear fashionable.

Although slightly disconcerted seeing Miles with this stunning woman, she joined in on the exchange of pleasantries as they all shook hands before Beau and Ellen excused themselves and walked off toward their car.

"You've had quite a shock," Diana said to Ariadne. "Burglary and murder are probably rare in a small town like Coowahchobee."

Rare as hen's teeth, as Judith would say, Ariadne thought as she agreed with Diana. They talked for a few minutes about the crime and then laughed when Miles flexed his rippling muscles and struck a pose in a blatant attempt to regain their attention. "If you feel the need for protection, doll, just give me a call."

Hearing the loudspeaker on the porch announce a table ready for "Duvall, party of two," Ariadne turned to go. "It's nice to meet you, Diana. Maybe we can have lunch sometime soon and get better acquainted."

"I'd like that." Diana's response rang sincere.

"And I'll join you. My treat." Miles hugged and kissed Ariadne good-bye.

As she walked across the parking lot, she rued her sporadic attraction to Miles, a notorious womanizer and more like some apparition from a Harlequin romance novel than a real person. He was certainly not anyone with whom she would want to become sexually intimate, although she enjoyed his friendship.

Ellen was already in the sheriff's car but Beau was waiting beside Ariadne's Beetle. "I almost forgot to tell you," he said, "that we've finished our examination of your house, so you can return tomorrow."

"Wonderful. I want to try to get back to normal as soon as I can," Ariadne said.

"Yes, well, I thought maybe I could come over there and help you reshelve the books. That's going to be the biggest job, I think."

Ariadne definitely wanted to see him again. "Thanks, I'd like that. How about late afternoon, about four? Is that a good time for you?"

"Great. Great. That's fine. I'll be at the station working on reports, so give me a call when you're ready."

Beau touched her shoulder as he held open the door of her car. My god, Ariadne thought, as the touch sent a small jolt through her system. What's happening to me? She tried to look unaffected as she told him good-bye and then drove back into town in a muddle. What did she know about Beau? Not much, really, just what she'd read about him in the *Courier*, especially in Tilda Kent's editorials around election time, praising his honesty and integrity and reminding voters how lucky they were to have him as their county sheriff. And, if Judith was right, he was divorced.

On the corner of Tallowwood and Ash Streets, Ariadne passed Julian Baldwin returning home after a long day at Rutherford, but, engrossed in thought, each failed to notice the other. Ariadne turned north toward Judith's and Suzanne's condo, while Julian continued south toward an area strung along the highway between Cottonville and the college campus, called "Po White Trash City" by many middle-class, would-be wits. Here he and Elizabeth rented a small dingy gray clapboard house they hated, having no money to upgrade.

In her kitchen cleaning up after the children's supper, Elizabeth was thinking about the newspaper story. How could Ariadne Caulfield afford her lovely home? Rumor had it that she'd inherited money, but Julian maintained that with two salaries it was possible to buy a nice house here in a decent neighborhood. A Utopian dream, though, because they had agreed that she shouldn't work outside the home while the children were small. Besides the fact that no suitable jobs would be open to her in this area, Coowahchobee had no acceptable day care center. Just Wee Willie Winkie's in an abysmal hovel surrounded by a dirt play yard where their children would catch god knows what. Not that she wanted to settle here in this backwater burg with its dismal stretch of pinewoods anyway; on the contrary, she hoped that Julian would eventually become attractive to a Northeastern university so they could escape to a city.

From the living room came a piercing screech that sent Elizabeth flying to her children. Baby Rosalind sat on the floor, squalling in a mound of spilled Goldfish crackers, which Miranda scrambled to pick up. "Mess!" Duncan yelled above the din, happy that for once he wasn't creating the problem. Elizabeth gritted her teeth and mustered her best motherly smile as she picked up the baby and herded the other two into the kitchen, where she fetched popsicles in three different flavors, making sure that each child received his or her favorite. Hearing Julian's car pull up in the driveway, she smiled in relief. Now *he* could cope with them for a while and she could get some much-needed rest.

8

*"Let us not burthen our remembrances with
A heaviness that's gone...."*
The Tempest

ON WEDNESDAY MORNING Ariadne drove home to Tupelo Court, pleased to see that the garish yellow and black crime tape had been removed from her white gabled house and spacious yard. She avoided the side door, where the intruders had entered, choosing instead to climb the broad front steps and cross the wide veranda to the front door. Everything was in its usual place. On either side of the door, framed by long narrow windows that allowed a view of visitors, stood two clay urns containing ferns, their fronds falling downward like green fountains. Off to the right a cluster of faded green wicker furniture—a sofa and two chairs with cushions bearing a fern motif on yellowed white canvas—huddled together near a group of potted plants. Ariadne hesitated, not wanting to enter the house but knowing that she had to do it. "Okay, Cassie," she told her cat, "we're going in."

Inside the house all was quiet. Ariadne paused in the foyer to let Cassandra out of her carrier before going upstairs to dress for class, the cat following close on her heels. The master bedroom overlooked the southeast corner of the yard, now bathed in early morning sunlight, highlighting the Spanish moss that festooned the gigantic oak tree outside. Inside, the pale yellow wallpaper glowed beneath a border of ivory magnolia blossoms and deep green leaves. Cassandra leaped onto the king-sized bed and stretched out like a black Rorschach pattern in the middle of the green and gold quilted bedspread, but then whined and pawed the bed as she heard a scratching overhead. Ariadne petted her. "Just a squirrel, Cassie my dear, and out of your reach."

At that moment the phone rang. Checking the caller ID panel, to avoid newspaper reporters, Ariadne was relieved to see her son's number. "Hi, David. You're up early."

"Couldn't sleep." His tone of voice suggested anxiety. "Judith told me you might be back in the house today. How are you doing?"

"I'm much better, thanks, though still a little shaky."

"Have the police told you anything more about the murder?"

"Not much. They had to send the body over to Tallahassee for an autopsy, but I expect to hear something soon. At least I can use my reference books again."

"That's great!" David paused. "Did you get the photo I sent in the mail?"

"Oh dear, I don't know. I forgot to pick up the mail. Let me look and I'll call you back."

In the mailbox at the end of the driveway Ariadne found a large manila envelope, tore it open, and smiled at her son's somber gaze. The photograph captured the rugged handsomeness that characterized David as a heartthrob, of the sort that abounds in Hollywood. She returned inside and called him. "The photo is wonderful, looks just like you. But I prefer you smiling."

"I do look pretty serious, don't I? But I think this pose will help me get some better parts." In his early thirties, David was beginning to realize that lead roles were more often than not going to younger actors.

"It's perfect, David." She didn't like the photo much but she knew it was important to David that she try to understand.

"Mom, how are you really coping?"

"I'm coping—what's the standard phrase?—as well as can be expected. My teaching keeps me occupied. Please don't worry about me.."

"Okay, I'll try not to. Keep busy, Mom. Love you. Bye."

After she hung up the phone, Ariadne thought about her lost husband. What had first attracted her to André was his deep voice drifting over from an adjacent table during a luncheon at the annual American History Association convention. Both were graduate students at the time, he at Southern Illinois and she at Berkeley, and both were presenting papers at the conference in preparation for the job hunt facing them as soon as they completed their doctorates. Mutual friends had introduced them, and their common interest in history and current politics had drawn them together. After a courtship carried on mostly by telephone calls whenever they could afford them, they had married and moved to Florida.

She stared at several framed photographs of Venice and its lagoon hanging in the hallway. André's accident had happened the summer they had spent six weeks in Italy the first time she had taught a history course at the American International College. She had begged her husband not to take a sailboat out on the Adriatic that day, when stormy weather had been predicted, but with a laugh, pointing to the clear blue sky and bright sunshine, he had gone sailing anyway. When a sudden storm swept into the area, André's boat had capsized, leaving her a shocked and distraught widow. Only after revisiting the Lido last summer, feeling his presence and then releasing him but keeping him close to her heart, had she been fully able to enjoy life without him.

Cassandra's sudden leap down the stairs jolted Ariadne back into the present. Realizing she was keeping students waiting, she wiped her eyes and hurried to change clothes.

LATE THAT AFTERNOON Ariadne returned home from the campus, where the stress of the last couple of days had continued to weigh on her spirits. She and Judith had answered their students' questions as best they could and tried to assure them that the investigating officers were doing all they could to catch the killer.

In her kitchen Ariadne fed Cassandra a snack, poured a glass of iced tea, and took it with her into the study. The sun now slanted through the west windows, bathing the empty bookshelves in a soft melancholy glow and accenting the row of family photographs along the green marble fireplace mantel. Ariadne avoided looking that way, not wanting to see the empty space in the tool stand where the poker had hung. She began to sort the stacked books.

By 4:30 when she realized Beau wasn't coming to help her, she felt rejected. She pictured the warm smile that brightened his craggy face and the undisguised admiration she had thought she'd detected in his candid blue eyes. Get a grip, she told herself, you're not given to fantasizing and at the moment you're overtired and in no condition to judge a man's signals (if there were any) or motives. Then she remembered she had been supposed to call *him* when she returned home. Maybe he'd been waiting all this time, thinking she didn't want him to visit her. But when she tried to phone him, the patrolman on duty said that Sheriff Hammell had been called out on a case. "He left in a hurry, ma'am." Without letting me know, she thought as she replaced the receiver.

An hour later she sat at her kitchen table staring at some leftover tuna casserole she had dug out of the freezer, knowing she should eat even if she had no appetite. Cassandra stood beside her, front paws braced against her chair, hoping for a handout. "Okay, Cass, just one piece of tuna but no noodles. They aren't on a plump cat's diet." She started as the doorbell rang. At the front door she was surprised to see Beau standing in a long patch of shade offered by a pair of porch pillars. She let him in before crossing the foyer to the living room to lower the volume on John Coltrane, blaring out of the stereo, Beau following behind. "Sorry about that," she said. "I was listening to it from the kitchen."

"No problem. I like jazz." For a minute he stood nodding to the rhythm, then he gave her a rueful smile. "I owe you a couple of apologies. First, I'm really sorry to be late. I was working on some reports at the office but had to go out on a call. We're shorthanded just now. Did you get my phone message?"

"Your office told me you were out, but I forgot to check the answering machine. I'm afraid I do that far too often. My family and friends get annoyed with me when I don't pick up on their messages. So you don't owe me an apology at all." She felt awkward, like some air-headed teenager. "In fact I should apologize for not calling you right away when I returned home. I just lost track of time."

His grin rewarded her contriteness. "Doesn't matter since I couldn't have come then anyway." He picked up a couple of plastic CD covers from the stereo, scrutinized them as if they were clues to something, and put them back. Glancing around the living room, he took in the elegant long shimmery gray drapes and the black tweed sofa piled with red and silver pillows, flanked by two gray and red plaid wing chairs with matching footstools. Graceful black wooden side tables held modern versions of Tiffany lamps with multi-colored glass shades patterned in geometric shapes. He'd examined it all during their inspection of the house but now he seemed to see everything with new eyes.

Ariadne watched him. "This was André's favorite room. He selected the colors—I like yellows and greens— and ordered the lamps ...Her voice trailed off. No need to go into boring and irrelevant details.

His smile lit up his blue eyes. "A beautiful room. It reminds me to apologize for the thoughtless remark I made about your house and lifestyle."

"Please don't apologize again, Beau. I realize that the house does suggest affluence. But all this furniture is old, except for the TV. I bought this one just last year, complete with cable, though I don't have time to watch very often." She paused. "The point is, I'm far from wealthy."

"I understand that. Maybe Medina died because whoever was with him misjudged the whole scene." That seemed vague to him but he didn't want to compound his mistakes by saying something offensive again. "At least our theory about the cause of death was on target. The autopsy confirms that a blow to the head by the poker killed Medina. He was hit right behind the left ear and died instantly."

Ariadne shuddered but nodded for him to continue.

"The lab's come up with nothing on the poker except blood, a strand of hair, and bone shards, all belonging to the victim. No fingerprints, except yours. Since Medina was wearing gloves, it's probable his assailant wore them also." He paused before adding, "We're not releasing information about the murder weapon."

She was a bit disconcerted by the intensity of his look but smiled as she said, "Of course. I appreciate your confidence in me and I won't say anything about this." Judith will be furious if she finds out I hid information from her, she thought, but I can't betray his trust in me.

"I never thought you would or I wouldn't have told you as much as I have," he said.

When he offered to help reshelve the books, she led him to the study. For the next hour they sorted and stacked the various volumes at her direction until Beau had to return to duty. "I'll call you again soon," he promised as he left.

When David phoned again later, she decided that since he wasn't directly involved, it was safe to tell him what the sheriff had said.

He laughed at her report. "Mom, whoever hears of murder by poker today? It's no longer a convention in mystery novels or films."

"This murder is all too real, my love, so I guess Oscar Wilde was right. Life does occasionally imitate art, even the outdated kind."

David laughed again. "At least it wasn't a bronze statuette."

"A what?"

"Statuette, Mom. Bronze. Raymond Chandler's weapon of choice."

"Sorry, you know I don't read mysteries."

"Or watch old movies?"

"Your dad and I used to watch them. He particularly liked those with Myrna Loy and the dog. What was its name?"

"Asta, Mom. Mr. and Mrs. North's terrier."

"That's right, I remember now. By the way, I agree with your suggestion to install a home security system."

"Good. Please do it sooner rather than later. Like *tomorrow*."

"Tomorrow is another day."

David laughed. "So you *do* know some movie lore after all!"

9

"Pure chastity is rifled of her store,
And lust, the thief, far poorer than before."
The Rape of Lucrece

"O HOLY NIGHT. *O Night when Christ was born ...."*

The Rutherford College Chorus tried as best they could to hit the high notes as they practiced songs for the annual holiday concert. It was only the fifth week of classes and the event was three months away, but the singers needed all the practice they could get. Allison McEnvoy, lead singer in the soprano section, wasn't much help to them this morning because she was desperately trying to keep from vomiting. Hands clasped over her mid-section and eyes downcast, she mouthed the words but emitted no sound.

Julian Baldwin, his hands in mid-air as he coaxed the difficult song from his protégées, frowned at Allison. What was her problem? He needed her strong voice to make this succeed and regretted tackling such a demanding piece of music. Why had he chosen it? He supposed it was pride in his ability to create splendid music with an amateur chorus. Pride in the way he was able to manipulate and modulate their voices. He jerked his thoughts back to Allison and glanced in her direction, but she was still staring at the floor, her face pallid, even a bit green around her mouth. He hoped she wasn't going to be sick.

How different Allison looked now from the way she used to look, prancing into his office in sexy little knit shirts, her pert breasts offering themselves to him. When she would plop down in the blue plastic chair beside his desk, her skimpy miniskirt would ride up her thighs to reveal a provocative glimpse of virginal white panties. She'd stare straight at him with that come-hither smile of hers, asking for it, begging to be taken. And he had complied, like every other red-blooded man would have done, given that kind of temptation. Yes, he had taken her once, but only once, and never again, he promised himself, never again.

When his musing caused him to miss a beat, Mary Matthews' frown brought his attention back to the chorus but only momentarily. Maybe he'd succumbed to temptation because he'd sought relief from the tension of following the rules, unspoken but clearly implied, that demanded sterling behavior on the part of those seeking tenure in academe. Too restrictive for someone with his manly urges, he told himself, but his hands shook slightly as he thought of how this incident, if not kept secret, could ruin him.

He struggled to keep the tenors on tempo. Hell, whatever his motive and the consequences, the deed was done and now he felt desire rising again just thinking about it. He hadn't taken her in various positions as he had imagined in his sexual daydreams, but softly and tenderly as she lay beneath him, smiling and gazing innocently and admiringly into his eyes. The sopranos were now lagging behind, so he waved his graceful hands in their direction to hurry them along. Damn, what was the matter with him? Didn't he remember just as vividly the aftermath of that seduction? How Allison had wept in his arms, apparently for the loss of the virginity he had claimed, judging by the blood that had ruined Elizabeth's blue afghan. There was no way he would be able to explain that stubborn stain, so he had stuffed the afghan into a garbage bag and then into the dumpster outside Lanark Hall . As he had dabbed a tissue over Allison's swollen, tear-stained face, no longer beautiful and appealing, feelings of regret, guilt, and fear had quickly crowded out desire.

"Long lay the world, in sin and error pining ...."

He stood straighter, lifting and widening his arms in an effort to gather the disparate voices together and shaking his head to banish the memory of that fateful day. At first he had despaired, shocked by a spontaneous act that could destroy his career and family. What if Allison told her friends or her mother? There'd be hell to pay if they exposed him to college officials, who would be hard pressed to consent to his promotion and tenure on the faculty. They wouldn't even need to debate moral turpitude since non-tenured faculty members could be dismissed without cause. And what if Elizabeth discovered his infidelity? She was already discontented with their marriage and unhappy in the small Southern town, so he feared she'd leave him in an instant. Take the kids, too, if she could. Worse yet, what if Allison accused him of raping her? That was certainly not true, but how would he defend himself? She was a foxy little number but nowadays the law tended to side with the victim no matter how provocative she was. He quickly ran his hand over his forehead, wiping off beads of sweat.

He took a deep breath to steady his nerves. He tried to convince himself that he had fully repented his carnal act, regarding it as the indiscretion of a contrite married man who deeply loved his wife and their three children, one still in diapers. If and when Allison ever tempted him again, he would tell her that their act of passion was a breach of his marriage and there couldn't be any second encounter. But over the past weeks nothing had happened to make him think his secret was exposed. Allison had avoided him, except for continued attendance in his music appreciation class, where she sat in the back of the room, head down, taking notes and leaving as soon as the bell rang. And she continued to sing in the chorus, coming and going hand in hand with her boyfriend Jason, to whom she had obviously confessed nothing.

Julian turned his attention to the chorus as they grappled with the hymn. *"O night divine!"* Everyone's attention was riveted by Ginny Gilsmith's earsplitting attempt to hit the high note.

Just then Allison felt her breakfast begin to creep up her esophagus. She fled from the rehearsal room across the hall into the women's restroom, where she vomited the half-digested remains of toast and jelly into the toilet.

Mary Matthews had followed her. "Hey! Are you okay?" she asked.

"I …I'm fine." Allison stood up and covered her mouth with a wad of toilet paper as she emerged from the toilet stall. "Really, it's just something I ate. I'll be better in a minute."

"What did you eat? It could be, like, food poisoning. You should go to the clinic."

Allison's knees began to buckle as she caught a glimpse of her pale, drawn face in the wavy mirror above the sink. When Mary reached out to steady her, Allison slumped into her arms and began sobbing.

"Please don't cry, Allison. You'll be all right." Mary patted her back and stroked her hair.

"I'll never be all right again!" Allison choked on a hiccup as she pulled her head away and tried desperately to stop crying. "Never again!"

"I'm sure it can't be that bad. Are you sick?" Mary held onto her friend's arm to steady her.

Allison's voice dropped to a whisper. "It's worse than that. I'm …I'm …p-p-p-pregnant."

"What?" Mary's astonishment was real. "But we agreed to remain virgins until we married. I mean, we, like, took that oath and all! Why did you and Jason—?"

"It wasn't Jason." Allison shook her head. "It was somebody else."

"Who?" Outrage raised Mary's voice a decibel. "Were you raped?"

"No, no, not that." Allison put two fingers over Mary's lips. "Not so loud, someone might hear you."

Like two does in the forest, both young women raised their heads to listen, but all they could hear, faintly from across the hall, were the singers' desperate attempts to master the hymn's impossible crescendo.

"I have to get out of here. See you later." Allison headed for the restroom door. She didn't want to discuss the matter any further for fear Professor Baldwin's name might slip out. She trusted her friend with most of her secrets, but this one was too enormous and would be too shocking for Mary to bear in silence. Before she and Professor Baldwin had …had …Allison didn't even want to think the words. She would have been surprised and shocked, too, if another student had told her she'd had sex (those were the words) with a professor. Professor Baldwin was the only one who could help her, so she'd have to tell him about being pregnant even if he'd be furious. Fearing discovery as the chorus finished rehearsal, she ran out of the classroom building and headed for her room in Doheny Hall.

On the way there, Mary caught up with her and asked, "Are you sure you're pregnant? Have you used a pregnancy test kit?"

"No way," Allison replied, "I'm afraid that if I go to a drugstore to buy one, someone from Rutherford might see me and that would spread all over campus. Someone in authority might call my mother. You know she wouldn't be able to handle it. I couldn't go home. But I might even get expelled!" Allision broke down again, sobbing as she began running toward the dorm.

"Gosh, Allison," Mary shouted, trying to keep up with her her. "You should at least find out for sure if you're actually pregnant."

"I can't," Allison cried. "No one can help me. Please don't tell anyone about this. Just leave me alone!!"

Once in the privacy of her room she peeled off her clothes, flung them on a pile of dirty laundry, and pulled on a white cotton nightgown. Pushing aside the top bed sheet and blanket, she lay down gently so as not to induce the nausea again.

How was she supposed to finish school now that this had happened to her? And how had it happened? One brief encounter, just a few minutes one afternoon on the couch in Professor Baldwin's office. Not that she had been thinking about sex at all when she went to talk to him about her grade in Music Appreciation, a course she had hoped to ace. But when she made a D on the first unit test, she realized that differentiating Brahms from Mozart or Haydn on an exam wasn't as easy as she'd thought it would be. She needed at least a B to keep her grade point average up and so she had sought out Professor Baldwin after his scheduled office hours, when there was less chance of meeting other students. She took pride in being a good student and was ashamed to have anyone know her grade was suffering. If her friends found out her reason for seeing him outside of class, they would tease her unmercifully about sucking up to a professor.

For a while they had discussed how she needed to develop better study habits and spend more time listening to the tapes he'd provided in the library. But then Professor Baldwin had come over to her, placing his hands on her shoulders, massaging them gently. When she arched her back in response, he slid his long fingers under her shirt and bra, where he cupped them around her breasts ("marvelous" he had whispered), rising and falling from the deep breaths she was taking to keep herself calm. For a moment he had caressed her as if testing her response. Then he had locked the door and after leading her to that ugly brown sofa and easing her onto the soft fuzzy blue afghan, he had edged himself down beside her.

Before this she had never yielded to the advances of the high school boys who had tried to fondle her in return for buying her a hamburger and a coke after school or the college guys who had treated her to movies and dinners in hopes of acquiring sexual favors. Although she relished male attention, she believed that guys dated just to get the sex they craved, an interpretation supported by her mother's fears and insistent reminders that sexual intercourse must be reserved for marriage. Only then, her mother had insisted, was it sanctioned by the church and by God himself. And Allison had up to now honored the abstinence oath she had taken at Wakulla Springs, along with Jason, who seemed even less interested in sex than she was. But Professor Baldwin's touch had undone her. The passion, gradually coaxed from her body by his finger strokes, had swept her away, especially when he had begun kissing her breasts. She had been amazed at the way her nipples had stiffened, sending ripples of excitement through her body, which intensified as he slipped off her underpants and positioned himself above her.

But then she tensed as he began pushing into her, hurting her. He just kept thrusting and thrusting and she was pushing on him and trying to say "stop," but he held his hand over her mouth and she knew she couldn't cry out because someone might hear and discover them.

Afterwards she had cried, quietly of course, so as not to alert anyone. At first he had been upset by her blood on his blue afghan. "She'll *kill* me," Allison thought she heard him mutter, as he pulled it out from under her, but she was too focused on her own predicament to bother about his. And then he was suddenly tender, holding her close until her sobs subsided, kissing her tear-stained face and stroking her matted, tangled hair. But she couldn't recapture the romantic feeling she had had before …before he …before they. …She couldn't put it in words. Except one that popped into her head out of the blue, one she had copied down from a lecture on Metaphysical poetry: "ravished." Before he had ravished her.

Reliving the experience seemed to quiet her anxiety and she lay still, drained and exhausted. With her spun-gold hair billowing out on the pillow and her small white hands crossed over her midriff, she resembled a Botticelli angel or a blonde Rossetti Ophelia floating down the river to oblivion.

10

ARIADNE LAY ON THE WHITE sugar sands of St. George Island, stretching her lean body out into the Gulf of Mexico, letting the warm ebbing and flowing waves wash over her, her eyes half closed behind green sunglasses. Stressed out after weeks of classes with hyper nervous students, she was exhausted. Out beyond the sandbar several students cavorted on plastic rafts, their distant laughter and bantering only occasionally penetrating her consciousness. She and Judith had organized this celebration of the rising of the spirit that haunts the Gulf in *The Awakening* for their combined class, but Ariadne was neglecting her duty in favor of being lulled into a blissful stupor by the soft plashing of the tepid water. She knew she ought to get up and refresh her sunscreen if she didn't want to get burnt by the late-afternoon sun, still blazing hot this time of year, but she was too lazy to move.

"What's this? A beached mermaid?" Miles's booming voice jerked her awake. "Why are you frying yourself to a crisp, Ariadne? Floridians have one of the highest rates of skin cancer in the nation."

When Ariadne stood up to greet him, Miles enveloped her in a hug from which she pulled away as quickly as possible. She wasn't altogether surprised to see him here because she knew he owned a house on the island, though she'd never been there. Whenever he'd invited her to join him for a day at the beach, she'd always turned him down, realizing that the romantic and isolated setting would only encourage his unwanted sexual advances. Stepping back, she noticed the tall, attractive woman behind him, Diana Macomb, dressed in a white bikini and a bright coral pāreu, wet from wading so that it clung to her slim legs. A tan straw hat with a floppy brim protected her glossy black hair and creamy complexion.

"Hi, Diana. Good to see you again."

"Thank you, you too." Diana's voice was as cool as her touch when they shook hands. Miles hugged both women close to him.

"Picnic time!" Judith's voice carried across the beach from the small cinder-block house she had rented for the weekend.

Ariadne extricated herself from Miles's arm. "Would you like to join us? There's plenty of food."

Diana hesitated, but Miles accepted immediately, as if he'd been waiting for her to invite them. They walked in unison across the sand, Miles cupping his hands under the women's elbows, although neither needed assistance. Shouting and laughing, the students splashed their way out of the water, surrounded the trio, and moved with them to a long wooden deck above the beach. There they all admired the table setting Judith and Suzanne had arranged to replicate Edna Pontellier's pigeon-house dinner party in *The Awakening*, which, as Judith had admitted to Ariadne, appeared much later in the book than the swimming evening. "But I guess Chopin won't mind if we combine scenes."

An assortment of deck chairs stood around a long picnic table covered with a yellow bed sheet to simulate Edna's satin tablecloth, adorned with strips of white crepe paper cut to resemble lace. Thick yellow candles marched up the center of the table in matching plastic holders meant to suggest Edna's brass candlesticks. Two clear plastic vases, the kind left over from florists' deliveries, held bouquets of orange and red lantana from Ariadne's yard, hinting at the red and yellow roses amassed on Edna's table. The overall effect, they all agreed, was charming. Judith and Suzanne beamed at their compliments.

"Not Chopin's opulence," Judith said, "but this kind of pastiche is an *homage* to her genius and creativity, even if it's not precise in its imitation."

Mary Matthews bounced over to Miles and Diana. "Hi Mr. Duvall and Ms. Macomb. I didn't know you'd be here." Her Raggedy Anne curls gleamed in the sun. "I work for these two now," she said to the others, "part-time in the law office. I run errands and file things and, like, do anything they want me to do."

She chattered on while Ariadne went inside to change clothes. When she returned, Miles seated her and Diana with exaggerated gallantry across the table from one another, and then eased down between them at the foot. Judith, Suzanne and several students joined them and soon everyone was happily eating hot dogs, ribs, potato salad, pickles, coleslaw, and chocolate chip cookies, washed down with lemonade.

At the other end of the table Jonathan Kennedy began arguing with a couple of women students about *The Awakening*. "It's decidedly *not* a feminist book but a novel about failed idealism in that Edna Pontellier wanted some impossible dream, one that she couldn't achieve and couldn't even articulate."

Trying to ignore him, the students busied themselves with passing food around the table.

"As is true of most women," he sneered as he leaned over toward Natalie Highfield, who scowled at him.

From across the table Alicia Maynor raised her voice to get his attention as she repeated a point Judith had made in class. "Edna had no chance to articulate her desires, given the social power of the Creole mother-women, who would have ostracized her if she'd spoken out." She and Natalie picked up their plates and glasses and moved to chaise lounges at the other end of the porch, where Allison McEnvoy and Mary joined them.

"Bitches," Jonathan muttered under his breath as he carried his chair around the table and wedged into a space next to Ariadne.

"So, is *The Awakening* a feminist book?" Miles asked the women with a wide grin.

"As I tell the students," Ariadne replied, "feminism is a lens that enables us to look at the world from the perspective of gender, race, and class issues."

"Exactly." Judith smiled at her as she said to Jonathan, "Thus a book may not be a feminist novel per se, but we can read and understand it now in terms of feminism and cultural studies in general."

Miles popped a piece of hot dog into his mouth. "Well, I haven't read the book but I'm enjoying your *homage* to it."

Turning toward Diana, Suzanne smiled. "You're from the South, aren't you? I like your accent."

"Thanks. Many people find a Southern accent irritating and indicative of stupidity. I'm from Marietta, Georgia, just outside Atlanta."

"But I discovered her working as a legal secretary at a friend's law firm in Baltimore," Miles said.

"And I asked to come here when I heard about the place from Miles," Diana added. "Baltimore is becoming unlivable, congested and polluted, like every other American city." As she spoke, Diana stared past a row of swaying sea oats out toward the Gulf. Her dark eyes seemed focused elsewhere and a slight frown creased her forehead. Then she abruptly excused herself and joined Alicia, Natalie, Allison, and Mary, who, impressed by her beauty and style, welcomed her eagerly. After a minute or two, Allison left the group to walk the beach. Diana looked as if she wanted to follow her but was held captive by Mary's animated chatter.

Miles consulted his watch. "Sorry to break up this delightful soirée, but it's time for us to go." He thanked Judith and Suzanne profusely for the food and repartee as he blew a kiss in Ariadne's direction. "Diana and I have to get back to work. We're preparing a case we have coming up in court a few weeks from now, and we haven't been together long, so we need time to establish a working relationship."

Ariadne thought that might not be the only kind he was aiming for but she smiled politely as Miles went to collect Diana. As the students scattered onto the beach, Judith and Suzanne joined Ariadne at the rail to admire the sun as it edged down into the Gulf, tingeing with gold the rosy pink clouds on the horizon. Judith lit a cigarette and blew a stream of smoke into the breeze. "Penny for your thoughts, Ari."

"I was thinking about Diana. She's quite lovely, isn't she? And intelligent."

"Just the type Miles likes, I suspect, present company *not* excepted." Judith's remark elicited only a small smile from Ariadne. "Aren't you even a bit jealous? That bikini top leaves nothing to the imagination and she and Miles seem pretty chummy."

"Typical Miles. Don Juan personified. I might be jealous if there were anything significant between us, but there isn't." Ariadne gazed out at the horizon between sky and sea, where the sun was just now settling into a golden pool.

"Diana is a looker but don't you find her strange in a way?" Judith continued.

"What way?"

"She seems sad, despondent even."

"That's maybe overstating it. Your interpretation is most likely affected by all that talk about *The Awakening*." Ariadne thought for a moment. "But I agree that she did seem distracted. Maybe just her discomfort being with academics talking shop."

"Hmmm. You could be right. And I admit I'm preoccupied with Edna Pontellier tonight. Still, something about Diana wasn't quite right. A hint of desperation in her manner?" Judith began to tuck her errant curly hair back into a ponytail. "I'm going to clear away the supper mess. You look tired. Why don't you go on inside and have a nap and I'll wake you when we're ready for the midnight swim."

"I'll help you," Suzanne said, wanting time alone with Judith. Ariadne felt a twinge of guilt for not having helped more, but realizing that she was suddenly very tired, she thanked them and agreed to rest awhile.

Out on the beach Mary strolled with Allison, who seemed wrapped in her own thoughts, occasionally kicking up blobs of sand. "Ms. Macomb is, like, a really neat woman, isn't she," Mary chattered, "very friendly and talkative. She wanted to know everything about me and my friends, especially about you and me, Allison, because she knows you are my best friend. I told her—"

Allison interrupted, glaring at Mary. "Why did she want to know about us? Why are we important to her? She doesn't even know me and I don't want to know her. You shouldn't tell her anything about me. Not *anything*."

Mary looked at Allison's frowning face, knowing she was afraid her secret would be exposed. But she hadn't told anyone about it and had promised she wouldn't. Now she'd have to try again to make up with Allison. She wished her friend would talk about her pregnancy, but Allison refused to discuss it.

Thanking Judith and Suzanne again for cleaning up, Ariadne went inside to the tiny bedroom she had claimed for herself, leaving the larger one for her friends. The students had brought sleeping bags for the deck or small tents for the beach. Her head was beginning to ache from too much sun and too many dark memories. She stood for a moment in front of the long wavy mirror mounted on the closet door, stretching out her arms and turning one way and then the other. Thanks to her devotion to daily walking, plus some lifting with David's old weights, her body was still firm. She pulled back the coverlet on one of the twin beds and lay down on the cool white sheets. As she listened to the ceiling fan droning overhead and to the muffled voices of the students who were helping their professors gather up the remains of the meal, she drifted into a sound sleep. Later, when Judith came to wake her, she was dreaming about throwing oranges at a group of people, Miles among them. The students' voices were louder now, just outside her window.

"Wake up, Sleeping Beauty!" Judith tossed Ariadne's bathing suit onto the bed. "We're off for our midnight swim in the moonlight, hoping to be the Gulf spirit's choice for semi-celestialhood."

"It's midnight? I feel as if I've slept a hundred years. Go on ahead and I'll join you as soon as I change." Moments later she heard laughter and shouting as the others ran to the beach and into the water.

When she was in her suit she followed them across the sand, stopping at the water's edge beside Jonathan, who sat hunched over, his sinuous body a pale white specter in the bright moonlight. "Aren't you going in with us?" she asked him.

"It's ridiculous to swim in that water, given the fact that the Gulf is notorious for treacherous undertows and teems with dangerous creatures. Sting rays and barracuda abound and encountering a shark is also a distinct possibility." Jonathan's pedantic response seemed tinged with defensiveness.

"I'm sure it's all right or Professor Sheridan wouldn't allow the students to swim here."

"Well, I prefer not to subject myself to the hazards of the deep." Jonathan turned away, not wanting to admit that he didn't swim well enough to brave the Gulf at night.

Ariadne waded out beyond the sandbar and then plunged into the warm water, swimming with a vigorous freestyle. Feeling confident and exhilarated and determined to test her skill by swimming out as far as she could, she headed toward the horizon. The golden moonlight highlighted the waves, ruffled by soft breezes, and she followed its trail into the deeper water. Then, as she began to tire, her attempt to go farther seemed to her more foolhardy than intrepid.

Turning toward the shore, she saw that she wasn't very far out, just beyond the sandbar, but drifting away from where she had entered the water. She made an effort to swim back, following the shoreline, but her arms and legs felt heavy and unresponsive. Off to her left she could hear the faint voices of the other swimmers, their bobbing heads dark against the moonlit water. For a moment she panicked and flailed about, choking and coughing as she inhaled a mouthful of brine. So this is the way it feels to drown, said a voice in her head as she desperately fought the current. She went limp, suddenly exhausted with her efforts.

In the next moment she was relieved to realize that the salty seawater was buoying her up, so she shifted over onto her back and floated, letting the current carry her down along the sandbank and into shallower water near the shore. She lay there in the white foam, pushed to and fro by the waves breaking on the beach, until she could muster enough energy to roll over and stand up. Orienting herself by the moon's glimmering path, she walked back through the shallows, weaving and panting a bit from exertion until she returned to the spot where she had begun. She accepted a towel from Jonathan, who had apparently found his niche as a cabana boy, and sat down on the sand beside him.

"I was afraid I might drown out there."

Jonathan was not sympathetic. "You weren't very far out, you know. Probably just ten feet beyond the sandbar, by my calculations, where you should have rested instead of panicking like you did. Besides, I was observing you the whole time."

Fat lot of good you would have done me, she wanted to reply, suspecting that he couldn't swim well enough to save anyone from drowning, but she refrained from insulting him.

"Thanks." She smiled. "I appreciate your vigilance."

Jonathan cleared his throat as he leaned toward her, a bit too close for her comfort. "Professor, I've been meaning to inquire about the investigation into Randall Medina's murder. I thought you might be coaxed into imparting information you have acquired from the sheriff."

Ariadne stood up. "I have no information but I'm sure the details of the investigation will be made public as soon as the sheriff's office decides to reveal them." Wrapping the beach towel around her, she started for the house, Jonathan striding beside her, lifting his stork-like legs and thin feet carefully to avoid sand spurs and crabs.

"Students can't be trusted," he said. "I venture to say that not one of us has an air-tight alibi for that dreadful night. Those officers interviewed several of us again, so I know they regard us as suspects, but some of us are more likely to have been involved than others." He paused to assess her reaction; when none was forthcoming, he continued, "Taciturn Lyman, for instance, undoubtedly knows more than he's admitting, though it's hard to fathom his thoughts. If he has any worth considering."

Ariadne walked a little faster, trying to ignore him but annoyed with herself for continuing to listen.

Jonathan picked up the pace. "And poor hopeless Jason, never having enough money for school or family. I cannot fathom what the beauteous Allison sees in that loser."

Aha, thought Ariadne. Could it be that Jonathan was a rejected admirer?

They climbed the stairs to the deck, where the moonlight highlighted the yellow table cover, flowers, and burned-out candles. Jonathan leaned against the deck rail. "Of course, we have to entertain the preposterous idea that one of our esteemed professors may have been the perpetrator of the dastardly deed. Professor Baldwin, perhaps? Or would he not jeopardize his tenure possibility by participating in a burglary? Professor Bannerman, then. He's a likely choice for thief and murderer, given his past record of violent behavior." Jonathan's smirk suggested his pleasure in having disconcerted her. "Surely you know about his dating students and his bout of fisticuffs with a grad student at Southeastern? It's common gossip around campus."

"I really don't pay attention to gossip, Jonathan."

"Of course not, Professor, why would you? However, I assume you're desirous of discovering the identity of the evil home invader and murderer, especially since he …"

Jonathan paused and closed his pale eyelids, simulating deep thought, then opened them wide as if a brilliant idea had struck him. "...or *she*? You know, a person presumably needs only a modicum of strength to bash someone's head in. Particularly if Randall were not anticipating violence from his cohort. And if his partner in crime were a woman, then he most likely would not have foreseen a lethal blow."

"Almost everyone's a suspect, Jonathan. But I think we should leave the sleuthing to the authorities. Excuse me now, I'm going inside." Without a backward glance she went into the bedroom to change into dry clothes.

When she returned to the deck, Jonathan was gone. She stretched out in a hammock set on a metal stand, basking in the moonlight until its beauty restored her good mood. In a few minutes she waved to Judith, Suzanne, and the students returning from the sea, arguing and teasing one another about whose swimming feats had pleased the Gulf spirit the most. The students changed clothes and then dispersed in various directions into tents and sleeping bags. Suzanne and Judith hugged Ariadne good night and then they went inside, leaving her to her thoughts. Much later, as the moon began to drift toward the horizon and mosquitoes began to bite, Ariadne went to her own room and slipped into bed, soon lulled to sleep by the muffled rumbling of endless waves falling on the shore.

11

ON THE MONDAY MORNING following the beach weekend Ariadne headed for the fitness center, seeking the endorphin high she needed before a full day of classes and student conferences. In a strip mall on the highway the small cinder block building housing Exercise for You snuggled between a dry cleaner and a Hogly Wogly convenience store. The gym manager, Lance Crowley, a former student, greeted her warmly. "Morning, Professor. Not many people in today so you'll have peace and quiet. I'll bet you're still stressed out from that horrible crime. Nothing like exercise to relieve that!"

Ariadne selected a stationary bike, setting it for half an hour at a reasonable pace with a series of hills as an added challenge. Soon she was absorbed in peddling to the cool jazz Lance had obligingly put on the audio system. A couple of other patrons ignored her, lost in their own exercise routines, but soon a tall woman in green biking shorts and a sports bra, her hair pulled back into a ponytail, sat down on the bike next to her. "Hello, Ariadne, having a good workout?"

"Diana, hi, nice to see you again."

They exchanged a few more pleasantries and then concentrated on their pacing. Diana pedaled furiously as if heading for some imaginary finish line. Her fair skin was soon flushed from exertion and she began emitting soft moans. All right, Ariadne thought, I can push myself a bit harder too, and she stepped up her pace.

"Ouch!" Diana groaned and clutched a calf muscle.

"Are you all right?" Ariadne asked.

Diana climbed down and began flexing her leg. "Cramp." She clenched her teeth in pain.

Lance rushed to her side. "What happened? Are you hurt?" His worst fear was that customers might injure themselves and blame the equipment or, worse yet, sue the center.

"I'm fine now, it was just a cramp." Diana climbed back on the bike.

"Maybe you should take a break." Lance's anxiety was evident in his voice.

"I was pushing with my secondaries, not my quads, which I should have been using." Diana's explanation seemed to reassure Lance that she knew what she was doing, so he retreated into his tiny office behind the front desk.

The women resumed their exercise, propelled by a Fats Waller rendition of "I Ain't Got Nobody" from one of Lance's prized jazz CDs. After another ten minutes Ariadne slowed down when she too began to feel leg cramps. Time to stop, she thought, no sense in overdoing it. As she dismounted, she dismissed as extreme wishful thinking a vision of herself laid up with a leg injury, unable to attend the faculty meeting.

Seeing Diana slumped on her bike seat, clutching her towel to her chest, Ariadne stepped over to her. "Can I help?"

As Ariadne reached out to touch her shoulder, Diana looked up, shook her head, but suddenly began to sob into her towel.

Ariadne helped her off the bike and led her to a battered sofa in the far corner, removing a couple of fitness magazines to the low table beside it. She waited until Diana composed herself. "Would it help to talk about it?"

Diana shook her head again but apparently reconsidered as she gazed into Ariadne's friendly hazel eyes. "You remind me of my mother." In response to Ariadne's smile, the floodgates opened. "She was blonde too, but with sky blue eyes. I always wanted to look like her but I inherited my dad's dark hair and eyes. Mom always said I was a good baby, too, cheerful and obedient. We were a happy family then. In fact my childhood was *idyllic*. My mother played with me all day long, read to me and would lie beside me until I fell asleep." Diana frowned and shook her head. "Then she died. Killed in a car accident when I was twelve. She slid through a stop sign at a highway crossing and was smashed by a semi. Never had a chance. She died on impact. Today is the anniversary of her death." Diana buried her face in her towel.

A shocked Ariadne could think of nothing appropriate to say. All she could do was to offer Diana a bottle of water. "Here, drink some of this."

Diana ignored the offer as she raised her head and stared into space. "I was devastated. I felt guilty because I had refused to go grocery shopping with her that day. It was Saturday and I wanted to hang out with a girl who lived next door. When Mom asked me to go to the store with her to carry the bags, I had a tantrum and ran to my friend's house." Tears gathered in Diana's eyes. "If I'd gone with her I might have made her stop at the crossing and she'd have lived. Or we both would have been killed in the crash. At the time I wished I were dead, too. Sometimes I still do."

Ariadne felt overwhelmed, though she had in the past dealt with potentially suicidal students, usually by sending them to one of her colleagues in psychology. "Perhaps you need to talk to a therapist. I can recommend one."

Diana's response, a throaty gurgle, might have been either a laugh or a sob. "Don't think I haven't talked to therapists! Dad sent me to several after Mom died, but they didn't help much. Even later, when I tried again, I couldn't face my guilt or come to terms with his remarriage. The very next year he hitched up with Alice, an air-headed file clerk from his office. Soft and plump and blonde, too, like Mom, but neither gentle nor loving. Oh, she pretended to be, when Dad was around, but when we were alone, she was mean. I hated her." She began twisting her towel in her hands. "In all fairness, though, I was a pain in the butt at that age. I tried to hide my anger because I wanted money from Dad, lots of it, to run away. I didn't wait for his money, though, because I left sooner than I had planned. I had a bank account with some money saved up over the years, mostly gifts from my grandparents, so I emptied it and ran away when their baby was born the next year. Another girl for my dad to love instead of me. A baby, soft and cuddly. Not hard and ugly like I'd become."

Diana suddenly focused on Ariadne, as if seeing her for the first time. "Sorry, I shouldn't have said all this." She stood up and frowned, her dark eyes glittering. "Don't repeat anything I said to anyone. Do you hear me? Not to *anyone*." She turned and headed for the door, pushing past a group of laughing coeds loaded down with gym bags and water bottles.

"Of course I won't ..."

But Diana was gone.

Lance emerged from his office. "Is everything all right, Professor?"

"Everything's fine." Ariadne struggled to keep her voice even. "See you again soon."

As she drove home Ariadne wondered what to do next. She ruled out telling Miles anything about Diana's condition or story, but she thought she might try to help the poor woman if Diana would accept her offer.

12

SERGEANT ELLEN NOLLE sat in her office staring at the stack of papers on her desk, the squeaky ceiling fan barely moving the stale air around her. The county sheriff's department shared a crowded one-story building with the city police department on the corner of Fritillary Street and Hyacinth Way, near the County Courthouse. The officers desperately needed more space, but so far the city and county commissions had found other projects to fund with their meager tax revenues, while promising to renovate as soon as possible.

When Ellen had first been hired on the Coowahchobee police force ten years before, after earning a degree in Criminal Justice from Georgia State University, she had thought of it as a temporary position. She would learn the practical side of law enforcement here, she decided, and then move on to a larger city force. But gradually she had adjusted to the slow rhythms of small-town life. Her marriage to Darnell Nolle, who owned his own insurance business just up the street, had been one reason for her contented adjustment. The other was the satisfying routines of police work she found here, especially when teamed up with Sheriff Hammell, a man she had come to like and trust.

She was only five feet, six inches tall, but because she carried herself well, she appeared taller. Except when she stood beside Beau, who dwarfed her. Mutt and Jeff, some of the other officers called them, but never to their faces. Her thick black hair was cut short around her ears, in which she always wore the gold stud earrings Darnell had given her on their wedding day. Her dark skin was smooth except for tiny wrinkles that formed in the corners of her widely spaced black eyes when she laughed.

The front glass door swung open and the sheriff entered, letting in a blast of warm, muggy air. In the reception area he greeted Darlene Mapes, the officer on desk duty, then retrieved two small bottles of water from the tiny refrigerator in the corner and gulped one down. After grabbing a wet paper towel from the restroom, he crossed over to Ellen's office and plopped into a chair beside her desk. He handed her the other bottle, laid the towel over his forehead, and sighed. "It's already a scorcher out there. Three days with no rain and the temperatures soaring into the high nineties."

"Not unusual for September, Beau. How long have you lived in North Florida?" A teasing question, because she knew he'd been born on the Gulf coast, gone to school in Tallahassee, married his high-school sweetheart, and settled down in Coowahchobee. Years ago his wife had divorced him and left town. He rarely mentioned her anymore.

"Doesn't everybody grouse about the weather?" He knew that Ellen never did. She didn't complain about anything else either. He was lucky she'd stayed in Coowahchobee, although she'd had very tempting offers elsewhere. "How was the night shift? Anything happen I should know about?"

She straightened up in her swivel chair and rubbed a finger over her left eyelid, which was beginning to twitch from long hours of reading. "Just the usual. Mrs. Mosley called around one o'clock to report her husband Tom missing. I sent a patrolman to haul him out of Roger's Roadhouse and take him home. You know how Tom used to do that only on weekends, but I guess now that the lumber company laid him off, he'll be spending more time with his rowdy friends at the bar."

Beau shifted to the Medina murder. "I read the reports Mike and Dale wrote up on their door-to-door interviews in Ariadne's neighborhood. No one seems to have heard or seen anyone that night, but I guess that's not surprising seeing how late it was."

"They asked specifically about cars driving in or out of the cul-de-sac but no one remembers hearing any. It's possible that the intruders drove in quietly with no headlights, but they may also have arrived on foot. Maybe through the woods in the vacant lot next door or behind her house. We checked the perimeter of the yard very carefully but found no footprints."

"What about your talks with the Rutherford faculty and students we hadn't interviewed earlier? Learn anything new?"

"Only that nobody did or saw anything and didn't know the victim well."

Beau laughed. "That college campus is a closed community, isn't it? But we knew that already. Either nobody knows anything about Medina and his friends or nobody's telling us. What did you find out at Southwestern?"

"Not much. None of the graduate students liked Medina a whole lot. One said he was arrogant and had a violent temper when crossed." Beau pulled a small green notebook from his shirt pocket. "Macdonald Hastings, a professor in the English Department, said he knew nothing about Medina's private life, but he was a serious student who wrote a fine thesis on Byron's Italian connections."

"What were those?"

Beau grinned. "I didn't ask. Didn't seem relevant. Maybe I'll ask Ariadne about it." He avoided Ellen's eyes by focusing on his notes. "Hastings also mentioned that he'd loaned Medina money a time or two and that he always seemed to be in need."

Ellen pressed her half-empty water bottle to one temple and then the other, seeking whatever coolness remained in it. "His parents in Blountstown told me they wanted to help him out but they're barely making it." She consulted her notebook. "Randall went to community college, then got a scholarship and finished up at Florida State, with some help from an uncle who owns a trucking business over in Jacksonville. The uncle died of cancer the day Randall graduated and his widow moved up North, so that source of income stopped suddenly. One of Randall's professors helped him get a teaching assistantship at Southwestern when a graduate student applicant turned them down at the last minute. But those assistantships are minimal wage, and Randall didn't make much more at Rutherford, which helps explain why he'd resort to burglary.

"His parents had no idea who his partners-in-crime might have been. The Rutherford students from Blountstown knew Randall but of course they aren't admitting to any criminal activity with him." Ellen flipped over a notebook page. "When I asked Randall's mother about the guys we interviewed, she said that Lyman Litchgate and Jason Overstreet were always trailing after Randall when they were 'young uns,' as she put it, but Randall never talked about them after he left home. Apparently he never told his parents much about anything. In fact, they rarely saw him."

"That tallies with what Jason and Lyman told us about their contacts with Randall when they were kids," Beau said. "Jason mentioned recent encounters with him at Rutherford, but Lyman denied seeing him there. I wonder if he's hiding something."

Ellen raised her large dark eyes upward, conveying her annoyance at secretive suspects in general and Lyman in particular.

Leaving Ellen to her paperwork, Beau went to his office to eat his lunch, an apple and a baloney sandwich on white bread with mayonnaise, his favorite since childhood when his mother had prepared it for him every other day, alternating with peanut butter and tupelo honey.

He was just savoring a chocolate chip cookie when a call came from one of Ariadne's neighbors, Sam Johnson. "We left home Sunday, Sheriff, and just got back. Heard your officers were asking the neighbors if they seen anyone around here Saturday night. I gotta tell you I seen Elias Eppersley, that young man who takes care of Miz Caulfield's yard, drive up in his red truck around midnight. He got out and snooped around on her porch a bit. Don't know if he came back later but he might have."

Beau asked him a few questions, assured him they'd check it out, and thanked him for calling. Then he sat for a moment, thinking. Did he know this Elias? Must be the son of Enos Eppersley, who died some years ago in a hunting accident. He vaguely remembered the boy holding his sobbing mother when they'd gone to the house to tell the family. Hadn't been in any trouble that he knew about. But he and Ellen would have to talk to him. Before that, though, they should find out more about him. Maybe ask Ariadne for information? Invite her to lunch? But take Ellen along because …he hated to admit it, but he was nervous about having lunch alone with Ariadne. He felt like an adolescent trying to get up nerve enough to call a girl for a date. Just keep it professional, he told himself, but he knew he didn't want to do that. His fingers separated themselves from his brain and dialed the number.

"Hello." Her cool voice thrilled him. "Hello?"

He struggled to speak. "Hi Ariadne. Beau here. How are you?"

"Hi, it's good to hear your voice. I'm fine. Teaching every day has kept me so preoccupied I haven't had time to think much about the murder." She was surprised to find herself saying the word without choking on it. "How's your investigation coming?"

"We're making it a priority." He thought for a moment. Maybe he should just leave well enough alone? No. "In fact we've found a new bit of information I wanted to ask you about."

"Wonderful. I'm glad you're making progress. What is it?"

"I don't want to discuss it on the phone," he said. "Could you meet Ellen and me for lunch today?"

"Of course, I'd be happy to."

"Great. The Blue Cat around noon?"

"Fine. See you then."

Beau hung up grinning. Mission accomplished.

PROMPTLY AT NOON Ariadne parked her car on Courthouse Square and went into the café, where discordant chatter rose from the cheerful crowd gathered around small metal tables, crowded into booths, and lined up on stools at the lunch counter. Above them the ceiling fans struggled to move the tepid air, marginally cooled by the two window air-conditioning units. Removing her sunglasses Ariadne spotted the sheriff waving at her from a booth in the back, where he sat with Ellen.

"Hi Ariadne. Glad you could join us." Beau rose to greet her with a handshake and a wide smile.

Ellen slid across the red plastic seat to make room beside her. "How are you? Not so stressed anymore?"

Ariadne sat down and smoothed out the skirt of her yellow seersucker sundress. "I'm much better, thanks."

A skinny waitress with "Sheryl" on her name tag brought glasses of water to their table, took their orders, and hurried off to the kitchen. While they waited for their food, they chatted about Ariadne's teaching, the weather, and local news that didn't involve the murder. Clearly, Ariadne thought, they're trying to put me at ease. But what do they want?

Sheryl returned with three glasses of iced tea, salads for Ellen and Ariadne, and a large hamburger with fries for Beau. He saluted Ariadne with his glass and exaggerated his Southern accent. "To the Nawtheners among us." He wanted to say something about Northerners being sweet, too, and kind, and beautiful, but couldn't think of any clever or subtle way to do it. He didn't want to offend Ariadne or to risk any teasing from Ellen by signaling a romantic interest. Not that she didn't suspect as much already.

Instead he decided to cut to the chase. "We're still trying to make connections between Medina and people he knew. We think whoever killed him was someone involved with him in burglaries. So far, though, no one's talking straight to us. It's exasperating."

Ariadne dipped pieces of lettuce into the small cup of oil and vinegar dressing beside her plate. "I guess I could contact the students and faculty you suspect. Someone might be more willing to talk to me than to law officers. Maybe in conversation someone would let something slip."

Ellen frowned. "I don't think that's a good idea. It's too dangerous. Right now whoever killed Medina may not think you're a threat to them because you weren't home at the time. But if you start snooping around, they might get suspicious and come after you."

Ariadne bristled at "snooping" but she realized that Ellen was probably right.

"But we welcome your advice about the people at Rutherford," Ellen continued. "We just want to keep you safe."

She and Beau exchanged glances. "There's something else we want to run by you," he said, moving his empty iced tea glass around in a small pool of water on the black laminated tabletop. "We've had a call from one of your neighbors about the burglary."

Ariadne's hazel eyes brightened with interest. "Did someone see something that night? What was it?"

Beau ran his hand through his sandy hair. She was so lovely, staring at him like that. He looked helplessly at Ellen.

Why me, Ellen thought as she read his look as a plea for help. Because I'm African American and so is the suspect? But she dismissed the thought as beneath the man she knew and respected. More likely he was disconcerted by his attraction to Ariadne. "One of your neighbors said he saw Elias Eppersley's red truck in your driveway about midnight on the night Medina was killed. He said he'd never seen Elias there so late at night and wondered what he was doing prowling around on your porch."

"Elias?" Ariadne's surprise registered in her voice. "He and his mother both work for me and I've known him ever since he was a small boy trailing along behind Zora while she cleaned our house." She thought a moment. "If Elias was on my veranda that night, he certainly wasn't 'prowling.' He would have been looking for a check I'd left for him under a flowerpot. I owed him fifty dollars for lawn work so I called and told him I'd be gone that evening but he could pick it up from the left-hand flowerpot next to the front door. He said he would and I guess he did, though I haven't checked under the pot. In all the excitement I forgot about it."

"We tried to talk to Elias this morning but he's gone over to Tallahassee to be with his sick grandmother." Beau spoke quietly, not wanting to be overheard by anyone in the adjoining booths. "His mother says she's been going there as often as she can but he's spelling her today so she can catch up on her work."

"I can't believe Elias was involved," Ariadne insisted. "He's an honest and responsible young man. And devoted to his mother, who relies on him for all kinds of things. I'm not surprised that he's tending to his grandmother." She looked at Beau intently. "Which neighbor reported this?"

Beau closed his eyes for a moment before meeting hers directly. "I can't tell you that."

Ariadne realized his inability to reveal this information. Probably protects his sources like journalists do, she thought. "Why did he or she wait so long to tell you this? Why not say it right away?"

Beau looked uncomfortable, seeing that she was annoyed. "The caller said he'd left town on Sunday and just returned. He'd heard we were canvassing the neighborhood and wanted to report what he'd seen."

Ariadne nodded but didn't return his smile.

Sheryl brought their check and as Ariadne reached for her purse, Beau drew out his wallet. "It's on me, Ariadne, a business lunch. Thanks for taking time to talk to us. And please believe me, we're not accusing Elias of anything.

Both of us know him and know his good reputation. We just want to speak to him. Maybe he saw something out of place or unusual, a car on your street or someone in the woods behind your house." He hesitated. "It's even possible that he returned later, saw the intruders in your study, went in, and confronted them. Might even have fought with them."

"And killed Medina with the poker?" Ariadne's voice quavered. "I can't imagine that. Elias is kind and gentle, not at all foolhardy. If he saw people trashing my study he'd certainly call the police."

"You're most probably right." Ellen turned toward her. "Our scenario is just conjecture at this point. We just want to ask him if he saw anyone near your house at the time."

"I'm sorry if I upset you, Ariadne." Beau looked genuinely concerned. "But we have to think about all possibilities. I'm going now to talk to Elias in Tallahassee. Then we'll know more about how he figures into all this."

Ariadne gathered up her purse and sunhat. "I know you're just doing your job. But I'm sure Elias's explanation for how he happened to come by my house that night will tally with mine."

THAT NIGHT as Ariadne was turning out the lights to go to bed, the doorbell rang. Peering out one of the long glass windows framing the front door, she was surprised to see Beau standing there, his gold badge gleaming in the porch light. She let him into the foyer. "Is something wrong?"

The alarm in her voice made his throat tighten. "Sorry to be so late, but I just returned from Tallahassee and wanted to tell you about our talk with Elias." He pulled out a handkerchief and wiped the sweat beads from his forehead. "Still mighty hot out there."

"Would you like a cold drink? Some lemonade or iced tea?"

"Thanks, but I just downed a bottle of water on the way here. Have to keep hydrated in this weather." He stood near the door, feet planted firmly on the dark blue woolen hall rug, hands clasped behind his back.

An official stance, she thought. "What did Elias say?"

"The same thing you told us. That he drove over to your house late that night to pick up the check. Said it was probably around midnight, right after he'd finished restocking the shelves at Elkins' Hardware. Then he drove on up to Elliottville to visit his girlfriend. We phoned her and she said he arrived about one. Pretty fast driving, I think, but not unusual for a young guy eager to see his girl."

"So you believe he wasn't involved?"

Beau stared down at the geometric designs woven into the rug. "Well, the coroner's set the time of death between midnight and two, which puts Elias in the vicinity at the time."

"So he is still a suspect?" Ariadne sounded dismayed. "Why don't you believe me when I tell you he's an honest young man who would never steal from me?"

"We do believe you but we have to keep the options open."

She wasn't sure if she was exasperated with him or with the police procedures that at the moment seemed irrational to her. "You think what you have to think, Beau, but I know he's innocent."

He flinched at her tone. Where had this gone wrong? He had meant to reassure her that Elias was probably telling the truth and all he had done was annoy her. He squared his shoulders. They had to keep him on their suspect list. Didn't she understand investigative procedures? An image of his ex-wife in an irritated mood rose before him as he looked at Ariadne's solemn face. Damn. Did he need this now? The energy that had sustained him all through this exhausting day suddenly drained away. He closed his eyes for a second. "It's been a long day and I'm exhausted. Let's talk about this later."

Driving home a bit too fast, Beau began to worry about becoming too infatuated with a citizen involved in an investigation. He shook his head as he realized that it was already too late, that he was, as his father would have said, "smitten" with her and unwilling to back away unless he was sure his feelings would compromise his work.

Ariadne slumped against the door, brooding about Beau's reluctance to accept her confidence in Elias's character. How could he doubt her? Elias's account of his whereabouts on that night was straightforward and believable. Was it obligatory for law officers to suspect everyone, to question everything? She knew, of course, that it was.

Cassandra sauntered up and rubbed against Ariadne's ankles, mewing softly. "Okay, Cassie, time for bed. I'm so tired I can't think straight anymore." Or judge anyone impartially. As she thought about Beau's solid, direct manner and open, friendly face, her indignation drained away. But that night she slept fitfully, dreaming of bank checks swirling around her like the Nebraska blizzards of her childhood.

13

DINNER AT THE BALDWIN house was always a nightmare. This evening was no exception. Nothing seemed to soothe the tempers of the irritable children and weary parents, cooped up together over the weekend, all longing for Monday to separate them into their various routines. The meal began calmly enough, with everyone sitting around a wobbly wooden table quietly eating or picking at food they didn't want. All too soon, despite Julian's and Elizabeth's efforts to orchestrate a peaceful family "togetherness" time, the quiet dinner morphed into a Mad Hatter's tea party.

"Potty poop!" Duncan's comment as he thumped his spoon into his mashed potatoes sent Miranda into a paroxysm of laughter. In her high chair next to Elizabeth, Rosalind began to bang her plastic Barney cup into her plastic Little Bo Peep bowl, sending green peas flying into the air and onto the shabby, stained beige carpet. "Poopy butt!" screamed Duncan, encouraged by his sisters' reactions to his new vocabulary. Elizabeth clenched her fists in her lap as she glanced at Julian and spelled out their keyword for sound parenting, "i-g-n-o-r-e."

Unfortunately, precocious Miranda recognized her parents' code and began an off-key rendition of her version of the alphabet song. "A, B, C, D, E, F, G, H, I, G, N, O, R, E!" she sang at the top of her lungs. She jumped off her chair and began to dance around the room, flailing her arms about her head and parroting her mother's "i-g-n-o-r-e" over and over. Duncan slid down and joined her, adding his refrain, "Potty poop! Potty butt! Poopy head!"

Gripping their cutlery Julian and Elizabeth continued to eat, clinging to their resolve that having children would not disturb their equanimity or change their lives.

Suddenly Rosalind screeched so loudly that both older siblings halted in mid-performance and turned to stare at her. Her face turned beet red as she tensed her small body and then expelled gas in a loud report.

"Fart!" Duncan yelled, exercising the only forbidden four-letter "f" word he knew. "Fart, fart, fart!"

Elizabeth snatched the baby and headed for the changing table, set up in a corner of the master bedroom.

Julian tried to cope with the whirling dervishes. "Time out!" But they were off and running again, laughing and chanting, "Fart! I-g-n-o-r-e! Fart! I-g-n-o-r-e!"

"Time! Out!" His voice became louder as he enunciated each word separately, but to no avail.

Then, just as abruptly as they had begun to dance, the children came to a complete stop, eyes wide, as the doorbell rang. Who would be coming to their house at dinnertime? Miranda's playmates were forbidden to call or visit at that sacred hour, and she knew that her parents had also told their own friends to please not disturb them when they were creating and maintaining essential "togetherness." The children joined Julian at the door, peeking around his legs to get a glimpse of the intruder who didn't know the house rules. Or didn't care about them.

On the porch stood Allison, dripping water from her yellow slicker and black rain boots. Lank tendrils of wet blonde hair clung to her flushed cheeks, accenting the dark circles under her round blue eyes, which first focused on Julian and then lowered to his children peering at her from their parental refuge. She peeled back her rain hood and shook her head slightly to clear her thoughts, then looked back up into Julian's astonished face. "I'm sorry, P-p-professor." She stuttered in her effort to speak quickly,

perhaps afraid he might slam the door in her face. "I know you don't want students to come to your house. But I have to talk to you. Now."

The children shrank from her high-pitched, tremulous voice and Julian instinctively reached down to put a hand on each small head as he stared at the rain-soaked apparition on his doorstep. "Fuck!" He blurted it out without thinking.

In an instant Duncan had learned another f-word. "Fuck," he echoed as he backed away from his father's hand. "Fuck. Fuck. Fuck." His voice rose to a crescendo, startling Miranda, who was fascinated by this beautiful creature with the power to cause such an outburst in her usually calm and controlled father. But she realized that Duncan was going to be in very big trouble for using such a monstrously taboo word. So she clapped her hand over her brother's mouth to protect him from provoking his father's anger.

"You can't *be* here. I can't talk to you now." Julian tried to remain calm though his voice betrayed his anger at Allison's invasion of his protected turf. Of all the coeds who might dare to break his cardinal rule—all meetings with students must be in his office—she was now the most dangerous. A very real threat to his marriage and family. "You'll have to come to my office tomorrow."

"I have to talk to you *now*." The pitch of Allison's voice rose higher as she reached out her arms as if to embrace Julian, who took a step backward, nearly toppling his hovering children. Duncan began to work up to one of his famous howling fits.

Julian stepped forward, put both of his hands on Allison's shoulders, and shoved her away from him. Her eyes widened as she stumbled backward. Maybe he was going to push her off the rickety porch or do something even worse. Her next thought—maybe he would try to kill the baby—was irrational because he didn't know she was pregnant, but it shocked her anyway. Stifling a scream, she turned, lurched down the two low steps to the sidewalk and staggered back to the safety of her car.

"Julian! What's happening? Who is that? What are you doing?" His wife's questions rained down upon her husband, who was bent over, head in his hands, a tortured Rodinesque statue. Elizabeth glared at Allison piling into her Sentra, recognizing her as one of the nubile coeds who stalked her husband. How dare that little witch come here! She felt like bashing her fist down on Julian's bowed head. He was such a fool to encourage her!

Julian pulled himself up, one hand on the door frame, trying to meet Elizabeth's gaze, but she had already turned around as she shepherded the older children into the living room. "Come on now, show's over," she said in a bright, reassuring tone. "Let's have some ice cream before your baths and then I'll read to you." She rumpled Miranda's hair as she selected her favorite fairy tale book from the children's bookcase. "And one of the scary books, too, Duncan. Any one you want." She picked him up and hugged him to her, murmuring a drawn-out "booooo" in his ear, making him shiver and giggle in delight.

"I choose 'Snow White,' Mommy." Miranda turned to address her father, who struggled to regain his composure. "When the prince kisses her, you come and kiss me, okay?"

"You bet, Princess, but why wait that long. Here are a million kisses for you right now." Relieved that a potentially disastrous scene had been averted, Julian lifted Miranda into his arms and kissed her cheeks and neck. She giggled and hugged him but struggled to get down, sensing that seven was too old to be held like a baby. Grabbing his hand, she led him after her mother and brother into the kitchen for their bedtime treat.

◻️

ON MONDAY AFTERNOON Allison stood in the hallway before Professor Baldwin's open office door, wondering if she should enter when he wasn't there. She shook water drops off her collapsible pink umbrella, one scarcely large enough to protect her from the driving rains, but she hadn't wanted Professor Baldwin to see her again in that dreadful yellow rain jacket. She stood the umbrella upright against the wall so it would drip onto the pseudo-terrazzo hall floor rather than on his nubby blue-gray office carpet, and made some futile attempts to shake dry the long soft rose challis peasant skirt clinging to her round hips. Then she crossed the threshold and stood looking blankly at the empty desk chair, trying to avoid glancing over to the sofa along the wall.

"What are you doing here?" Julian's voice behind her made her whirl around and hold up her hands in front of her, as if to push him away.

"You, you ... told me to come to the office." Allison's voice became more emphatic as she stammered out the words. Stepping back, she allowed him to pass her, which he did with barely a glance at the beautiful breasts that had driven him nearly mad with desire.

"All right. Come in then." He pointed to the blue plastic side chair, which she slid into without a murmur, then seated himself across the desk from her.

"Well?" He found it difficult to be stern as he watched her, sitting there, eyes lowered, trying to compose herself. Her knuckles were white knobs against a small black purse she clutched in her lap. Her golden hair fluffed around her drawn face as it began to dry, triggering Julian's desire against his will. He grabbed a pencil and began tapping it on the desk.

"I have something to tell you. Something bad." Allison lifted her eyes to meet his and the pain in them caused him to push back his chair and bolt across the room to close the door. Clearly this was not anything he wanted a student or colleague to hear. She recoiled as he darted past her to and from the door, but he didn't pause or touch her.

"What is it?" His voice began to quaver. Had she reported their sexual act to someone? His wife? His chairman? The dean? Fuck! His anger rose up against her.

She flinched again and swallowed hard. "I'm ...I'm ... *pregnant.*" As soon as the words flew out, the courage to speak drained from her body and her shoulders drooped, followed by her curly head. She sat immobile, hugging her purse close to her body.

"Fuck! Fuck it!" Julian's face froze in a mask of fear and anger. How had that happened? Of course he knew the answer well enough. One careless moment of unprotected sex. No fear of STDs with this Christian virgin. But damn it, why hadn't he thought about pregnancy? His mind whirled and his eyes flashed hatred at Allison, who was now sobbing softly into a tissue.

"Did you do a pregnancy test?" He asked and then clenched his fists when she just stared at him with tearful eyes. "I suppose it's mine," he whispered bitterly, raising his eyebrows at her look of shocked surprise. "What do you want to do about it? I can give you some money if you want to get an ..." He struggled to articulate his suggestion.

Allison's eyes widened. "I can't do *that*. It's a sin." She blushed and hung her head as she realized that what they had done was a sin also. "I just can't do that," she repeated helplessly. "But I don't know what else to do. My mother will die when she finds out. She's had a hard time coping since my father died. She'll be no help at all." She began to cry again, silently, the tears making wet tracks down her pale cheeks. "Please, you have to do something."

Julian wanted to crush her, to make her disappear, anything to make this go away. But as he sat silently for a few minutes, eyes closed, his anger began to dissipate and he felt guilt wash over him, followed by a twinge of pity for her, forlorn and alone and so afraid. In a weak moment he had given way to his urges without a thought for the consequences—for her or for himself. He had to pull himself together and respond somehow to her plea. But what could he do for her now and how could he do it in secret? Because this could ruin his life, beginning with his marriage. When Elizabeth found out, she would leave him, taking away his children. His career would also suffer. He had been at Rutherford long enough to know that professional success with scholarly and creative accomplishments wouldn't guarantee his academic advancement if this reality were revealed. Neither his colleagues nor the administration would condone impregnating a student, even if he did take responsibility for his misdeed. He'd lose everything. God, what was he going to do? He needed time to devise a plan.

"Allison." He spoke gently, going around the desk to her side but not touching her. "I need some time to think about what to do." He reached into his pocket for his wallet and pulled out a twenty-dollar bill, all he had with him. "Here's some money for some good food or vitamins or something you need. I'll get you more. But I need time to think, to plan—"

She shook her head, shoved his hand away, and headed for the door. She let out a sharp cry when she opened it and saw Chris Bannerman standing there. He stepped aside to let her pass and then called after her, "Hey, you left your umbrella." He waved it in the air to get her attention, but she had already rounded the corner, heading for the elevator.

"Never mind, I'll keep it for her. Another student upset about a grade." Julian hoped Chris believed him.

"She's a looker," Chris smirked. "Wouldn't you love to get into *her* panties!"

Julian cringed but clapped his hand on his friend's shoulder in a gesture of male solidarity. "Hey, sorry, I have to go. Elizabeth is picking me up to run errands downtown." He tried to smile as he steered Chris out the door.

As he emerged from the building, Julian was relieved to see Elizabeth waiting in the station wagon, where Rosalind and Duncan waved to him from the back seat. He tickled and tussled with them a minute before climbing in beside his wife. Soon they were off down Magnolia Way to Main Street. For the sake of family peace Elizabeth had decided not to reveal that she had seen Allison emerge from Julian's building and dash across the quad toward the girls' dorm. But her thoughts swirled around Julian and that impulsive young girl, who was threatening to become more than just an annoyance in their lives. Julian really needs to get tough with her, Elizabeth thought, before something dreadful happens.

14

"What great men have been in love?"
Love's Labour's Lost

AS IS USUAL IN LATE SEPTEMBER, North Florida was invaded by clouds of velvety black love bugs, coupled together for the duration of their short lives, dizzily mating in the fetid air. Drivers cursed these tiny two-headed kamikazes as they bombarded windshields, hoods, and bumpers, coating them with a sticky residue. When Ariadne noticed several on the bumper of her silver Beetle, she made a mental note to have the car washed soon. Then she drove out onto the highway and headed for the Tallahassee airport to pick up Judith and Suzanne, returning from a weekend trip to the Minnesota Historical Society archives in St. Paul.

A half-hour later, having encountered very little traffic in mid-morning, she waited in the airport lobby, just outside the security barriers, catching a glimpse of the jet as it landed on the main runway and taxied to a gate. Soon she spied Judith and Suzanne pulling their carry-ons and waving to her. After hugging them both, she asked Judith, who was researching Meridel Le Sueur for a proposed critical biography, "Did you find new useful material?"

"The Le Sueur archive was unbelievably comprehensive. I collected information going back to her early days in Iowa, where she came in contact with radicals, labor organizers, and Marxists through her stepfather, who founded the IWW. But the most fascinating was material about her life in Hollywood, where she was a stunt woman in *The Perils of*

Pauline. I was lucky to find so much biographical material I can use to flesh out my critique of her literary works."

As they drove out of the airport onto Capital Circle, Judith, always attuned to Ariadne's mood, squinted at her. "Something bothering you?"

"Beau and Ellen think Elias Eppersley might be a suspect in Medina's murder because he was seen at my house that night. Both Elias and I told them he'd come over to pick up a check I'd left for him on the porch but I'm not sure they believe us." Ariadne gripped the steering wheel. "That really upset me and I'm still nervous about it."

Suzanne chimed in from the back seat. "They probably have to consider everyone a suspect who was there around that time."

"That's exactly what Beau told me." Ariadne said. "And I know you're right. But I've been mulling it over and have decided to try to do everything I can to convince them they're wrong about Elias."

"Don't get involved. It's too dangerous," Judith said. "They'll find the real culprit soon enough."

Ariadne was doubtful about that result but to mollify Judith, she agreed. When she pulled into the Sycamore driveway, her friends thanked her for the ride and promised to call her later. At home she settled down at her desk with a pile of notes for an article comparing the activities and political philosophies of Emma Goldman and Crystal Eastman, two progressive activists from different class strata at the turn of the 20th century. During her summer break she had completed her research and was now ready to begin writing. She shuffled her notes and stared at her computer screen, waiting for the first sentence to come to her, but she couldn't concentrate. Elias didn't kill that man, she thought. He just couldn't have done it. But who did? And how could she help find the culprit? She pressed the icon for spider solitaire and began to play the most difficult version with four card suits, a process that usually calmed her nerves. As the red and black cards clicked into place, it came to her. Clues. She needed to find clues the officers had missed. After all, she knew her house and yard better than they did.

She grabbed her straw hat and headed outdoors. Two yellow butterflies pursued each other in spirals over the orange and red lantanas planted for a splash of color at her side door. She crossed the back yard to a blanket of purple hearts that separated her lawn from the pinewoods. Where had the burglars entered and exited her yard? The officers had searched the yard for evidence, especially footprints, but maybe they hadn't ventured into the woods, thinking it a useless task after the rainstorm. Who knew what kind of evidence might be lurking there? Maybe an untrained eye like hers could spot something significant. Probably not, her rational mind told her, but she refused to just stand by and do nothing.

The metallic drone of crickets and grasshoppers rose and ebbed around her as she entered the woods, pulling aside the masses of kudzu covering the low bushes and stretching up and over the tall slash pines, creating gigantic green monster topiaries. Trying to scout around for anything unusual or out of place, she threaded her way deeper through the tall weeds, some knee-high with tiny white flowers, others swaying their fragile plumes over her head. She ignored soft kisses of drifting love bugs and the whine of hovering mosquitoes, but she swatted at a dive-bombing deer fly because she knew from experience how painful its sting could be. Here and there she brushed away the wispy webs of minuscule iridescent green spiders with vampire red eyes. And once she almost tore through a gigantic silken labyrinth woven by a two-inch-long banana spider, its lengthy legs splayed out as if to hold its fragile world together.

Although she had been in the woods only a few minutes, she was soon panting for breath in the close air. The persistent insect chorus suddenly ceased and then began again, but in that split second of quiet, she heard a noise, as if someone had muttered a curse or a threat. She turned but could see nothing through the dense thicket of foliage. Please curb your imagination, she told herself. If you keep on hearing phantom noises, you'll soon wind up in the loony bin. She plunged on, pausing occasionally to look around her, though she had begun to realize how futile her quest for evidence was since she had little idea of what she was looking for, broken branches, perhaps, or hacked-away vines. But nothing seemed disturbed.

Beginning to think her search for clues hopeless, she moved toward the vacant lot next to her property. A rustling in the underbrush made her stop in fear of the rattlesnakes her neighbors had warned her about, though she had never seen one in all the years she'd lived here. She was relieved to see a fat white opossum, its diurnal sleep disturbed, waddling off through the undergrowth, its ratty tail held high. Looking behind her and listening intently, Ariadne heard something larger crashing its way through the woods, headed in her direction. Maybe a deer, she thought, except that they were shy creatures who only now and then ventured to the edge of the woods to nibble lawn grass and dashed away if a human approached them. Thinking it might be one of the homeless people who often camped in the woods caused her a moment of fear, though the ones who occasionally came to her door for a handout seemed harmless. She reached into her pocket for her cell phone and realized she'd left it at home. Suddenly panicking, she began to run downward toward the highway, where she could hear the roar of a semi. She rushed headlong, desperately pushing the tall weeds aside and trying to maintain traction on the slippery pine straw underfoot. As close as she was, she would have made it to the edge of the woods if she hadn't tripped over a tree root. Down she plummeted, dragging kudzu vines with her, banging her right knee into a moss-covered rock and thudding into a pine tree trunk. She lay stunned for an instant and then shuddered as she felt a hand on her arm. She sucked in her breath before it could emerge as a scream and, gathering every ounce of strength left in her body, she rolled over.

"Hey Beautiful, are you all right?"

She stared at the face swimming before her eyes and, as her adrenalin rush dissipated, she sank back against the tree. "Miles. You scared me half to death! What are you doing here?"

"The guy next door saw me ringing your doorbell and told me you'd gone off into the woods, so I decided to follow you. I should have called out right away but I got disoriented tearing through those darn vines. Why anyone in their right mind would be tramping through this jungle is beyond me."

"But why did you come?" she began, and then realized what day it was. "Oh Miles, I'm sorry, I completely forgot our lunch date. I got to thinking about the murder of poor Randall Medina and how whoever did it probably fled off into these woods, so I decided to search for any …" She trailed off, looking sheepish and thinking that "clues" sounded too much like mystery fiction. "I've found nothing."

She winced as she tried to stand up. "And now look what I've done." She rubbed her left elbow and tried to put her weight on her right knee, but it buckled beneath her. Miles caught her around the waist and held her upright against him.

"Be careful, I'm all sweaty," she warned him.

"Horses sweat, women glow. Though I do admit that just now you look more like a scarecrow than a woman."

Just then another figure broke through the trees and vines. "Beau" and "Sheriff," the couple exclaimed together.

The sheriff looked both annoyed and embarrassed. "A neighbor called in a report that a man had followed you into the woods. I came over to make sure you weren't in any danger." He looked away. "But I guess you're not."

Miles laughed and hugged Ariadne to him. "It's not what you think, Sheriff, though I wouldn't mind having a tryst with this fair damsel in distress, but not out here in this oppressive insect-infested jungle. I came to pick her up for lunch and was surprised to see her hacking her way through the underbrush. I'm afraid I frightened her into falling and maybe injuring her knee."

A twitch around Beau's mouth signaled his unease as he turned to Ariadne. "Let's get you out of here and have a look at it. You might have chipped a bone."

"I'm fine, really. It hurts but I'm sure it's just a bruise." All she wanted to do was get out of the heat and lie down. A bit dizzy, she staggered as she tried to take a step.

"Take it easy," Miles said. "That was a nasty fall. Here, put your arms around my neck and I'll carry you out."

"I don't *think* so." Ariadne's tone hovered somewhere between amusement and indignation. "You'd never make it back through this morass without falling and I don't want both of us to be injured."

Beau spoke into his radio and then took Ariadne's right arm. "We'll both help her and we're better off going to the highway rather than back through the woods. My deputy will meet us with his car."

Soon they pulled up into Ariadne's driveway where Gladys Jespersen broke away from a group of neighbors and rushed over. "Ariadne, are you all right? I called for help when *he* went into the woods after you." She glared at Miles.

"I'm fine, Gladys, just bruised a little from a fall. Do you know Miles Duvall, my lawyer?"

Miles began to charm the woman with his smile and patter.

"Maybe I should drive you to the doctor's office to have that knee examined," Beau said, taking Ariadne's arm again, as Miles grasped her other elbow. They seemed oblivious to Ariadne's growing exasperation with their solicitude.

"I'm fine. Or I will be as soon as I take care of myself."

"I'd be delighted to help you do that, my dear." Miles made an exaggerated, sweeping bow. "Perhaps some expert massage might help."

Ariadne pulled away. What on earth was she doing standing here like some wounded doe in the forest, while the males circled around her, pawing the ground and shaking their antlers. She limped to the door and opened it. "I really just need some rest. I'll see you both later."

The bucks pawed the ground one last time before heading out.

Two minutes later the doorbell announced Beau's return. She didn't protest when he put his arm around her shoulders, propelled her to the kitchen, and, seating her by the table, propped her right leg on a chair. Without a word he opened the refrigerator freezer door, rummaged around, and emerged with a large plastic bag of peas. "Most people have some kind of frozen vegetable that's useful in these situations," he said as he wrapped the pea packet in a kitchen towel and laid it on her knee, tucking the ends underneath. Then he pulled out another chair and sat down across from her. "Are you comfortable?"

"Thanks, it feels better already," Ariadne said with a wan smile.

Beau drummed his fingers on the table. "What did you think you were doing out there? Don't you know how dangerous it can be to go tromping around in those woods? Homeless men, wild animals, rattlesnakes, who knows what else."

She started to say that the only wild animal she'd seen was the harmless opossum but thought better of it. His concern seemed genuine, if extreme. "You're right, Beau. I'm sorry to have caused so much fuss. The break-in and murder haunt me and I want to help."

His demeanor softened. "Please believe we're doing all we can to solve this crime. Just leave the investigating to us, okay?"

Holding the cold package to her knee, Ariadne shifted to a straighter position. "I know you're doing your job. But I'm afraid you don't ..." She searched for the appropriate words. "You don't appreciate my concern."

A smile flickered around his eyes as he folded his arms on the table and leaned toward her. "I know you're upset with me about Elias. But please understand our position. Ellen and I have to try to remain impartial until something breaks and we determine who killed Medina. But I don't want that to hurt our friendship."

"Me neither." She smiled at him. "I'll try to understand."

After Beau left she phoned Judith, who laughed at her rendition of the afternoon's adventure. "That sounds like the typical dumb-woman ploy in suspense films, where the audience thinks, 'No, stupid, don't go wandering down that dark haunted hall by yourself, especially in high heels!'"

"I was wearing sneakers, thank you. But yes, I realize now that it was a ridiculous thing to do, though I really was only trying to help."

"Probably your best bet is to lie low and let the police do their job. I'm sure they don't need your assistance and horning in will only get you into trouble, maybe even real danger."

"Now who's sounding like a bad movie," Ariadne laughed. "But you're probably right."

"You bet I am. So stop trying to be a detective!"

15

"But I will wear my heart upon my sleeve. ..."
Othello

"YOU'RE GOING ON A DATE with the sheriff?"
Judith's voice on the phone a few days later brimmed
with laughter. "What are you going to do, play with his
handcuffs?"

"It's not a date," Ariadne insisted. "He wants to continue
talking about academic life in general and the students
in particular in order to get a better perspective on the
murder. We're going on a nature walk over in Torreya State
Park."

"A nature walk?" Judith snorted her contempt for the
outdoors. "Your recent escapade in the wild should have
convinced you of its perils."

"You have a point but I'm looking forward to seeing
the park and getting outdoors in this lovely weather. My
knee is fine again so I can hike a bit."

"Well, you deserve some fun in your life and it's about
time you started dating again. I'll call you later to get all the
juicy details! Bye."

"It's *not* a date ..." Ariadne tried to protest but Judith
had already hung up.

"Hi," Beau said when she answered the doorbell, his
grin revealing his sexy overbite. The present stage of their
relationship placed them somewhere between a handshake
and a hug, so she just smiled back and stepped aside to let
him enter.

He followed her down the hall to the kitchen. "Should I have brought some food? Maybe we can pick up something on the way."

She shook her head as she pointed to a large blue cooler standing ready on the table. "Of course not. I said I'd make the lunch and I did. Fried chicken, homemade potato salad, cucumber pickles, apple pie, iced tea, the works. Never let it be said that a college professor doesn't know her way around a kitchen." Her assertion of culinary expertise was, however, tinged with hypocrisy because a neighbor had given her the homemade pie and pickles, though the chicken and potato salad were her own.

Beau picked up the cooler. "Can't beat home cookin', ma'am." He accentuated his Southern drawl to tease her and was rewarded by her low mellow laugh as she followed him out to his tan Jeep Wrangler. "Your chariot awaits you, my lady." He held the door open for her and stowed the picnic cooler in the back. "I hope it won't be too windy with the top down but I wanted us to enjoy the sun."

Last night a cool front had crept down from Canada through the Midwest, veered eastward over Texas, and slipped overnight into the Florida Panhandle, bringing blessed relief from the heat. "It's wonderful to be out in the open air." Ariadne stretched her arms out as if to embrace the fine weather. They drove slowly out of town, savoring the play of sunshine into the green pine forest around them as they descended into the plain beneath Coowahchobee's hills. As they picked up speed, the wind whipped Ariadne's short pageboy around her face.

"Too breezy?" Beau's words streamed into the wind.

She shook her head. "It's invigorating!"

How beautiful she is, he thought as they skimmed under I-10 and slowed down onto a back road, where Ariadne admired a profusion of white, yellow, and purple wildflowers along the roadside. "I didn't expect to see blossoms this time of year. Except for the ragweed, of course, and goldenrod. I remember my mother complaining about how those gave her hay fever in the fall."

"You're not originally from around here, are you?"

"No, I grew up in northeastern Nebraska, near the Missouri River. My mother knew the names of most of the area's wildflowers and trees, birds and insects, and taught me about them."

Beau nodded. "I've never had the time or money to travel much. I've lived all my life in these parts. Grew up in Eastpoint."

Ariadne smiled. "I remember the piers and the shrimp boats along the highway there but not the town itself. Just a few houses and fish shacks. No tourist attraction to rival Carrabelle's 'world's smallest police station.'"

"You mean that little phone booth near the road? Years ago we took a picture of David beside it," she said. "Why didn't you stay in Eastpoint?"

"Too small. I liked playing around the fishing boats and the beach when I was a little kid, but by the time I got to high school, I wanted a bigger town with more excitement. My folks let me live in Tallahassee with Memaw—'Grandma' to you Northerners—so I could go to a larger high school and then, wouldn't you know it, I began to miss home. So I returned every other weekend, especially in the spring, when there weren't any football games to keep me in Tally. After college I became a cop and settled in Coowahchobee, just the right size town for me."

They crossed a highway and continued on a stretch of gravel road until they arrived at the Torreya State Park entrance, where a sticker on Beau's windshield allowed them to sail on by the small wooden box containing entrance fee envelopes. They wound around to a small parking lot in front of a large white plantation house with green shutters at the windows and tall pillars holding up the porch roof. It stood in a clearing surrounded by several species of lofty trees. Beau pointed upward. "That one's a torreya, a type of evergreen conifer tree; and according to the plaque over there, this is the only place in Florida where they grow. You can tell the species by its narrow needles, tinier than those of the pines."

She gazed upward along the tall gray trunk of the evergreen to its branches spreading high over them and then nodded, although she couldn't really tell the difference. "Why does it grow only here?" she asked.

"A botanist over at Florida State told me that no one knows the answer to that. Another Florida mystery, I guess."

They strolled up the path to the mansion and under the white wooden roof connecting it to the park ranger's small office and souvenir shop, where Beau took a map from the box on the door. Then they crossed the lawn sloping down to the cliff overlooking the Apalachicola River.

"Magnificent!" Ariadne exclaimed. "Breathtaking!"

"You got that right." Beau might have been commenting on the view of the river or of Ariadne as she gazed at it and he at her. "Let's do the River Bluffs Trail," he said, showing it to her on the map. "It's about a forty-five-minute comfortable hike with a good view of the river."

They found the beginning of the trail and began to climb up and down the wood chip path lined with dark green ferns and fledgling magnolia trees under towering pines and oaks, some sporting patches of blue-gray lichens or tawny mushrooms, others bearded with Spanish moss. Ariadne spotted a large black bird with a brilliant red crest hacking away at a dead tree trunk. "Now there's a bit of nature I know. A pileated woodpecker. I see one occasionally in the woods behind my house."

Beau beamed at her as if she'd identified an albatross, but she didn't notice as she cautiously followed the trail, hanging on to tree trunks and vines when the hill plunged downward through groves of palmettos to the water's edge. Almost an hour later, when they returned via a steep climb upward to the back of the souvenir shop and office, Ariadne was glowing from exertion but she seemed oblivious to Beau's admiring glances as she said, "Let's spread the blanket at the edge of the cliff. We'll have a room with a view for lunch. I'm famished."

Nodding his agreement Beau brought the cooler and blanket from the Jeep and they laid out their feast overlooking the river. But just as they began to sample the fried chicken, a loud sharp screaming and crashing of branches in the treetops brought them to their feet. A park ranger emerged from the office and pointed up into the cloudless blue sky where a large bald eagle soared across the clearing, followed by another. Ariadne gasped in delight at her first sighting of these majestic birds in the wild.

When she turned around with a wide smile, Beau drew her to him and kissed her, an act that surprised her as well as the park ranger, who recovered first and ducked quickly back into his office.

Ariadne drew back, hesitated, and then suddenly threw her arms around Beau's neck and kissed him back. A few minutes later, growing self-conscious, they began looking around for the eagles, but they had vanished into the trees.

When Ariadne suggested they eat, Beau readily agreed and was soon lavishing praise on the food. Ariadne laughed. "I have to confess that I exaggerated a bit about my cooking. I fried the chicken and made the potato salad, but my neighbor bought the pie and the pickles at the county fair."

Beau took her hands in his. "Lying to the sheriff is likely to incur a penalty. Fortunately, though, you won't have to go to court to make payment. I'll be happy to collect right here." He drew her close and kissed her again.

This is probably going too far too fast, Ariadne thought, but after they cleared off the remains of the lunch and settled again on the blanket, she relaxed into the circle of his arm, where, she realized, she felt very comfortable indeed.

"Tell me more about yourself." She decided that conversation might keep the mood while cooling things down a bit.

"Nothing much more to tell, I'm afraid. I went to community college in Tallahassee and then got a degree in Criminology from Florida State." Looking out over the river as if sorting out his memories he continued, "I got married my senior year. And divorced not much later."

She smiled at him. "You don't have to discuss it since it's really none of my business."

He traced a finger around her lips before kissing her again. "We were married too young, I think, and we didn't really know each other as well as we thought we did. I was happy to become a deputy sheriff in Coowahchobee but Etta Mae wanted a big city. She tried to talk me into moving to Jacksonville or Orlando but I wouldn't budge. We were both too stubborn. After our divorce she moved to Miami. That was years ago and I don't hear from her very often anymore."

They were silent for a while, listening to bird calls and the wind rustling the live oaks high above them. Beau hugged her closer, wanting to say something romantic but reluctant to do so for fear of rejection. Maybe she preferred that slick lawyer who obviously desired her. He winced at the possibility.

Ariadne, who had been studying his face for a sign to explain his silence, slipped out of his arm and shifted around on the blanket. "Are you all right? Not a stomach cramp, I hope. I think the cooler kept the food cold enough but you can't always be sure when mayonnaise is involved."

"I'm fine and the food was great." Beau certainly didn't want her to guess what had been on his mind. "Especially the fried chicken and potato salad." He winked and gave her a hug.

Gradually they gathered up the picnic things and made their way back to the Jeep, holding hands.

THAT EVENING, sitting in a rocking chair on Ariadne's spacious veranda, Beau began to talk about Medina's murder. "Ellen and I are both stymied. We had very little evidence to begin with and have uncovered nothing new. He was probably killed by a companion but we can't shake the alibis of those who knew him at Rutherford."

"Isn't it possible that Medina's cohorts weren't even from here? They might have been his graduate-school friends or others we don't know about."

Beau rocked slowly back and forth. "Sure. That's possible. But we've pretty much interviewed everyone he knew at Southwestern and earlier in Blountstown. No luck there either. Everyone seems to tell a plausible story about where they were that night, and some check out, but others just can't be verified."

"Whoever broke into my house must have had a compelling need for money. Anybody you interviewed fit that category?"

Beau's laugh was quick and short. "Who doesn't? No wealthy people in the group of suspects and a couple of downright poor ones. Especially the graduate students, who seem to live from hand to mouth."

Ariadne fingered the long fronds of the potted fern beside her. "The faculty and students are decent people, so if one of them succumbed to the temptation to burglarize my house and fell into murder in the process, he or she must now be suffering from guilt. Maybe someone will eventually crack under the strain and confess."

Based on his many years in law enforcement Beau was convinced that spontaneous confessions happened as often as spontaneous combustions, but he didn't want to hurt or insult her, so he refrained from commenting on the remoteness of that possibility. He glanced over at her lovely profile, barely visible in the shadows, with a stray strand of blonde hair falling over her cheek. Here was another chance to tell her how he felt about her, he thought, but what on earth should he say? Words weren't so much the problem as getting them said. And he didn't want to pick the wrong time or say something that might be misconstrued. He decided to play it safe. "Can I ask you a personal question?"

Ariadne was a bit startled and a fleeting image of Pandora's Box crossed her mind. "Of course. What do you want to know?"

"I was wondering about your name. I knew Ariadne was mythological, so I looked it up on the Internet and found the story of Ariadne and the Minotaur. How she saved that guy Theseus by giving him thread to find his way out of the labyrinth and a sword so he could kill the beast."

Ariadne was charmed at his thinking this a personal inquiry and flattered by the thought of his researching her name. And was it reserve or consideration that he didn't mention the Cretan princess's love for the Athenian hero? No way was she going to retell that part of the story and thank heaven her name didn't come from mythology anyway. "My parents didn't get the name from the myth. My mother was an avid mystery reader, so she chose 'Ariadne' from Agatha Christie's Hercule Poirot novels."

"Really?" Beau hoped he wouldn't have to read any mysteries, a genre he detested. Those authors hardly ever had the police procedures correct, even when they named a series of law enforcement experts in their acknowledgments. He was certain he could write a novel that would accurately reflect how real-life detectives solved crimes. If he could sit still at the computer long enough, that is. "What kind of character is she? A detective?" he asked.

"No, Ariadne Oliver is a mystery writer who helps Poirot solve his cases through her imaginative and intuitive conjectures."

Beau smiled. "You seem to be like her, both imaginative and intuitive."

"Thanks." Ariadne shrugged. "But if I have those traits, they don't seem to be working now when I'm trying to help you solve the Medina murder. All I really seem to have in common with Ariadne Oliver is her love of privacy, comfortable shoes, well-cooked meals, and green apples. I really like Granny Smiths."

Beau laughed as he reached out and took her hand. "Don't be too hard on yourself, Ariadne. You've helped us a lot in assessing the responses we've gotten from the faculty and students we've interviewed." Her smile and the slight pressure she returned on his hand encouraged him to reveal his more personal thoughts but he found himself tongue-tied again. Why was he brave enough to raid a meth lab and articulate enough to persuade an unruly suspect to come along quietly but cowardly about moving this relationship to another level? He caressed her hand and then stood up. "It's getting late and I still have casework to catch up on."

Ariadne stood up, feeling disconcerted, and looked into his deep blue eyes, trying to read them. Why didn't he kiss her good-night in this idyllic setting—warm breezes wafting the sweet scent of honeysuckle on the veranda trellis, a bright half-moon gleaming above, the soft hum of insects in the grass? Had she misunderstood his intentions in the park?

Then she brushed uncertainties aside and, relying on her intuition, threw her arms around his neck and kissed him. He held her close, returning the kiss, and then, reluctantly and apologetically, went off to do his work. Seeing movement in the next-door neighbors' windows, Ariadne cringed at the thought of being a new topic of Coowahchobee gossip, but she smiled at the memory of a romantic day.

16

"'Tis one thing to be tempted, …
Another thing to fall."
Measure for Measure

THE FIRST MONDAY in early October Julian Baldwin woke with a start. This was the day he had to turn in his promotion and tenure file. Dean Vernon Giddings had requested the binder by noon, but Andrew Holrood, Julian's chairperson, wanted to review its contents this morning before sending it to the dean's office, where it would also be made available to the tenured faculty. The ascent from assistant to associate professor at Rutherford required a majority of their positive votes, coupled with the dean's approval, leading finally to President Osborne's decision. Downstairs in the tiny living room he found Elizabeth perched on the sofa watching the weather channel on TV. She held baby Rosalind on her lap with Miranda and Duncan cuddled up close beside her. Without taking her eyes from the screen she said, "Where are you going? The hurricane is already in the Gulf and headed north. It's expected to land somewhere on the coast early this afternoon, maybe sooner. It's been upgraded to a three and is expected to do a lot of damage. If it hits south of here it could roar right on up through this area like Michael did. Coowahchobee still hasn't recovered from that. It'll be dangerous out there. You really need to stay here."

The children stared at their mother and then at him. Miranda echoed her mother's advice in precisely the same tone of voice. "Dangerous. You should stay home, Daddy."

"Stay home, stay home, stay home," Duncan began to chant, his voice rising in pitch with each utterance.

Julian struggled to calm his nerves, already frazzled from a restless night, as he pulled a package of gum from his pocket and gave pieces to Miranda and Duncan. "Daddy has to go to the office. It's important. But don't worry. I'll be home as soon as I can."

He blew kisses at them but no one noticed as their eyes swiveled back to the screen where a meteorologist was explaining the intricacies of hurricane motion.

As Julian drove over to campus he spied a mother pushing a stroller across the intersection causing him to panic again. What if Allison decided to keep the baby, his baby? Feeling nauseous he pulled over and laid his sweaty forehead against his clenched hands clasping the steering wheel. A honk startled him as a car speeding past nearly clipped him. He grasped his promotion and tenure material, bound in a black ringed notebook on the passenger seat. Get a grip, he told himself, you'll think of something.

When Julian reached Holrood's office just after nine, his mentor was pacing up and down. "About time, Baldwin. I've been waiting an hour." His glaring look softened as he read the younger man's face. "Well, if you have everything in order, we can still get it to the dean by noon." He glanced out the window. "No classes today. We need to prepare for this 'cane. You should go home as soon as we finish here."

Andrew's anxiety fueled Julian's own angst, but he tried to remain calm as he watched the dean leaf through his portfolio. Finally Andrew approved Julian's materials and dismissed him with assurances that his record was impeccable and certain to impress Vernon, who knew how much the music department valued his contributions and how much the students appreciated his dedicated teaching. He patted Julian on the back and shook his hand. "Soon you'll be a tenured faculty member with all the privileges and responsibilities that position entails."

Julian hoped Andrew couldn't read the anxiety likely evident on his face. As calmly as he could, he thanked his mentor, shook hands, and returned to his office where the phone was ringing.

"Where are you?" Elizabeth's querulous tone set his teeth on edge. "The wind's going to blow this crappy house away and the kids are scared silly."

BY MID-DAY nearly every shop and office in Coowahchobee had closed, allowing people to return home to secure their patio furniture, pick up objects lying around their yards, and round up their children and pets. Anyone with a beach house or a boat docked at the Gulf had already done as much as they could to prevent wind and water damage before the area had been evacuated early that morning.

Downtown in Miles's law office Diana Macomb sat at her desk staring out the windows at the gray sheets of rain obscuring Courthouse Square and flooding the streets. She thought about going back home but she felt safer here. Even though she stashed away every penny she made as a legal secretary, she couldn't afford a decent house, even here where mortgages were low, and she had resisted renting an apartment in a building with snoopy neighbors. So she was stuck in a tiny rented shack that could just as well be blown down or washed away for all she cared about it. She shifted around in her chair as she surveyed the neatly arranged desk, file cabinets, and bookshelves. The law office of her dreams. But not hers yet and maybe never. Always a bridesmaid and never a bride. Her laugh was hoarse and choked with tears. Being a lawyer was her goal, the career she had struggled for years to attain. And now she could see it as a real possibility. Except that her meager savings wouldn't finance law school.

Diana reached for the thermos of coffee she'd brought along to keep her sustained if the power went out. Her hand shook as she unscrewed the red plastic cup, so she screwed it back on and set the thermos aside. Obviously she'd had enough caffeine already. A wave of loneliness swept over her and she buried her head in her hands.

Suddenly she remembered her talk with Ariadne that day in the gym. Why had she confessed so much? Was she mad? She had held her secrets tightly within her for such a long agonizing time and then they had burst out in a moment of weakness. Emotions held in check for years and then released because Ariadne reminded her of her mother. Shit. All that nonsense about feeling guilty over her mother's death and her anger at her stepmother. What had come over her?

A moment later she sat upright and set her jaw. Get a grip, she told herself, straightening her shoulders and wiping her eyes on a tissue. All these years of being on her own, of struggling to keep afloat and to get ahead in the world, and now an emotional breakdown? She couldn't, wouldn't, let that happen.

She thought about those early years, after she had left home at thirteen. She had taken a bus to Baltimore to see her mother's older sister, Aunt Agnes, a librarian, single and living alone in a small apartment. Her aunt, who had never liked her brother-in-law, blaming him for thwarting any possibility of her sister's having a career, welcomed her niece into her life. Diana had slept on her couch for some months while she attended a local high school, which she hated because the other students were snobs who ostracized her from their cliques. Of course, her father had ultimately found her and had ordered her to return home. When she had refused, he'd told her he would no longer be responsible for her until she agreed to his terms. Years later she had learned from Aunt Agnes that he'd continued to send her money for Diana and had wanted updates on her welfare in return. But by that time it was too late for any reconciliation. The bitter anger and jealousy she felt toward his new wife and daughter continued to eat away at her.

But she had succeeded well enough without them. After earning a community college degree, working part time with a professional maid service, she had attended the University of Maryland, graduating with honors. While there she had enrolled in drama courses and became entranced by the theater. For a time she hoped to become an actress, but after landing several minor roles but never a lead part, she realized that playing the nurse but never Juliet suggested a lack of theatrical talent. Then a couple of lawyers she met while cleaning office buildings in Baltimore encouraged her to enroll in law school, a plan that intrigued her, but one she couldn't afford. Undaunted, she got a job as a receptionist in a law office, attended secretarial school at night, and became a legal secretary.

So here I sit, Diana thought, trying hard to please Miles, while all the time wishing I were in his shoes. She clenched her hands on the chair arms and fought tears. To be or not to be. Her hoarse laugh echoed in her head as she stood up and began to pace up and down between the desk and the window. What she really wanted was revenge on those who stood between her and her dreams, but she was no Hamlet. She shook her head to clear away the notion. But she wasn't Ophelia either. Maybe not a hero but definitely not a victim. She'd come too far to break down now. She straightened her shoulders and stared through the window at the lightning flashes above the courthouse, illuminating the large green leaves of the magnolia trees, glistening with rain as their branches swayed violently in the wind.

DURING THE NIGHT Hurricane Ross, downgraded to a tropical storm, veered westward, soaked the coast between Pensacola and Panama City, and then abated as it moved inland. For the most part damage was slight, a few washed-out roads and flooded yards in low-lying areas. The next morning in Coowahchobee the sun shone bright again. The townspeople arose to find manicured lawns and dirt lots alike littered with pine branches, brown palm fronds, clumps of green pine needles, and gray Spanish moss. Here and there along the wet streets skinny dogs and cats scavenged for garbage spilled from toppled trash cans. The citizenry prepared for a clean-up day as their lives returned to normalcy.

17

"…when you do dance, I wish you
A wave o' the sea, that you might ever do
Nothing but that…."
The Winter's Tale

MILES DUVALL'S VOICE on the phone was smooth, sexy, and compelling as he worked to persuade Ariadne to go with him to a cocktail party that evening.

"But I wasn't invited," Ariadne protested. Miles had introduced her to Judge Davidson and his wife at Chez François one evening, but she'd never been to their house.

"No problemo, Doll. They told me to bring a date."

Then why didn't you ask me sooner? Ariadne wondered. But because she was feeling lonely this weekend while Judith and Suzanne were at the Cape San Blas beach and Beau was on duty, she was more susceptible to Miles's blandishments than she'd been in quite a while. Might as well get out and enjoy the party, she told herself, even if she were Miles's second (third? fourth?) choice. You're pathetic, she said to her image in the hall mirror.

Most of the guests at the Davidsons' house were professional people from the community, some of whom Ariadne knew quite well and was glad to see again. Miles's lawyer friend, Jeff Rood, an amiable guy who livened up even the dullest party, greeted them at the bar, set up on the dining room buffet table. His companion, Diana Macomb, had metamorphosed from a professional legal secretary to a sexy partygoer in a long, slinky, black sequined dress, her lustrous dark hair arranged in an elegant French braid. "Hello," she said, acknowledging Ariadne with a slight smile. "How have you been?"

Ariadne again regretted not having invited Diana to lunch as she had intended to do. She wasn't sure she was ready for more confession, but she had to admit she was curious about the woman. When the guys began to talk shop, Ariadne led Diana to the food spread out on another table. "Let's help ourselves to hors d'oeuvres. They look delicious."

Ariadne selected a stuffed mushroom and a cracker with Gorgonzola cheese from the sumptuous buffet. And then, because she seldom beat around the bush, she said, "You might feel embarrassed by your outburst at the fitness center, Diana. So I want you to know that what you told me will be held in strictest confidence. We professors hold to a confidentiality code much like that of lawyers, which I extend to others beyond students."

Diana stopped gathering up carrots and celery. "I'm not worried about that, Ariadne. But you're right that I'm embarrassed about my outburst. I don't know what came over me because I pride myself on being self-controlled."

"I've been told that a strenuous workout can trigger release from mental and emotional stress. Perhaps that accounts for it."

"I was pushing myself pretty hard that day. And I've been stressed out by my new job," Diana said as they both accepted glasses of champagne from their host. "I love the work but Miles is an exacting taskmaster."

"I hadn't known that. I've only known his jocular public persona," Ariadne replied. "I've always wondered if that might be a mask over a more serious nature. Why don't you tell him how stressful the work is for you?"

Diana shook her head. "I can handle it, really. I want to learn as much as I can about being a lawyer. Until I can afford law school, this is the best way to do that."

Balancing their fragile glasses and small plates of hors d'oeuvres, the two women sat down on a magenta brocade sofa in a relatively quiet corner of the spacious living room. Ariadne leaned toward Diana. "What about family members? Do you have someone you could visit for a respite?"

Diana stared into space. "My family is dead. All dead." She refocused her eyes on Ariadne. "Dead to me, anyway. I cut all the ties when I left home." She set her plate on a side table with a clatter and wiped her hands with a paper napkin embossed with a gold crest.

"Out, out damned spot?" Miles joked as he wedged himself between the women and took Diana's hand in his.

Ariadne lifted her eyebrows. "Not funny, Miles. Diana is hardly Lady Macbeth."

Diana stiffened as she pulled her hand away and placed the napkin on her empty plate, but she said nothing.

Undaunted, Miles grinned. "Jeff and I are boring each other with guy talk. Why don't you come and entertain us?"

"In a minute, Miles. We need a bit more time to finalize our solution to world peace. Would you mind refilling our glasses?" Ariadne smiled at his chagrin as the women handed him their champagne flutes.

He stood up and bowed. "Happy to oblige with any contribution I can make to such a worthy cause, oh beautiful ones." On his way to the bar he was waylaid by Judge Davidson and they were soon engrossed in conversation.

Ariadne turned to Diana. "As far as I know, no one has ever discovered a resolution of global conflict at a cocktail party. I'd rather hear more about your life. Historical narratives are my forte after all."

"I'm afraid my story is too personal for a historian like yourself. Emotions don't appear in history, at least not in the kind I studied in school."

"Fortunately, scholarship has changed, for the better I think. Historians are now intrigued by the emotions preserved in memoirs and diaries, stories of how people make sense of the world by recording their personal experiences. Even diarists from previous eras, more restrained than contemporary ones, often described acute pain and anguish, along with regret, jealousy, anger, and other distressing human emotions. And, of course, also joy, happiness, love, compassion, and a host of other positive feelings that characterize human experience." Ariadne began to fear she was lapsing into a boring lecture but Diana appeared to be listening intently.

"Any memoir I might write would make for some pretty bleak reading," she said. "Very little joy, happiness, love, or compassion in my history."

Ariadne hoped Diana wasn't going to cry again. "I usually advise stressed-out students to try keeping a journal," she said, "writing down anything that comes to mind, then later reading and reflecting on their musings. Some have told me that it helped tremendously. A few even sought out professional help later."

"I doubt ..." Diana was interrupted by Jeff, balancing two full flutes, which he handed gingerly to the women, followed by Miles carrying a plate of petits fours from the buffet.

"Sweets to the sweet. Or tarts to the ...Oops, sorry about that," Miles said. "My wit often trips me up."

Annoyed with Miles's crude humor, Ariadne wanted to ask him to take her home but he gave her no chance to talk as he set down their glasses and swept her across the hall into the Davidsons' dining room, cleared of furniture for the occasion, where a local jazz trio had struck up a dance number. They danced well together, occasionally switching partners with Jeff and Diana. Miles was an excellent dancer who led Ariadne through several intricate steps she couldn't have done without his guidance. She began to relax and enjoy herself, despite resisting and resenting Miles's persistent attempts to nibble her ear during the slow dances. Finally, feeling dizzy from the champagne, the stuffy room, and her proximity to Miles, she decided she'd had enough. "I think I'd better go home now. I'm feeling queasy."

Sometime later, after fending off Miles's advances, Ariadne was preparing for bed when she heard a car in the drive. Recognizing Judith's Escort from her window, she ran downstairs to turn on the porch lights and welcome her friends. "Why are you back so soon? I thought you were staying over at the beach until tomorrow night."

"Rain," Suzanne said. "Rain, rain, rain. It began this afternoon and is predicted to continue through tomorrow. Nothing as dreary as being at the beach in a downpour."

"We saw your light on and thought we'd come to hear about your evening at the party," Judith said, hugging Ariadne. "When you texted me, I couldn't believe you were going out with Miles again."

The three women moved into the kitchen, where Ariadne poured glasses of ice water and set out a plate of chocolate macaroons. "I probably shouldn't have gone with Miles since that only encourages him to keep asking me out when I'm really not interested. But I did have a good time. We ate delicious canapés, drank champagne, and danced." Ariadne sat lost in thought for a moment and then added, "I spent some time talking again with Diana Macomb."

"How's her job with Miles going?" Judith asked.

"She said it stresses her out and she seemed very depressed, but she also seemed quite obsessed with tragedy and guilt in her childhood. I suggested a therapist but she said that hadn't helped her so far." Ariadne was cautious because she wanted to honor her promise not to talk about the poor woman's troubled life. "The only other thing I could think of was journal writing. I told her that my students have responded well when I've proposed it to them. I'm not sure, though, if it's really useful for combating depression"

"A friend of mine who teaches at the University of Minnesota told me about a case of a suicidal student who wrote about her fears in a journal for her freshman English class," Suzanne said. "The instructor was concerned enough to send her to a therapist and as far as I know she's fine now." She shrugged. "But of course that's only one isolated case."

Judith glanced at the clock. "Oops, it's later than I thought and I have an early class tomorrow morning."

She and Suzanne hugged Ariadne, agreeing to continue the discussion of how to help depressed people at another time, and then left for home.

In the car Judith said, "Diana's problems may be very serious ones. I suspect Ariadne thinks so, but I hope she doesn't get too involved in the woman's life and history. She's often too sympathetic for her own good."

18

"Love's feeling is more soft and sensible
Than are the tender horns of cockl'd snails …."
Love's Labour's Lost

"A DAY AT THE BEACH with Beau? Sounds like fun,"
Judith's response to Ariadne on the phone was wistful.
"Suzanne's at a sociology forum in Tallahassee so I'm alone
all day. Just as well because I'm preparing a test for my
American Lit students. Five short essay questions. That'll
endear me to them since they hate to write more than
two sentences per answer. Between you and me, I hate to
read more than that too, but demanding some substantial
writing is the only way to get them to think. And to judge
how well they can express their ideas."

Ariadne glanced at the clock. "Sorry, Jude, I have to
get ready but why don't you two come over for supper
tonight, if Suzanne gets back in time? We'll be home by
late afternoon because Beau's on duty at six."

"Sounds good. She'll be here by then, too. I'll stop at
The Delectable Deli and pick up some lasagna and a veggie.
Have fun."

Beau arrived promptly at ten. He stood in Ariadne's
doorway for a moment, looking at her, then shut the door
and took her in his arms. His kiss was passionate and she
gave way to it just a shade longer than she intended. When
she moved back, her hands sliding from around his neck
to take hold of his, he pulled them to his lips and kissed
her knuckles. Her radiant smile encouraged him to kiss
her again and they stood together, bodies entwined, until
a loud meow from the kitchen caught Ariadne's attention

and she drew away, laughing. "Cassie's hungry, as usual. I have to feed her before we go."

In the kitchen she fed the cat and handed Beau the cooler with sandwiches and lemonade she'd prepared earlier. "Let's get out of here before Cassie begins begging for more," she said and led the way out to his Jeep.

Soon they were driving south along a country road, enjoying the scenery. Overhead a hawk wheeled around searching the ground for field mice. "Broad-winged," Beau said. "You can tell by the white bands on the tail. A bit early for it to be here. It's usually found in North Florida only in the winter."

"It's beautiful," she said, welcoming a conversation that didn't focus on the murder, a topic they'd agreed not to discuss on this outing.

They drove through Blountstown and at Bristol turned south into the Apalachicola National Forest, identified by a large brown wooden sign on the shoulder of the road. Broad oak trees yielded to slender pines surrounded by dense underbrush. Beau pointed east. "We could go on over to 319 and then south through Crawfordville and Medart, but they're doing a lot of road work over there and this is prettier anyway."

"It's lovely here." Ariadne was entranced by the sunlight flashing through the trees, highlighting the bright green fan-shaped saw palmettos clustered among them and mirroring the cloudless sky in brackish pools of water at their roots.

In no time they passed through Panacea with its several small cinder block seafood stores set back in the pines, painted in cheerful pink and green pastels, their signs spelling out the catch of the day. Beau pointed left just before the bridge over the Ochlocknee Bay. "Mashes Sands is down that way. Have you ever been there?"

She nodded. "A couple of times when David was small. It's a pretty beach."

"Yes it is, but I want to show you a new park near Alligator Point."

Turning left after the bridge, they drove down a stretch of road lined with tall pines. Houses began to appear through the trees on the right side and Ariadne caught glimpses of the water beyond. She knew that Alligator Point stretched like a gator tail westward for a few miles between the Gulf and the mainland. Turning left again, they drove down a road between tall sand dunes lined with sea oats. A few large houses rose up on the gulf side and then an expanse of white beach dotted with shrubs led to the Bald Point Park gate. Beau parked the Jeep and helped Ariadne out. "Look at this lovely flower," she said, bending down for a closer look at a single stem of fat, yellow, oblong blossoms spiking out from a clump of shiny green leaves.

"That's a showy crotalaria. I don't see any others around here. This one must have survived the bulldozing for the new park buildings."

"It's showy all right. I thought it was a snapdragon. Maybe they're related?"

"Could be," Beau said. He didn't think so but he didn't want to argue either.

She adjusted her canvas hat to shield her face from the sun, now high overhead and they held hands as they walked past the cinder block restrooms and the two picnic areas set up on concrete slabs under pointed wooden roofs. When they stopped in the shade of a small gnarled water oak, Beau took Ariadne in his arms and said, "We're lucky today, no one around."

Ariadne hugged him. "Look at all the different shades of blue out there." The broad expanse of light blue sky contrasted with the darker blue water at the horizon. The tide was out, leaving brown patches of sand dotting the azure sea closer to shore, where here and there small gray and white sanderlings dashed ahead of the waves, pecking for food in the shallows. "It reminds me of the paint-by-number sets we used to love as children. Especially one I did of a sailing ship in a sea of various blues."

"I'll bet it was a masterpiece."

"Hardly. And it certainly didn't compare with all this natural beauty." She smiled at him. "What did you like to do when you were a boy?"

"The usual 'guy stuff.' Baseball, football, fishing. And magic." He grinned at her surprised look. "I got a magic kit for my twelfth birthday and I practiced tricks for years. Got real good at it too. I used to perform at little kids' parties to earn extra money all through high school and college."

"Can you still do it?"

"I have a few tricks up my sleeve."

"I'll bet you have!" Ariadne laughed. "That reminds me of the play Judith and I saw over in Tallahassee the night of Randall Medina's murder. *The Tempest.* Do you know it?"

"Sure. I read it in college and was intrigued with Prospero as a magician."

"Some say he's a magus, dealing in white, not black magic."

"Please don't remind me of that," Beau said, grinning. "I wrote an essay on his magic and got a C- because I didn't research the difference between 'black' and 'white.'"

He drew her close to him as they strolled down a wide gray ramp toward the water, where the ebb tide had left clumps of brown seaweed on the sand dunes and exposed sandbars near the shore. Peeling off their sneakers and socks and rolling up their pants legs, they strolled along the shore, occasionally wading across a shallow pool to a sandbar farther out. Through the clear Gulf water they could see small patches of seaweed covered with tiny white barnacles and occasional sand dollars. Beau reached down, scooped up one of these from a raised circle in the sand, and carefully placed it in her hand. "It's gray and spiny when alive but white when it's washed out on the sand and bleached by the sun."

"David used to collect these when he was young," she said. "Beautiful things in various sizes, some as small as a shirt button. I don't know what happened to them."

"They're very fragile and crumble like sugar when broken, so it's hard to keep them very long." Taking the creature from her, he gently placed it back in its briny home.

They returned to a bench at the end of the ramp and sat watching a slender blue heron stalking fish in one of the tide pools. Now and then, farther out in the Gulf, a large white fishing boat sped in from the ocean toward the bay. Gradually the tide began to return, sending rippling waves of water toward the shore.

"I love to fish," Beau said. "Someday I'll take you out in my motorboat I keep in Carrabelle across from Dog Island where I have a small house. Someday soon I want to take you there." Beau drew Ariadne close to him. Turning her face toward his and lifting her sunglasses onto her hair, he kissed her, softly at first, then more passionately. He slipped one hand under her tee shirt and began to caress her breast through her thin cotton bra. She yielded, feeling aroused and drawn to his warmth.

Moving his hand to her lips, she held it there for a minute and then said, "I think I'm in love with you."

"I know I love you." Beau wrapped his arms around her and began kissing her again.

"Beau, wait. Not here …in public." She hesitated. "Let's eat lunch and then go back to my place." As he pulled her closer, she thought how very much she wanted to be alone with him.

In the Jeep on the way back to Coowahchobee they barely noticed the scenery, smiling at each other over nothing but their happiness.

But just as they reached Ariadne's driveway, Beau's cell phone rang. "It's Ellen," he said after talking for a minute. "She needs my help at a convenience store robbery over in Bristol." He looked forlorn. "I have to go." They kissed good-bye and Ariadne entered her house thinking that this is the way it would often be in a relationship with an officer of the law, whose job necessarily would come first. But she knew she wanted him no matter what the frustrations of their relationship might be.

📖

THAT EVENING Ariadne opened the cartons of deli food Judith had brought for supper and slid large pieces of lasagna onto dinner plates. Beside them she piled generous helpings of green beans smothered in mushrooms. As the three women ate, listening to Suzanne describe the forum in Tallahassee, Cassandra hopped up onto the chair beside her mistress, stretching as far as she dared toward the tempting odors. Despite Ariadne's frowns, Judith and Suzanne slipped the plump cat a morsel now and then.

After they finished eating Judith tapped her cigarette box on the table, stared at it for a moment, glanced over at Suzanne, and stuffed it into her shoulder bag. "I meant to ask about your date, Ari. Did you finally get to third base?"

Ariadne grimaced. "Third base? I haven't heard that one since David was in Junior High. And I'm not about to reveal any salacious details."

"Salacious?" Suzanne raised an eyebrow. "Sounds like someone got lucky today. That Beau is eye candy I'll admit, but is he your type? What do you talk about?"

"We have lots in common. Movies, TV programs, sports."

Judith snorted. "Since when have you been even remotely interested in sports? Not since you watched David's high school soccer games. And even then you were never sure about the rules. We used to tease you about that."

"Okay, we *don't* talk about sports much, but we've had interesting discussions about movies we've seen together."

"*Interesting*? That's a word I tell my students to avoid at all costs. It's so vague it turns the intended meaning around. So I'm assuming your discussions are actually fairly boring," Judith said.

"Do we really need to pursue this *un*interesting topic?" Ariadne retorted, rubbing Cassandra's furry belly as the cat lay upside down on the chair beside her. "I'll admit I'm falling for Beau, probably faster than I should. I'm trying to be cautious about getting too committed before I'm sure I'm ready."

Judith had observed the toll on Ariadne's emotions that grieving for André had taken, so she spoke softly with no sarcasm, "Seriously, dear friend, it's time to move on with your life."

"I know, Jude, but I'm just not sure if an outdoorsy sheriff can make an indoorsy academic happy," Ariadne quipped, seeming determined to keep a sense of humor about her future.

Suzanne changed the subject. "What does the sheriff say about the murder? Any new evidence?"

"No, not that he's told me about. He's particularly annoyed with the way the faculty and students have clammed up and are sticking to their original alibis, although he's convinced someone is lying." Ariadne sighed. "I'm trying to help but the students all pull the sympathy routine with me, and our colleagues stop just short of telling me to mind my own business. Some, like Chris and his pal Julian, make me believe they're hurt by my probing, as if they should be above suspicion."

"Chris is an ass par excellence, and I wouldn't be at all surprised to hear that he was involved," Judith retorted. "But you've got to sympathize with poor Julian these days. Remember how excruciating it was to wait for news about tenure and promotion? Puts a real strain on anyone and particularly, in this case, on a sensitive musician-type. Gossip has it that his home life isn't so rosy either. Elizabeth is unhappy here and who could blame her. Stuck in a small town and a small house with three small children."

Suzanne, who had never wanted offspring, gave a mock shudder and then yawned. "I hate to break this up, but I'm exhausted."

"Yes, it's time for bed," Judith said, turning to Ariadne. "We'll leave you to dream of warm beaches and warmer sex."

"We didn't—" Ariadne stopped short, realizing she had fallen victim once again to Judith's teasing. She laughed as she walked them to the kitchen door and flung it open, executing a low curtsy. "Parting is such sweet sorrow but I need my rest to face the morrow."

Judith laughed as they headed for the door. "Maybe one day we should team-teach Shakespeare, dear friend."

"As You Like It," replied Ariadne with a grin.

19

"I will a round unvarnish'd tale deliver
Of my whole course of love. …"
Othello

"WHAT A GLOOMY DAY." Ariadne spoke aloud as she stood at her kitchen window, gazing out at the fog-shrouded woods. "But at least the rain has stopped." It had been raining for two days and nights, slight drizzles and sudden downpours, saturating the earth into sponginess and plastering a mosaic of leaves and pine straw on the sidewalks and streets. Ariadne felt vaguely depressed, not so much because of the weather but because she was alone on her birthday. As if to mock her loneliness, Beau's craggy face came to mind, smiling at her as he held her in his arms. He hadn't been able to get off duty for any length of time since their beach trip and she missed him terribly.

"Get a grip." She was talking out loud again. "Can't stand around all day feeling sorry for yourself. Not with student essays awaiting grades." She crossed over to the study, Cassandra in her wake, where she piled wood into the fireplace and lit it carefully with a piece of fire starter. Soon the dancing yellow and red flames cheered her as she sat down at her desk across the room. Time to get a new rug, she thought. The old bloody one lay rolled up and locked in the evidence room at the sheriff's office. She had been trying to forget the gruesome crime although it hovered like a marauding tiger at the edges of her mind, threatening to spring upon her at any minute. She no longer spoke to anyone except Judith, Suzanne and Beau about the crime because, as they often reminded her, if the murderer was someone she knew, then she could be in danger if she probed too much or even inadvertently exposed someone's secret.

She shook her head, not wanting to believe that any of Rutherford's faculty or students could have killed Randall, although Beau and Ellen seemed to think it possible. However, they also suspected it might have been a gang of thieves believed to be responsible for a series of break-ins in several other small towns—Greensboro, Gretna, Quincy, Midway—between the Apalachicola River and Tallahassee. Beau had explained to her that several stores, houses, and trailer homes in those towns and others had been ransacked in the months preceding the crime in her home. His and Ellen's theory was that this "gang" (of maybe only two or three persons) had gone on a burglary spree but disbanded after the murder. If Medina's death had been unintentional, it would undoubtedly have frightened them. Any one or all of them could have been college people.

Cassandra curled up on the hearthstones until she had absorbed as much heat as she could stand, and then stretched, yawned, and swished over to the bookshelves, leaping high up to her favorite hiding place, a shelf from which she could survey the room. As Ariadne settled back in her desk chair and picked up the next paper, the phone rang. "Hi Mom, happy birthday!" David said. "What are you doing today? Sorry I can't be there, but I hope someone's taking you out to celebrate."

Keeping her tone light to conceal her depressed mood, Ariadne thanked him for the lovely card and said she was fine with just Cassandra for company.

"Okay, Mom. I'll try to make it up to you when I can get home again."

After his call, which had lifted her spirits somewhat, Ariadne returned to her grading task. With a small sigh she picked up a research paper from her Western History class, entitled *The Importance of Oxen in the Westward Expansion*, a topic she hadn't approved beforehand and one that sounded both banal and boring. But soon she was deeply engrossed in the essay, made compelling by her student's clever arguments and engaging rhetoric.

Several minutes later the phone rang again. "Happy birthday." Judith's voice sounded groggy. She and Suzanne had planned to return from a Boston trip in time to celebrate with Ariadne. "We're still stranded at the airport because all planes to Atlanta are being held here until the heavy storms abate there. I'm at a coffee kiosk, waiting for more to be brewed. They sold out just before I got here. We're really sorry to miss your birthday."

Ariadne mustered all the cheerfulness she could. "Don't worry, we can celebrate when you return."

"Oops, sorry, I have to go," Judith said. "It's my turn at the counter and I've got to free up my hands to buy coffee. Hope to see you soon! Hugs!"

Whatever enthusiasm Ariadne had managed to dredge up for paper grading was now lost, so she added another log to the fire and settled into an armchair. Watching the capering flames, she thought about her childhood birthdays when her father would take her and her friends on a hayride with his horse and wagon. In later years André and David had made her birthday cakes together. She smiled as she remembered a lopsided two-layer chocolate one David had been allowed to make by himself.

Stop feeling sorry for yourself, she thought, as she got up and went over to her desk. In the bottom drawer, behind a set of grade books, she found her memento box, stuffed with birthday cards from previous years. Taking it back to the armchair, she began to read them, savoring every word, especially "To Mom I love you," scrawled in David's childish hand. She lingered over those from her husband, too. She smiled. André had often reproduced poems or quotations from his favorite authors. When she opened a note card with the Venetian Grand Canal on the cover, she gasped as she read the poem she had been trying to remember.

"As an unperfect actor on the stage
Who with his fear is put beside his part,

Or some fierce thing replete with too much rage,
Whose strength's abundance weakens his own heart; ..."

In a flash she remembered that André had copied the Shakespearean sonnet onto the card the year they had traveled to Europe before David's birth.

"So I, for fear of trust, forget to say
The perfect ceremony of love's rite,
And in mine own love's strength seem to decay,
O'ercharged with burden of mine own love's might."

She brushed sudden tears away at the memory of André's love for her, thinking that she didn't need to be reminded of her loss today when she was already depressed. She got up and stirred the fire until the flames danced again. When she started to put the card back into the box, the next lines caught her eye.

"O, let my books be then the eloquence
And dumb presagers of my speaking breast,
Who plead for love and look for recompense,
More than that tongue that more hath more express'd.

"O, learn to read what silent love hath writ:
To hear with eyes belongs to love's fine wit."

"A book that speaks of love." André had said that about his gift to her that year. She remembered seeing it last in the upstairs bedroom, where she now found it buried in a basket under a pile of books she was going to read when she had time—a slim leather-bound volume with paintings of Venice. She sat on the bed engrossed in its watercolors of the canals, bridges, and *palazzi* they had both loved. Then she thought of something else. The small blue and green striped Venetian glass vase André had bought for her on the island of Murano. She'd been afraid to use it for fear of breakage, so for years it had sat empty on the mantelpiece. But when she went back down to the study to look for it now, all she found were the framed family portraits, with

a space where the vase had been. The intruders must have stolen it. Have to tell Beau, she thought, but as she picked up the phone, the doorbell rang and rang again. It kept ringing as she crossed the foyer to the front door.

"Hi ya, Babe!" An ebullient Miles grinned at her as he carried a large food box from The Delectable Deli into the dining room. He returned to his car for a cake box and a bottle of champagne in an ice bucket. After setting the table with her good dinnerware, retrieved from the sideboard as if he owned the place, he dished out the food and steered her to the table, where he pulled back a chair with an exaggerated flourish and seated her, kissing the nape of her neck in the process. Then he opened the other box and set before her a round cake, its vanilla frosting decorated with pink roses and two red entwined hearts.

"Happy birthday, Beautiful!" Miles leaned over her, lifted her face to his, and kissed her.

"Miles, it's ..."

"Tacky. I know. Especially the hearts. But at the risk of perpetuating an old cliché, it's the thought that counts."

"It's lovely, really lovely. And I'm flattered that you went to all this trouble on my birthday."

Miles made a sweeping bow. "No trouble, Milady." He busied himself opening and pouring the champagne, and then toasted her beauty, brains, and sexy body, in typical Miles fashion. Ariadne found her spirits rising with each sip. Bending over the table Miles sniffed the aroma of quail, scalloped potatoes, and julienne carrots with black mushrooms. "The Deli people outdid themselves with this special order," he said. "It smells delicious." Then he drew Ariadne up from her chair and began to nibble her neck. "But not as delicious as you."

Ariadne resisted his attempts to steer her upstairs to her bedroom. "Miles, the food will get cold." She tried to wriggle out of his arms, becoming more annoyed as he persisted.

"Hot desires are more compelling than hot food." He continued kissing her as he nudged her across the room. "Cold food is a small price to pay for passion."

"Miles, I have to tell you something," she started to say, when the doorbell jangled.

Miles whispered into her ear. "Let it go. It can't be important."

Ariadne shook her head and, pulling free, crossed the foyer and opened the door. Standing before her, holding a small cake box, was Beau, in his dark green uniform, looking a bit sheepish. "Hi. Happy birthday. I thought you might like this cake." He opened the box to reveal a round vanilla-frosted cake covered with pink roses around two red entwined hearts and the words, "Happy Birthday, Ariaden."

They both stared at the misspelling.

"Damn!" Beau looked stricken. "I didn't see that."

His chagrin made her heart lurch. "It's beautiful. Never mind the mistake. Come on in."

"Who is it, Doll?" Miles came up behind her, put his arms around her waist, and pressed his face against her hair. "Oh, hi Sheriff, what have you got there?" He raised his eyebrows at the cake. "Well, well, great masculine minds seem to run in the same channels. But what's with the misspelled name?"

"Never mind." Ariadne tried to avert tension. "Two cakes are better than none. Come in, Beau, and join us for a gourmet lunch. Miles brought plenty of food."

The sheriff looked dismayed by the lawyer's presence and apparent intimacy with Ariadne. "Sorry, I can't. I'm on my way to the office to relieve Ellen. She's been there since dawn."

Ariadne turned to Miles. "I need to talk to Beau alone for a moment." She stepped out onto the veranda and put her arms around him. "This isn't what it looks like. I mean, what it must seem to be to you. Miles is just an old friend who came to celebrate my birthday. I really want you to stay."

Beau looked skeptical but hugged her back. "I'm sorry, but I really can't."

"Wait a minute," she said as he turned away. "There's something I need to tell you. When I was looking at a Venice book, I realized that my green and blue Venetian glass bud vase is missing from the mantelpiece. I guess it's just too familiar, something I had stopped noticing. It's what the Shakespearean sonnet about books speaking for the lover was trying to tell me."

Beau looked puzzled, trying to make a connection between books, vase, and poem.

"I'm sorry, I ..." Ariadne tried again to explain.

Just then Miles emerged, looking peeved. "Seems to me you have more than you need for a successful birthday and I just remembered I have to return an urgent phone call." He grabbed her a bit roughly, kissed her cheek, and strode over to his Jaguar standing in the drive.

When Ariadne again began to stammer out an apology, Beau kissed her and held her close. "It's all right, I understand. And I want to hear more about the vase. And the book and the poem. But right now I really do have to get to the office." He kissed her again, on her lips and then on her forehead, and left.

Back in the dining room Ariadne gathered up the food and refrigerated it because she didn't feel like eating. She smiled as she stared at the two cakes and the misspelling of her name on Beau's, realizing how much she desired him. She vowed to break off with Miles as soon as possible.

An hour later, Beau returned, enveloping her with hugs, kisses, and happy birthday wishes. "I got lucky," he grinned. "Mike Gregson came in to spell me because he needs the extra hours."

She grabbed his hand and led him to the kitchen. "Are you hungry? I have lots of food. Or do you want to hear about the Venetian bud vase now? I'm so embarrassed about not realizing it was missing. Funny how you said that the poem I couldn't remember might be a clue and then it was. It led me to the Venice book and then to the vase. Or rather the place on the mantelpiece where the vase should have been."

Beau took her in his arms and began kissing her again, then whispered in her ear, "I don't want to hear about any clues just now."

She felt her heart beating against his as she held him tightly against her and then led him up to her bedroom. "Neither do I."

LATE THE NEXT MORNING she woke from a dream in which she'd been carrying a large chocolate cake down a long passageway, trying to keep its heavily frosted layers from slipping off one another onto the floor. Turning over to the middle of the bed, she reached for Beau, but he was gone, leaving the imprint of his head on the pillow. Next to it was a note in his large, sloping handwriting, "Didn't want to wake you. I'll call later. XXX"

Ariadne lay back and thought about how she had responded to Beau's fervent lovemaking with passion she had long suppressed. "And where were you, old girl?" she asked Cassandra, who had jumped onto the bed, meowing for breakfast. "Decided not to join us here, I guess. Just as well. At times like those three really is a crowd."

The bedside phone rang and a more cheerful Judith said, "Hi, we're back. Got into Tallahassee after midnight. We're exhausted but I wanted to call to see how you're doing. You seemed kind of depressed yesterday."

"I'm much better today," Ariadne said, not wanting to say how much, much better she felt. "And I hope you'll come over to eat with me tonight." Judith's positive response prompted Ariadne to add, "Is it all right with you if I ask Beau to join us?"

"Sure. We both like him."

The evening went better than she had expected. During dinner they all avoided any mention of the Medina murder, but the sheriff entertained them with stories of unusual crimes he'd encountered in his long career. They discussed local and national politics, recent movies, and books they wished they'd written. After they had toasted Ariadne's birthday with the rest of Miles's champagne, they laughed and chatted as they washed the dishes and cleaned up the kitchen.

Finally Judith and Suzanne, nearly asleep, put on their coats, said warm good-byes to Beau, and thanked Ariadne for a delightful evening. She accompanied them to the door, where Judith hugged her and whispered, "I love that guy!"

"Good," Ariadne said, "because I do too."

20

"...the wolf...thus with his stealthy pace,
With Tarquin's ravishing strides, towards his design
Moves like a ghost...."
Macbeth

UNDER COVER OF DARKNESS with just the sliver of a new moon high overhead, a figure dressed in black jeans, jacket, and knit cap creeps out of the woods and onto the Rutherford campus. Up in the tall pines an owl hoots and toward town someone's dog howls, breaking the eerie silence. Moving around the walls of the women's dorm, seeking entrance, the shadowy figure discovers a back door propped open an inch or so by a wooden block. One hand reaches up to unscrew the dim bulb lighting up the small stoop. Slipping inside, the intruder climbs the stairs to the second floor, pulls open the fire door, and glides through. Pausing to listen for signs of life but hearing none, the invader moves from door to door, checking the nameplates. Most of the doors are decorated for Halloween with black silhouettes of witches flying on broomsticks over yellow smiley faces drawn to resemble pumpkins. At number 22 a gloved hand reaches out to adjust the witch dangling over that smiley's black shiny eyes, then taps the nameplate below: Allison McEnvoy.

Pushing open the door, the interloper steps inside, moves over to the bed, and looks down at Allison, lying supine, her gauzy white nightgown outlining her body. Her slightly opened dark-rimmed eyes reveal white half-moons beneath her pale gold eyelashes and her pink lips flutter with each shuddering breath. Gloved fingers touch her blonde curls, tugging one forward on each side of her head to form a ring under her chin, but then pull back as a loud snore erupts from Allison's rosy mouth. Apparently she has taken a sleeping pill, evidenced by the small bottle on the bedside table, so this is going to be easier than expected.

A flat pink child's pillow lies beside her. Some loving hand has embroidered "Rock-a-bye Baby" on it in rainbow colors with fluffy white lambs gamboling beneath a cradle suspended from the branch of a slender tree. The gloved hands seize the pillow and lower it onto Allison's face, then bear down as she begins to struggle. The hands press the pillow harder while Allison's body flails around on the rumpled sheet. Her assailant climbs onto the bed and straddles Allison to hold her down, smothering her with the fluffy lambs, but Allison's struggles suddenly dislodge the pillow and her mouth opens in a potential scream. The murderous hands grab her throat and squeeze until Allison jerks and then lies still. The killer, eyes averted, slides off the bed, empties the pill bottle into a jacket pocket, replaces the bottle on the table, and then, clutching the pillow, steals out of the room, down the stairs, and out the back door.

"Hey, watch it, dimwit!" Bob Stanforst protests as the heavy door slams into his girlfriend, Ginger Berline. A dark-clad figure brushes past them, lopes a few feet across the parking lot, and veers off into the woods. Bob pulls a small flashlight from his pocket and aims the beam in that direction but the person has vanished. Bob turns back to Ginger, squashed up against the brick wall. "Are you okay?"

"I'm fine, just fine." Ginger's voice registers her annoyance. "Who was that?" She adjusts her clothing and moves toward the door.

"Probably one of your friends let her date in," Bob says, wishing she'd do the same.

"It's really late and I'm tired." Ginger likes Bob but not enough for serious lovemaking. "Call me tomorrow." As she enters the dorm, she removes the wooden prop and locks the door behind her to ensure herself and her dorm sisters a night of safe and restful sleep.

21

"Chaos is come again."
Othello

"**NOOOOOOOO.** Oh, noooooooooo." Mary Matthews' plaintive cries woke the young women sleeping late on Saturday in the dorm rooms adjacent to Allison's. Her screams followed her discovery of Allison's body lying atop wrinkled sheets, her hair like spun gold flaming out on the pillow, her eyes closed in perpetual sleep. Mary had reached out to shake Allison awake, but when the golden-crowned head rolled off the pillow at a distorted angle, Mary screamed and fell to her knees on the braided rug beside the bed.

By twos and threes other dorm residents rushed into the room.

"Help her."

"Get Peggy."

"Call 911."

"Just *do* something."

Peggy Blake, the resident dorm assistant, a young woman barely older than her charges, rushed past them and paused in shocked silence before the bed. She fumbled her cell phone out of her jeans pocket and dialed 911. "One of our students looks …like she's dead." She glanced around. "There's an empty bottle next to the bed. Maybe she took too many sleeping pills?" Her voice shook as she gave the location of the dorm, but she remained calm. The stunned and frightened students, some weeping, followed her to the first-floor lounge.

The ambulance arrived just ahead of several police and sheriff cars, their red and blue lights flashing. Trying to keep calm, Peggy met the officers at the front door, introduced herself, and indicated the way to Allison's room before returning to the lounge. After the coroner, who had arrived with the ambulance, pronounced Allison dead and suggested strangulation to the officers as a possible cause of death, Silas Henley and his crime scenes crew began to process the room.

Officer Darlene Mapes met Beau and Ellen as they returned to the foyer. "The dean is demanding to see you."

They went outside, where Vernon Giddings stood waiting. "Terrible, just terrible," he groaned. "I was told a student killed herself. Who was it?"

"The student is Allison McEnvoy, but we don't want her name released until we notify her family," Beau told him. "Would you get that information for us, please?"

"Of course, of course, right away." Vernon's agitation was apparent in his wavering voice.

"We won't know the cause of death for sure until we've investigated, maybe not until after the autopsy. But we think she might have been attacked."

Vernon blanched. "Attacked? Oh dear, how could that happen? It couldn't have been one of the students who live here. Nice girls, all of them, from good families. Must have been an intruder, don't you think?"

"We're checking into that possibility."

Vernon ran a hand through his thinning white hair. "We pride ourselves on the safety of this dorm, Sheriff. Now parents will be demanding that we immediately install the alarm system we've been promising." He wrung his hands. "There's just never enough money...."

After thanking the dean Beau conferred with Darlene, who reported that the deputies had found all the doors and windows securely locked and undamaged. Then he summoned Tommie Lee Graham, the security guard, who followed Beau into the foyer. "Awful thing, Beau, awful. You think she kill't herself?"

"We don't know for sure but by the look of things, she might have been attacked."

"Attacked? By who? One of the girls who live here?" He shook his head. "Can't think one of them woulda done that. Nice girls. Always nice to me. And Peggy, too. Heart of gold she has."

"Sure, I understand, Tommie Lee." Beau paused. "Could someone else have gotten inside last night?"

The security guard looked surprised, then defiant. "Don't see how. Peggy's careful about not lettin' anyone in 'cept the ones that live here. And I checked all the doors last night just after the one o'clock curfew, Beau. None of them was open, not one. And your own deputies found nothin' broken into. Can't see how someone coulda got in. Unless somebody inside let 'em in."

"That's possible. Or could an outsider have entered earlier and hidden inside?"

Tommie Lee furrowed his brow. "Coulda done. But Peggy or one of the seniors is s'pposed to be at the front desk until curfew. Not part of my job to check on that. Just to make the rounds at night and be on call day and night. I got my cell phone on me all the time." He pulled it out from his pocket and held it up for Beau to see.

"I'm sure you do your job well, Tommie Lee. When you made your rounds last night, did you see anyone lurking about? Or anything unusual?"

"Seen some students comin' and goin' but nobody I didn't know." He furrowed his brow. "Nothin' unusual, I guess."

"Where were you after you made your rounds?"

Tommie Lee looked defensive. "In my apartment 'cross the street from campus. Ever'one knows I'm there all night and they have my number if they need me."

"Thanks, Tommie Lee. I appreciate your help and I'll get back to you if I need anything else."

They shook hands and Tommie Lee started for the door, but then returned. "Beau, maybe I shouldn't be sayin' this. Don't want to get them nice girls in trouble or nothin', but jist after school started last fall, I had to come back over here real late in the night, and I found the back door propped open. I reported it to Peggy and she told me later that she'd really laid into those girls, tellin' 'em they'd be in big trouble if they ever done it again. Didn't think they did, but now I ain't so sure."

After Tommie Lee left, Beau called Peggy out into the foyer. "I saw the empty pill bottle by her bed," she told him, "but I can't believe Allison would commit suicide. Why would she do that?"

The sheriff looked deep into her anxious eyes. "We're not sure yet how Allison died but there are enough signs of a struggle to make us think someone may have attacked her."

Peggy shook her head. "No one would want to hurt Allison. The girls all like her. She's friendly and kind and …" Her voice trailed off.

"If she was attacked, her assailant could have been someone from outside the dorm. Maybe even a random intruder."

Peggy's eyes widened. "Like a Ted Bundy?"

Everyone knows the story of Bundy's assault on Florida State University coeds in the 1970s, Beau thought. How he had gained easy access to a sorority house in the early morning winter darkness, then bludgeoned two coeds to death and mutilated their bodies before slipping out unnoticed to continue his killing spree.

"I don't know how anyone could have gotten in, Sheriff. I lock up after curfew." Peggy looked apologetic. "I know that 'curfew' sounds odd today when schools are not as strict and protective as they used to be. But Rutherford parents insist on it because they want security for their girls. The guys' dorm doesn't have hours, but we have a strict one a.m. curfew for the girls." Her scornful tone suggested she thought the discrepancy unfair.

The sheriff pulled out his notebook. "Do you stay at the front desk until all the students are back?"

"Yes I do. Last night a group arrived just at one o'clock and signed in as usual. I checked the list and everyone was here, so I locked the doors and went to bed."

Beau led her back to the lounge, where the students were quieter now. Peggy introduced the sheriff and the students swiveled their heads in his direction as he addressed them. "You've had a great shock and I can see how distraught you are. But it's very important for us to get as much information as quickly as we can." The young women nodded but no one spoke. "We'll be talking to each one of you individually as soon as we can, but now I need to ask you an important question and I need the truth. Were you all in the dorm by one o'clock this morning?"

Most of them nodded again, but two of them looked at each other and then down at their hands clasped in their laps. Beau spoke to Peggy, who then approached Ginger Berline and Rebecca Swit. "The sheriff wants to talk to you." They trouped out to the foyer where Peggy introduced them to the sheriff.

"If you know something about last night, you need to tell me," he said.

Ginger's eyes filled with tears. "It's all my fault. Bob Stanforst and I drove over to a new club in Elliottville that doesn't even open until eleven. We intended to stay just an hour but we lost track of the time." She swallowed hard. "I called Rebecca on our way home and asked her to sign me in and prop the back door open."

Rebecca shook her head. "It was my fault, too. I knew I shouldn't have done it, but I didn't think anything bad would happen. I mean, we've done it before and nothing did."

Unfortunately, not everyone remembers the Ted Bundy story, Beau thought. Or they figured it couldn't happen to them. He let Rebecca return to the other students. "Now, Ginger, tell me the rest of it."

"We saw someone come out of the dorm. But I couldn't identify him or anything. It all went so fast. One minute he was bumping into us and the next minute he was gone into the woods."

Beau took out his notebook. "Slow down, Ginger. This is important. I want you to tell me exactly what happened last night between the time you arrived from Elliottville and the time you entered the dorm. Try to remember every detail you can."

Ginger nodded, suddenly aware of the significance of their encounter with the shadowy figure. "After we came back from Elliottville Bob parked the car and walked me to the back door. The one Rebecca had propped open. We stood there a minute talking and suddenly the door opened and slammed me into the dorm wall. A guy ran by and headed into the woods. Bob shined his flashlight on him but I didn't see him really well. Maybe Bob did, but we didn't talk about it."

"Do you remember what the person was wearing?"

"A jacket, I think. And a knit cap. Both dark-colored."

"Could it have been someone you know?" Beau knew he had to be careful not to lead her into saying something she didn't actually recall, but he hoped she'd remember some significant detail.

"I don't think it could have been because he would have stopped to see if I was all right. Don't you think so?"

Beau nodded and thanked her for her help, telling her they'd take her statement later and to call him if she thought of anything else; then he let her rejoin the others.

Ellen then brought Mary to sit with them around the coffee table. "I know how shocked you are and how difficult this is for you, Mary, but it's especially important that we talk to you now because you were the one who found Allison."

Mary plopped her limp body into a worn easy chair and peered at them with her red-rimmed black eyes, like two raisins in her puffy tear-stained face. "I ...I just can't believe it. You know what I mean? Allison dead. Why did she do it?"

Ellen glanced at Beau. "Why did she do what, Mary?"

"Take those sleeping pills. I saw the empty pill bottle on the nightstand. Why did she do it? I didn't think she was, like, that desperate. I thought she was getting help. You know what I mean?"

Ellen waited to tell her about their attack theory because she wanted to hear more about Allison's psychological state. "Why did she need help?"

"She was pregnant. She told me a while ago but I don't think she told any of the other girls. She didn't want anyone to know. You know what I mean?"

"Mary." Beau raised his voice slightly to get her attention. "She may have overdosed on the sleeping pills, but we won't know that for sure until the autopsy. But we think she may have struggled with someone who attacked and killed her."

Mary was stunned. "Autopsy? Attacked? Killed? Who would do that? Who would kill Allison? Why?"

Beau gave her a minute to recover. "Let's talk about Allison's room when you found her. Did you notice anything unusual?"

"Well, the bed was all messed up and everything. But I was so upset I didn't look around much." As she thought for a moment her shoe-button eyes widened. "Hey, I didn't see her baby pillow there on her bed. She always slept with it. Maybe it fell off when …" She couldn't finish the thought.

Ellen and Beau exchanged glances. "What pillow?" The sergeant asked.

"Her pink baby pillow. The one her mother had embroidered with 'Rock-a-bye Baby' and a cradle about to fall out of a tree. Sometimes we'd laugh about how that cradle would, like, crush the lambs under the tree when it fell. You know what I mean? But Allison loved that pillow and slept with it, like, every night, especially after her father died."

"What else did you see?"

"Just that empty pill bottle. But Allison would never kill herself!"

"We're sorry for your shock and loss, Mary. We'd stop now but we have to get as much information as we can as quickly as possible so we can proceed with our investigation." Beau hoped he didn't sound too official and insensitive.

Wiping her eyes with a tissue, Mary nodded, so he continued. "Where were you last evening?"

"At the Baldwins' house. I took an overnight so I could babysit their kids."

"Where did they go?"

"Professor Baldwin was over in Tallahassee for a two-day meeting or, like, seminar, or something. So Mrs. Baldwin went to an art exhibit over in Elliottville. She stayed for dinner and a movie and then overnight at a motel because she didn't want to drive home after dark. That seemed sorta weird to me. I think she just, like, wanted to get away from those kids." Mary frowned. "They're very smart and fun sometimes but they're exasperating too. I think they're spoiled. You know what I mean? They're, like, very demanding and not very polite. I keep trying to get them to say 'please' and 'thank you' but they don't do it very often. And sometimes they make me mad when they mimic me. If I'm too strict with them, they do things like dance around singing my name until I think I'll go crazy. You know what I mean?"

"What time did the Baldwins return?" Ellen asked.

"Mrs. Baldwin came back about eight this morning. The kids had been up, like, two hours already, and Miranda and Duncan were hopping all over the place shouting at each other while I was changing Rosie's messy diaper for the *second* time."

"Did Mrs. Baldwin drive you back to the dorm? Or was the professor back by then, too?" Ellen asked.

"I never saw him. I drove my own car back. And then I went to Allison's room and found her …" Mary's black eyes filled with tears and she hugged her arms to her shuddering body.

Ellen and Beau read each other's glances as Ellen pulled more tissues from a pocket pack and handed them to Mary. "We're sorry to keep you so long, Mary. Just one more question and we'll let you go back to the others. Did Allison ever say who the father of her expected baby was?"

Mary squirmed around in the chair. "She was, like, 'It wasn't Jason.' Her boyfriend, Jason Overstreet. I thought she was, like, maybe trying to protect him. You know what I mean? But I don't really think so because she told me they'd never had sex and I believed her. And I'm sure Jason would have married her if it'd been him." She leaned forward and spoke in a whisper. "I think she might have been raped or something. She was, like, 'I wasn't raped,' but I don't think she'd do it with anybody. You know what I mean? She didn't like any other guy. Except those professors she had, like, crushes on. But that wasn't anything important."

Ellen nodded to encourage her to continue.

"All she did was flirt with them a little. We all do that. It's fun and they seem to like it." Mary frowned. "Doesn't help our grades any, though."

"What professors do you flirt with?"

"Oh, we all adore Professor Baldwin," Mary said. He's so, like, handsome and nice. But Allison was having trouble in his class in music appreciation, trying to get her grade up. She was so proud of her grade point average and that D was going to, like, ruin it. She went to see him about it but he wasn't very helpful, I think. Anyway, she was, like, mad at him about it."

"And the others?"

"She sorta liked Professor Bannerman. He's popular because it's easy to get a good grade in his class. But I think he's a jerk." She lowered her voice though no one else was around to hear her. "I know for a fact that he got into a fight with a guy up at Southwestern. Over a *girl*. Nobody, like, talks about it anymore but everyone was laughing about it when it happened. He likes to date students and he even dates some from here, but they, like, go out of town so no one will know. But we do." She thought for a moment. "Oh, I almost forgot Mr. Gooch, the new basketball coach. He's always, like, willing to tutor students with math. Allison is a whiz at math, so she didn't need help like I do, but she thought he was cute."

Mary shook her curly head when Ellen asked about other professors Allison flirted with. "Can you think of anything else we should know?"

Mary thought for a moment. "Well, I'm not sure this is important but Allison was upset about her father's will. It should have been settled by now, but it wasn't and she was like, 'I *really* need that money. And I *deserve* to have it.' But they've been searching for her older sister. Her half-sister. Allison was, like, 'I never knew her because she left home when I was just a baby.' Sometimes when she'd get a letter from her mother, she'd get mad. Once she tore the letter up. But I don't see how that would have, like, anything to do with her death." Mary's voice shook as she said the word she dreaded.

"Thanks for your help, Mary" Ellen said. "We're very sorry this happened to your friend."

Mary continued to sob as Beau and Ellen returned her to Peggy's care.

The officers assured the students that they would soon be allowed to return to their rooms and that counselors would come to help them cope with their grief and shock. Before leaving the dorm Beau and Ellen consulted with the deputy taking individual statements, left Silas and his crew to finish processing Allison's room, then checked the crime scene tape there and in the back-door area. At the front door they were met by Sestina Soporis, the dean's secretary, with the information that they needed to contact Allison's mother. In the parking lot Beau spoke briefly with the reporters, giving them only as much information about the crime as necessary. Later he and Ellen would prepare statements for the television crews that were probably already on their way to Coowahchobee from Tallahassee and Elliottville.

Beau turned to Ellen. "After we speak with her mother, we'll grab some lunch and then round up as many more students as we can find. Not too many here on a weekend, I suspect, but we'll want to talk to them ASAP."

22

"...my heart is drowned with grief,
Whose flood begins to flow within mine eyes...."
II Henry VI

THE NEWS OF ALLISON'S DEATH spread quickly across the Rutherford campus and beyond. By late afternoon several students who hadn't gone home for the weekend had gathered in the cafeteria. Jason sat at a large round table with his friends, his head hidden in his folded arms, his shoulders quivering whenever a sob escaped him. On the table several plastic-wrapped sandwiches and small unopened bags of potato chips were strewn among cans of Coke and Pepsi but nobody was eating.

His friends felt helpless but tried to comfort him. "Hey man." "Come on now." All of them had experienced the death of others, including Randall Medina and their own grandparents, but no one their age and as close to them as Allison had been.

Lyman Litchgate and Bob Stanforst looked up and then back at Jason as Beau and Ellen approached them. "Police, Dude," Lyman informed the huddled shape. Jason raised his head and pushed back from the table, his tear-stained face a blank.

"Allison was his girlfriend. He loved her," Lyman told the officers, who were surprised to hear him articulate this message in complete sentences without being prompted. They saw that today he was dressed more plainly in jeans and a faded gray sweatshirt, though his hair was still striped pink and purple and his various jewelry piercings were all in place.

Ellen's voice was soft and reassuring. "We need to talk to all of you about last night. You understand that we can't wait longer if we're to get to the truth about what happened to Allison."

Jason hung his head as if he couldn't bear to hear the news again, and he gripped the table edge as his hands began to shake. "I didn't kill her. I love her." He swiped tears away with his flannel shirtsleeve.

Bob's voice trembled. "It wasn't Jason. I saw who it was. I was there and saw it wasn't him. Ask *me* about it. Not *him*. He's suffering, man. Let him alone."

"Let's go over to that other table in the corner," Beau said to Bob and then looked over at Lyman and at Jonathan Kennedy, sitting alone at a nearby table. "We'll want to talk to you two also. You can wait over there by the windows."

When they were all rearranged, Ellen opened her notebook and encouraged Jason to continue. He spoke rapidly, as if he had to get it all out at once. "I know it looks bad for me, her being my girlfriend and all. But I swear I didn't kill her." Like you didn't kill Randall Medina, Ellen wanted to say but restrained herself. They couldn't prove anything about that murder, and she didn't want to compromise this investigation by linking it to Medina's death. Even if they might be related. And even if Jason was a suspect. She chose her words carefully. "When did you last see Allison?"

"Yesterday about suppertime. I wanted to get hamburgers at the drive-in but Allison said she felt sick. Eating would make her worse, she said, so we just sat in the dorm parking lot and talked." Jason's muffled voice was barely audible.

"How long did you sit in the car talking?"

"Not long. I don't know." He shook his head.

"What did you talk about?"

He avoided her eyes. "Nothing much."

Ellen waited until he glanced at her again. "We were told she was pregnant. Did you know that?"

Jason's eyes narrowed. "She told me."

"When did she tell you?"

"Then. In the car."

"How did you feel about her being pregnant?"

Jason squeezed his elbows close to his sides. He hung his head and spoke almost in a whisper. "I hated it. I yelled at her but she started to cry and then I felt sorry for her."

"Did you ask her who the father was?"

"Yes, but she wouldn't tell me. She said it was a mistake and she didn't love him." His voice broke on the word "love" and the rest of the sentence was barely audible.

"What else, Jason?"

"We talked about getting married but we have no money. She said she'd get some as soon as her father's will was settled but that's taking a lot of time." Jason slumped in his chair. "When I get money I have to give it to my dad. He needs it bad."

Ellen wrote this in her notebook but decided not to pursue the topic just then. She wanted to keep him focused on Allison. "How did she feel about that?"

Jason wiped his sleeve across his eyes. "Allison said it was hopeless and started to cry again. I reached out to her but she pulled away, like she was afraid."

"Afraid you might hit her?"

"I guess."

"Had you ever hurt her before?"

Jason stood up and looked directly at Ellen. "No. And I didn't hit her then either. I wouldn't hurt her. I love her."

"Sit down, Jason. I'm not saying you did anything to her." Ellen waited until he took his seat again. "What happened next?"

"She got out of the car and ran into the dorm before I could stop her. I didn't want to see any of the guys so I drove home. To Blountstown."

"When was that?"

"About seven. Mom was glad to see me and made me some supper, but then my dad started in about how he needed money and I was no good because I was wasting my time in college instead of getting a job to make money to help them out. Same old story." He looked straight into Ellen's soft dark eyes. "I get scholarship money for school but nothing extra for Dad."

"I understand how difficult that is for you, Jason. What did you do when he confronted you like that?"

"Same thing I always do. Got out of there. Have to when he gets like that."

"So where did you go?"

"I drove around town for awhile and then out in the country. But I didn't want to waste gas so finally I came back to the dorm. That's where the guys found me this morning and told me about Allison. I wanted to go over to her dorm but they wouldn't let me. Told me the police had taken her away. Then they talked me into coming with them to get something to eat." He looked down at the sandwiches and chips in front of him. "But I can't eat."

"What time did you get back to the dorm last night?"

"I don't know. Around three, I guess."

Ellen debated about how far she could or should push him. He seemed calmer now but the effects of Allison's death showed in his trembling hands and bleary eyes. "Did you stop anywhere or see anyone while you were driving around?"

"No." He bowed his head as tears welled up again. "I know it looks bad for me. But I didn't kill Allison. I wouldn't do that."

Over at a table in the corner Beau asked Bob about what he had done and seen the night before. "It's very important that you remember exactly what happened while you were standing with Ginger by the back door of the dorm."

"Yes sir, I know that. The guy I saw was about Jason's height, I guess, but I'm pretty sure it wasn't him. I think I'd recognize him even in the dark." Bob's tone was defensive.

"Just tell me what happened."

"Yes sir. Well, the door flew open and banged into Ginger. I tried to help her but she said she was all right."

"Did you get a good look at the person who came out the door?"

"The light was out so we couldn't see much," Bob said, trying to focus his thoughts. "He was wearing a jacket and a cap. And I think he was carrying something, but I couldn't tell for sure. By the time I shined my flashlight on him, he was already running into the woods."

"What was he carrying?"

"I don't know. Too hard to tell in the dark."

"Did you get a look at the face?"

"No sir. His head was down and it all happened really fast."

"What about the jacket and cap. Can you describe them?"

"A black jacket and the cap was one of those knit things. Black, too, or maybe dark blue?"

Beau noted it down. "There's something I'm wondering about, son. Didn't you or Ginger think it strange that someone was exiting the dorm at that time of night? If it had been one of the residents sneaking out, wouldn't she have stopped to apologize for bumping into you? Or just to say 'hi' or something?"

"We thought it was maybe somebody's date who'd been in the dorm after hours."

"And you didn't call the guard?"

"Tommie Lee? No, no sir, we didn't. We didn't want to get anybody in trouble."

"But didn't you think it was strange when the person ran off into the woods?"

Bob squirmed around in his chair. "I guess so. But we just didn't say anything about it." He noticed the sheriff's stern look. "We were arguing."

"Thank you, son, for being so cooperative. We'll be back to you if we need more information."

"For a line-up maybe? Like you see on TV?" Bob asked.

"It may come to that and we'll notify you if it does." But Beau suspected there was little or no chance that either Bob or Ginger would be able to identify the person they saw—or didn't really see.

After questioning the loquacious Jonathan, the reticent Lyman, and a few other students with no relevant results, the officers left the cafeteria.

"Same damn story this time around," Beau said. "They look you straight in the eye and beat around the bush about their whereabouts. We need to put more pressure on them."

For the next several hours he and Ellen were kept busy hunting down the three professors mentioned by Mary as being objects of Allison's crushes. They found the coach, Adam Gooch, playing basketball in the Rutherford gym with some of his team. He appeared to be shocked and bewildered when they told him about Allison. "I just started working here a few months ago so I don't know any of the students very well yet."

Beau checked his notebook. "One student mentioned that you tutored her and others in math. She said they had crushes on you."

Adam blushed and brushed a lock of sandy hair off his forehead. "Yes, I tutor students twice a week in the early morning. Mostly girls. But I never think about them in the way you're suggesting. They're so *young*, just kids, really. And no way would I harm any of them." When asked where he'd been overnight, Adam told them he'd been at his mother's house, three blocks from the college, where he lived with her and his younger sister.

On their way back to their car Beau said, "He seemed genuinely surprised that we might think he was in any way involved with Allison or any of the other girls."

Ellen agreed. "Or that we might consider him a murder suspect. He seems honest but you never know. Might be an act. I'll check his story with his mother."

When they questioned Chris Bannerman on the city golf course, where he was waiting to tee off, he folded his arms across his chest and frowned at them. "I suppose you know my reputation by now, so no wonder you might suspect me. But I never dated Allison. And there's no way I would get a student pregnant. I can't imagine any of my colleagues impregnating students either, much less killing them. Why would we jeopardize our careers? This is the twenty-first century, the technological age. Any semi-sophisticated person would be able to find a solution to an unwanted pregnancy short of murdering the woman." When asked to account for his whereabouts the night before, he readily told them he'd been with Delana McAndrew, the new physical education instructor, until the wee hours. He winked at Ellen as his foursome was announced over the loudspeaker. "Now if you'll excuse me, I have important business to attend to."

Ellen adjusted her seat belt as the officers left the golf course. "I don't trust that guy farther than I could hit one of those little white balls."

"Maybe you can take up golf when you retire." Beau grinned at her.

"I doubt it. Besides, I'm too young to think about retirement."

"Nor would I want you to. Your judgment of human character and motives is the best I've ever seen in a law officer."

"But you must have thought about retiring, Beau. What are your plans?"

"Yeah, I've thought about it. Especially with two difficult murder cases on our hands. Tires me out." He smiled at her. "I'd like to move out to Dog Island where I could relax, fish, and read those nature books my relatives give me every Christmas and birthday."

"Sounds like a plan." Ellen wondered if he would ever do it. Active guys like him often had problems retiring from their jobs.

Ellen jotted down a couple of items in her notebook as they turned south on Ash Street, heading toward the Baldwins' house. "Bannerman bears watching," she said. "I've made a note to check with Delana McAndrew about that date."

"Yes, he's high on my list of suspects. Judging from the story about his fight with the guy in Elliottville, he can be violent if provoked."

Ellen tapped her pen on her book. "Fighting over a woman may seem romantic to some, but it just spells trouble to me."

At the Baldwin house the officers found a frazzled Elizabeth carrying a screaming Rosalind. She ushered them into the tiny living room while she paced up and down, jostling the baby and patting her back. "She's teething." Elizabeth raised her voice to be heard over the din. "I'm at my wit's end trying to quiet her."

Ellen asked for an ice cube and a piece of paper toweling, which Elizabeth fetched from the kitchen. Taking Rosalind on her lap, Ellen carefully pressed the paper-covered ice to the baby's gums while crooning a soft tune. Rosalind stopped in mid-wail, her eyes fixed on Ellen's. Elizabeth motioned the sheriff into an armchair and sat down on the sofa. "Ice. Of course, I should have thought of that. My other two never had teething problems, though god knows they had everything else."

Beau cleared his throat. "We came to talk to your husband."

"Julian's taken our son to the park. He's been away a couple of days and now is trying to get in some quality time with each child separately." She paused, thinking. "What do you want with him?"

"Allison McEnvoy died in Rutherford's dorm last night and we're questioning everyone who knew her."

"We heard," Elizabeth said. "Our neighbor heard it from her cleaning woman who heard it from god knows who. Gossip spreads like wildfire in this town. Do you think the girl was murdered?"

Beau nodded. "All signs point to it, ma'am."

"Horrible, just horrible." She crossed and uncrossed her legs, smoothing out a wrinkle in her cotton slacks. "But I seriously doubt that Julian knew the student very well. Just one of those girls who stalk professors." She decided not to mention Allison's visit to their home or Julian's panic and subsequent silence about the reason for her visit.

"Stalk?" Ellen handed over Rosalind, who had fallen asleep. "Was she stalking your husband?"

Fearing to disturb the baby, Elizabeth lowered her voice. "Well, 'stalk' is perhaps too harsh a term for her hanging around Julian. He says all coeds have crushes on their professors and it means nothing. To him, anyway, but I suspect that others take advantage of their adoration."

"But you don't think your husband does?" Ellen spoke softly too.

Elizabeth's eyes narrowed. "Of course not. He's a devoted husband and father. And a highly principled professor. With a lot to lose right now during his tenure process. Why would he put his career in jeopardy just for a few jollies with a bim—" She broke off and bit her lower lip. "With a student."

The sheriff opened his notebook. "Your babysitter, Mary Matthews, says that you were away last night and didn't return until this morning. Where were you?"

Elizabeth shifted a sofa pillow, resting it under her elbow to ease the weight of Rosalind on her arm. "Why do you want to know that?"

"Just routine questions we're asking everyone."

"I drove up to Elliottville to see an exhibit of Etruscan art. It's touring the country just now and that's the closest city for us. Heaven knows, it wouldn't come to this burg."

"Did you go alone?"

"Yes, Julian was at a music conference in Tallahassee. And it's not like I have any close friends here who might have gone with me."

"Elliottville's only a couple of hours away, so why didn't you come back yesterday?"

Elizabeth stiffened. "Why are you asking me all these questions? Surely you can't suspect me of murder? Or Julian either. That's ridiculous."

Beau's straightforward look met hers. "Like I said, just routine questions. We're asking them of everyone who knew Allison."

"Well, Sheriff, I didn't *know* her at all. Nor did I have any wish to know her. I stayed over in Elliottville to have dinner and see a film. A documentary on the enormous power the corporations wield over American politics. Not something that Coowahchobee's *one* and *only* theater would book. I got Mary to stay overnight so I wouldn't have to drive home after dark. I was at the Magnolia Motel." She stood up, carefully balancing Rosalind in her arms, looking defiant. "Now, if that's all you need to know, I have to start dinner."

Outside in the car Beau grinned at Ellen. "I didn't know you were maternal. Where'd you learn that ice-on-the-gums trick?"

"As the oldest of six kids I learned a lot of tricks to keep them happy. My grandmother taught me that one, along with dipping a corner of a napkin in a glass of beer and letting them suck it when they were fussy with colic. But I didn't think Mrs. Baldwin would appreciate that remedy."

Beau laughed. "She didn't seem to appreciate our visit at all. I thought she was nervous under that cool façade."

"She's an icy one. Hard to read. Yes, nervous and high-strung, too, in my opinion."

"Doesn't it seem strange that a devoted mother would decide to stay away from her family all night?" Beau asked. "It's really not that long a drive from Elliottville."

Ellen shrugged. "Maybe she just needed some quality time alone. It's not easy for women to cope with young children all day. And she doesn't seem like a happy woman. If her husband was fooling around with coeds, that might be motive enough for murder. Especially if he was the one who got Allison pregnant and she knew it. I'll check that motel to see if she really stayed there."

They found Julian at Three Sinks Park watching his son scramble up and down the monkey bars. He was edgy, but cooperative when they told him about the assumed murder. "This is dreadful. Who would want to kill Allison? She seemed like a nice girl." When they asked about the last time he'd seen her, he replied, "I saw her often, in class and chorus practice. Duncan! Come down from there." He rescued his son from atop the rounded hood covering a twisting slide and then returned. "Sorry, he's always testing the waters." He kept his eye on Duncan, who was now sitting on a miniature ditch-digger, trying to move a pile of sand from one spot to another.

Beau looked up from his notebook. "Where were you last night, Professor?"

Julian kept his eyes on Duncan. "I was at a music conference at Florida State. Last night I went to a recital there and then stayed overnight at the Holiday Inn. Attended an early conference session this morning and then drove on home."

Frustrated with the digging equipment, Duncan screwed up his face and started to howl.

"I'm sorry, Officers, I'd better see to my son." Julian picked Duncan up and patted his back to quiet him.

"Just one more question, Professor. Your wife mentioned that Allison was maybe 'stalking' you. That's her term for it. Is that what was happening?"

Julian frowned. "Elizabeth is jealous without any cause. Of course, these young women get crushes on us male professors, but it amounts to nothing. We don't think anything of it. At least I don't." He set Duncan on the ground, where the boy clung to his father's leg as he gazed up at the sheriff.

"We'll contact you again, Professor, if we have more questions."

As soon as Beau and Ellen had left the park, Julian hurried Duncan into the car and drove home, his hands trembling on the steering wheel. He felt a desperate need to gather his family around him.

"Daddy. Did you know that Gorge Washingman never told a lie? *Never!*" Duncan's emphasis revealed that he stood in awe at the impossibility of such a feat.

As Julian glanced in the rear view mirror at his son's earnest face, his knuckles whitened on the wheel.

"Daddy. I'm gonna be like Gorge Washingman when I grow up and never, never, never tell a lie." Duncan gazed out the window, kicking his feet against the back seat and humming to himself, "Never, never, never, never" until

Julian yelled "Stop!" Duncan's eyes widened and he opened his mouth to howl.

"Hey, let's sing another song. How about 'John Jacob Jingleheimer Schmidt?'"

Soon father and son were singing at the top of their voices the repetitive song that usually drove Julian crazy. Today it seemed far less irritating than the "never, never" refrain.

LATER THAT DAY Ellen found Beau in his office. "I checked out the Baldwins' accounts of where they were when Allison was killed," she told him. "Julian was registered at the Holiday Inn in Tallahassee and Elizabeth at the Magnolia Motel in Elliottville, just like they said. They both checked out this morning, but those towns are close enough for either one of them to have driven here, killed Allison, and then returned in the early morning hours."

"We'll keep them on our list of suspects."

"I spoke to Delana Andrews about Chris Bannerman," Ellen continued. "He may not have been honest with us about the time they parted Friday night. She says he took her home around midnight and urged her to let him come in but she pleaded a headache and sent him on his way."

"We need to speak to everyone again, see if we can shake out some discrepancies in their stories," Beau replied.

Ellen agreed. "Maybe we'll get lucky this time. Lord knows, we're due."

23

"Truth will come to light; murder cannot be hid long."
Titus Andronicus

EARLY SUNDAY AFTERNOON Ariadne, Judith and Suzanne were summoned by Vernon Giddings, along with other faculty, a grief therapist, and a couple of local doctors, to counsel and console the bereaved and frightened Rutherford students. Allison's death, now known to be murder, had frightened them badly. They felt as if some new unknown evil had entered their sheltered lives, rendering them all vulnerable. The assembled counselors tried to assure the students that they were safe, that whoever had committed this atrocity was probably long gone, but no one, themselves included, was convinced. By early evening everyone was exhausted, drained of emotion but still edgy.

The three friends stood talking in the faculty parking lot.

"Did you hear them say Allison was pregnant?" Judith asked, lighting up her seventh cigarette of the day. "I suppose the father was Jason Overstreet, her boyfriend?"

Ariadne nodded. "I guess. But they'd taken that crazy abstinence oath."

"Why anyone thinks that would stop young people with raging hormones from copulating is beyond me," Suzanne said, frowning at Judith's cigarette.

"If Jason knew she was pregnant by someone else, he'd probably be furious, but would that motivate him to kill someone he obviously loved?" Ariadne asked.

"Love is wasted on the young, along with everything else that requires maturity," Judith said. "What about others she might have slept with?"

"I don't even want to think about that if it suggests people we know."

"You mean 'men' we know? Like our esteemed colleagues, especially those who chase skirts? Even co-ed skirts, a practice I find despicable. Power-mad idiots, driven by their libidos instead of their brain cells or their sense of decency. Probably even trading good grades for sexual favors." Judith caught Ariadne's raised eyebrow. "I know, I know. We don't have any evidence at all that sex fiends like Chris play that game, but I don't put it past him. And like I've said before, I wouldn't put murder past him either. Raging hormones aren't confined to the young."

"They aren't just sexual either. They engender other emotions as well, like envy, licentiousness, avarice, and all those other deadly sins," Suzanne said.

Judith ground her cigarette butt under her shoe. "Could there be a connection between the murders? Both Allison and Randall were at Rutherford. I wonder if they knew each other."

"When Beau and Ellen questioned her, she said she knew him slightly. But of course she could have been lying." Ariadne stifled a yawn. "I'm exhausted. Let's go home."

"Want to join us for supper at The Blue Cat?"

"Thanks, but I think I'll just eat some leftovers and go to bed early."

"Okay, then. See you tomorrow."

An hour later Ariadne sat at the kitchen table with a cup of cocoa, trying to relax enough to go to bed. The doorbell startled her but she was relieved to find Beau on the veranda. She pulled him inside and wrapped her arms around him, while he caressed her hair and kissed her gently. "It's horrible," she said. "I can't stop thinking about that poor girl murdered in her sleep when she had no chance to escape. What monster could do that to her?"

Beau slipped off his jacket and laid it on the wooden bench against the foyer wall. He put his arm around her as they walked to the kitchen. "It's a gruesome crime, that's for sure. And especially for the Rutherford students. A killer in the dorm has shattered their sense of safety, but even worse is the fear that someone close to them might have strangled Allison."

"A student? I hope not. Do you suspect anyone?"

"I can't discuss that just yet." Not even with you, my new love, he wanted to say but couldn't get the words out.

Ariadne made more cocoa and they sat together at the table.

"Did you find the pink pillow?"

Beau frowned. He'd wanted to keep that bit of evidence secret, but Mary Matthews had told everyone she knew about it. "No, but we'll keep looking of course." He looked at her intently. "Did you hear that Allison was pregnant?" When Ariadne nodded, he continued, "Well, the autopsy showed she wasn't."

Ariadne's eyes widened. "What? How is that possible? Mary Matthews told us this morning that Allison was really upset about being pregnant and that it wasn't her boyfriend's child."

"The gynecologist we consulted said it was undoubtedly a false pregnancy or more technically a 'pseudocyesis.' Bloating and cessation of menstruation are two characteristics."

"What causes it?"

"Stress, they say." Beau shrugged. "But isn't everything chalked up to that these days?"

Ariadne nodded. "Yes, but stress can be serious. It's been cited as a cause of suicide."

"Allison's stress may have been caused by a sexual encounter. Mary Matthews told us that she thinks Allison may have been raped, though Allison denied it."

"That's terrible. I wonder why she wouldn't have reported such a crime." She thought for a moment. "Unfortunately, rape victims are often too embarrassed or ashamed to say anything. Or they're afraid of the repercussions if the guy finds out, especially if it's someone they know and perhaps love."

"It's also possible Allison was seduced into a sexual act and was afraid to report that to anyone," Beau said.

"Do you think she accused someone of being the father? If she did, then he might have decided to do something about it." She frowned. "Though murder is a pretty radical reaction to an unwanted pregnancy."

Beau just shook his head, too weary to speculate on motive. He worried about how much more he ought to confide in Ariadne and tried not to think about how Ellen would counsel him not to continue. But he trusted his new love and hoped she could advise him about her colleagues. "Mary mentioned some professors Allison had crushes on. Apparently, that's not uncommon with the coeds."

"Not uncommon with students generally. We women professors have our share of admirers, too, male and female. Students often develop crushes on professors for various reasons, not all of them overtly sexual. They tend to idolize us as substitute parental figures and guardians of the knowledge they need for success in life."

"Would you tell me more about the professors Mary mentioned? Adam Gooch, Julian Baldwin, and Chris Bannerman."

"I doubt whether any of them would dare to have sex with a Rutherford student, much less murder her, considering how much they'd have to lose if discovered," she said. "Especially Adam and Julian, who don't have tenure yet. I don't think that Chris, despite his temper and his tenure, would kill a woman." She frowned. "I just can't picture anyone I know doing that."

Beau studied her drawn face. "You look exhausted, my love. It's bedtime."

She grasped his hands tighter. "Can you stay with me?"

"I thought you'd never ask." His grin lit up his face as he folded her in his arms.

◫

ON HIS WAY TO THE OFFICE the next morning, Beau heard from Ellen that the owner of Forte's Gun and Pawn

Shop in Elliottville had reported a green and blue Venetian glass vase resembling the one in Ariadne's description. He turned the car around and headed for Georgia.

24

"I am surprised with an uncouth fear;
A chilling sweat o'er-runs my trembling joints...."
Titus Andronicus

IT WAS ALREADY EVENING evening by the time Ariadne and Judith returned from shopping in Tallahassee. In Ariadne's driveway they sorted through their packages, with Judith transferring hers into her car. "You're sure you don't want to come for dinner? We're going to have plenty," Judith encouraged.

Ariadne shook her head as she pulled one of two large potted mums from her car. "I have some leftovers that need to be eaten. Plus, I want to sort through all the Halloween decorations I bought. I think I went a little overboard."

Judith smiled at her friend. "Maybe Beau can help?"

Ariadne returned the grin. "I'm sure he's working tonight."

After making her promise to join her and Suzanne if Ariadne changed her mind, Judith headed home, her Escort packed with her new purchases.

Thankful for her bright porch light illuminating the front walk, Ariadne carefully carried the mums from her car to her veranda and set them down next to a cluster of other plants she planned to put in the yard this week—green cacti and aloes, red kalanchoes and multi-hued begonias. A few more trips to her car were necessary before she had all of her bags piled in the foyer. "Cassie, girl, I'll have dinner soon!" Ariadne called into the house. Probably sleeping, she thought, as the phone rang.

"Forgot to charge your cell again?" Beau teased as she picked up the call in her kitchen. "You know me so well," Ariadne laughed. "Is everything all right?"

"Finally got a lead on your break-in. We found your blue and green glass vase in Forte's Gun and Pawn Shop in Elliottville." A meow from the top of the stairway alerted Ariadne that Cassie was awake. She pulled out a can of food as Beau continued. "Someone brought it in just yesterday. The shop owner called us as soon as he recognized it from the description we sent out."

As Ariadne moved to the stairway to call for Cassie, she saw that the light in her study was on.

"Unfortunately, the ID the guy used was a fake, but we have a description of him now."

"That's fantastic," Ariadne mumbled as she looked down the hall.

"You okay? Do you need to call me back?" Beau reacted to her distracted response.

"I thought I turned the lights off in the study," Ariadne mused as she padded past the guest bath toward the study.

The tone in her voice snapped Beau into cop-mode. "Get out of the house, Ariadne."

"I'm sure it's nothing, it's just—" Ariadne gasped as someone suddenly lurched from the bathroom and clamped a gloved hand over her mouth.

"Ariadne!" Beau's voice was barely audible as the phone tumbled to the floor.

"Don't scream and I'll take my hand away," a muffled voice whispered in her ear. Nausea crept in as the intruder pressed something hard into the small of Ariadne's back. "I really don't want to use this."

Ariadne instinctively held up her hands as if surrendering and nodded in compliance. The attacker removed the gloved hand from her mouth and squared it firmly on her back just between her shoulder blades. With the other hand pressing the gun into her spine, he propelled her forward. Together like Siamese twins they moved into her study.

"Where's the money?" The harsh whisper was insistent.

Ariadne tried to keep alert and focused. "What money? I have some cash in the kitchen but—"

"The money you have stashed in this study! Show it to me now."

The thought that this must be the burglar who had killed Randall Medina sent a wave of terror through Ariadne and she began to slump to the ground. A hand jerked her upright. "I'm not going to hurt you if you give me the money. But if you don't—" A jab to her backbone reinforced the murmured threat.

Ariadne's heart was beating in her throat as possible moves flashed through her mind. Keep insisting she had no money? Pretend she had it hidden somewhere else in the house? Maybe stall for time until …until what? Surely Beau was on his way, but he might have been calling from Elliottville. That drive could take thirty minutes.

Trembling and almost breathless, Ariadne tried to calm her fears as the raspy voice again demanded the money. "I know it's in these books somewhere. Stop stalling and get it for me."

In the books? The burglars must have been searching for a safe as Beau and Ellen suspected. How pleased they'd be to know they're right. Ariadne almost laughed at the irrelevancy of that thought but quickly sobered up at the realization that she had no safe and no money, a fact that was likely to arouse the anger and frustration that had already fueled a murder.

A loud meow and a scurry of paws emanated from the hallway, startling both of them. Later Ariadne would have to admit that she couldn't remember what exactly happened next, just that events occurred almost simultaneously and, for her, fortuitously.

"Cassie!" Ariadne blurted out. It was a knee-jerk reaction. Of course she knew her cat couldn't save her.

And yet …with a whir of widespread wings, a large palmetto bug skimmed between the two of them, causing Ariadne to shriek and her captor to swear. Following the bug, *her* prey, Cassandra tore down the hallway and lurched into the two figures in her way. The shocked intruder stumbled, giving Ariadne time to whip around and knock the gun from his hand. She snatched it up and pointed it at Jason Overstreet, whose face she could see for the first time. He stared at her and then sank onto the floor.

With both of them in stunned silence, the insect's hissing was clearly audible. The two-inch long flying cockroach whirled around the room, pursued by Cassandra, who emitted low-pitched yowls as she pounced upon it each time it bounced against a wall or a piece of furniture.

Ariadne remained focused on Jason as the roach and Cassie finally flew past her and back out of the room. Muffled thumps indicated their progress down the hall. Jason continued to stare at Ariadne and the gun. "Don't move or I'll shoot!" she blurted out. In her later retelling of the scenario she would laugh as she compared herself to an actress mouthing some very bad movie dialogue, but at the moment all seemed very serious.

"Don't shoot me," Jason whimpered. "I wasn't going to hurt you."

Ariadne felt a flash of anger. "You could have fooled me, pushing me about like that with the gun in my back. You were the one who broke in here with Randall Medina weren't you, Jason." She said it as a statement, not a question.

Jason hung his head. "I need money real bad and he said we could get lots of it here."

"But I don't have money in the house. Why did he think that?"

"Everyone talks about the money you have hidden away. They say you've been hiding it for years and it must be a fortune by now."

"You mean the story I told students years ago about hiding money in our books?" Ariadne was astonished. Jason managed a meager nod. "But it was a few dollars here and there," she stammered. "The students would laugh when I said we always forgot to take the money out before donating the books. I never meant the story to be taken seriously." She exhaled at the ridiculousness of the rumor. Then she gasped, "That story is why you killed Randall?"

Ariadne tightened her grip on the gun but Jason didn't look like a threat. He looked utterly defeated. His voice was hoarse and ragged. "It was an accident, I swear. I didn't mean to kill him. He was furious when we couldn't find the money. He kept pulling out the books and throwing them around the room. Then he grabbed the poker and was swinging it around like he was going to break up the furniture. When I tried to pull it out of his hand, he dropped it and turned on me. He knocked me to the floor. I got the poker, jumped up, and swung it at him. I didn't mean to hit him so hard. I was just trying to scare him away from me."

"Not another word, Jason, you're under arrest." Ellen Nolle stood in the doorway, her gun drawn, and a sheriff's deputy right behind her. "Put the gun down, Ariadne."

"How—Why are you here?" Ariadne squeaked out as she laid the gun on her desk.

"Beau called me," Ellen said.

Of course he did, Ariadne thought. She should have figured that. She watched Ellen handcuff Jason, read him his rights, bag his gun, and hand him over to the deputy before sitting down to take her statement.

After about twenty minutes of detailing the events, Ariadne was exhausted. But she managed a weak smile when Beau finally arrived. "I drove as fast as I could" he said, enfolding her in his arms. The stress of what had happened finally released itself as she sank into his hug, absorbing his warmth and concern.

25

"Rumor is a pipe blown by surmise, jealousies, conjecture...."
Shakespeare, Henry IV, Part II

THE NEXT MORNING Beau arrived at the office early, but Ellen was already at her desk staring at a stack of paperwork. He winced as he took a sip of bitter coffee and slid into a side chair. "Good work last night."

Ellen could tell he meant more than just the arrest, but didn't want to embarrass him. "I think we should deputize the cat and the cockroach." Her facetious comment elicited a short laugh from her boss.

After a few moments of silence, Ellen looked up. "I think it's great that you two have found each other," she said softly. The look on Beau's face told her that he agreed. "But she needs to get a house alarm."

"She's calling the company this morning," Beau reassured her.

"I'm half-way finished with the report."

Beau nodded and, taking in her dark bloodshot eyes, replied, "Why don't you take the day off and get some sleep. I'll finish it up and then go check in on Jason."

Ellen raised an eyebrow.

"And yes, Ariadne."

"Give her my best," Ellen smiled as she stood, gathering her things.

Later that day in Ariadne's foyer he pulled her close and kissed her several times. "How are you feeling?"

"A little jittery yet and I have a million questions," she said as she led him down the hall to the kitchen. "I just made fresh coffee. Want a cup?"

"No thanks. I've already drunk a gallon today." He eyed a plate of chocolate chip cookies on the table. "But I could eat a couple of those. With a glass of milk if you have some."

Ariadne impatiently watched him wolf down a cookie before asking, "What's happening with Jason?"

"He's at the county jail with a lawyer who won't let him talk much. Just claims you have a fortune hidden in your house but not in a wall safe like we thought. He says you stashed money in your books."

Ariadne frowned. "Apparently he and Medina believed a story I told years ago, when I first started teaching at Rutherford. Some students in one of my history courses complained about the required texts being too expensive, so I made a lame joke about how they could find other uses for them after the course was over. I said my husband and I were stashing our money away in my old set of Shakespeare's plays." She shook her head. "We were doing that but it was never more than just petty cash."

"Jason said they'd heard about your hidden fortune from students who had heard it from others. Sounds to me like your comment just snowballed."

"That seems ridiculous, doesn't it? But I realize that in a small-college world gossip flourishes and history is distorted into rumor," Ariadne said. "I just feel so responsible. I see well enough now how even the most innocuous remark can be misconstrued; but when I made that little joke, I had no idea it would escalate and backfire on me and harm others. Poor Randall Medina was lured into a crime by a rumor and it cost him his life. And poor Jason must have been desperate for money."

Beau reached over and brushed his hand over her hair, resting it for a moment against her cheek. "Jason admitted to stealing your Venetian glass vase to give to his mother. He told her he'd bought it at a flea market and that it wasn't valuable. But his teenage brother Josh thought otherwise and decided to pawn it up in Elliottville. Used an ID he made on the Internet. Darn close to the real thing. When I faxed a copy of it to the office, Ellen recognized Josh from her visit to the Overstreets in Blountstown. We put out a description of his car and a deputy spotted it across the street from here and called for backup. Jason must have been driving it. Ellen got here sooner because I called her when I heard your distress."

Ariadne grasped his hand. "I've never been so scared in my life. But at least I didn't panic."

"No, you didn't." He smiled but his voice was stern. "But grabbing the gun and turning it on Jason wasn't a wise move. You might have killed him."

"I know. But in the heat of the moment I just reacted without thinking. I was lucky Ellen came so quickly." Then she added, "Did Jason kill Allison, too?"

"He swears he didn't and seems truly upset about it, but he's still our prime suspect."

"What else do you know about Jason? I feel so sorry for him."

Beau was glad Ellen wasn't there because she'd probably have a reason why he shouldn't say more, but on his own he couldn't think of one. "Jason admired Medina as they were growing up in Blountstown and did pretty much everything he could to please his idol. It looks to us like Medina took advantage of the younger kid's adulation to get him to do anything he suggested. Like sending Jason into the Hogly Wogly to snatch candy bars and gum balls. Later on he'd position him as lookout while the older guys broke into houses at night to steal whatever they could get. Mostly petty cash."

"Why did Jason need the money that desperately?" Ariadne asked.

"Ellen learned early on that the Overstreets live on the edge of poverty. Worse yet, the father's been an alcoholic for years, and the Blountstown police said that Jason's mother often calls them in to calm down her husband when he goes on a rampage and threatens her and the kids." Beau took another cookie. "He claims he was never the same after a car accident in which he hit his head. He attributes his anger to brain damage and the fact that he's been unable to collect any insurance money because the accident was his fault. Driving under the influence. All that happened when Jason was in high school, so he came to depend more and more on Medina, who was good to him even as he used him."

"Poor guy. I'm not excusing what he and Medina did, but I can see why they did it."

"Poverty is a major cause of crime. At least in our experience that's been true," Beau said. "Jason was smart and lucky enough to get a scholarship to Rutherford, a college he otherwise wouldn't have been able to afford. Everything went well for him until this year when his father lost big in a poker game with some guys from Jacksonville, who threatened to kill him if he didn't pay up. His mother was hysterical, begging Jason to do something, so he went along with Medina's latest scheme to burglarize houses in Coowahchobee and other small towns around here."

Beau carried his empty milk glass to the sink and rinsed it. "Jason has admitted to breaking into several houses before yours. They got frustrated when they couldn't take stereos or TVs because they had no way to fence them and they found little or no cash. He claims he only half-believed the story about money hidden in the books, but his family's urgent needs compelled him to participate in the burglary. And even to come back and try again on his own."

"Do you believe he killed Medina in self-defense?"

"It's possible. Of course it's up to his lawyer to convince a jury. But from what I know of Miles Duvall, he'll be up to the task."

"Miles?" Ariadne caught Beau's grin.

"Yes. And he's doing it pro bono. Turns out he's been something of a benefactor to Jason, as well as a couple of other students, by contributing to the scholarships they need to stay in school."

Ariadne had difficulty picturing the slick lawyer as a patron of poor students, especially because he had often talked about hoarding his money for a trip around the world when he retired. But she was glad to hear otherwise.

Beau came around behind her, kissing her softly as he massaged her shoulders. "I'm sorry but I have to get back to the office. I don't want the other officers criticizing the sheriff for fraternizing with citizens when he should be tending to business."

"Well, this citizen doesn't want to be arrested for kidnapping so I'll let you go. Thanks for coming by and filling me in. I'll see what I can do to help Jason because I really do feel sorry for him, especially if Medina's murder was self-defense." She hesitated. "And, of course, if he didn't kill Allison."

"Does that mean you'll have to spend time with his lawyer?" Beau kissed her, more firmly this time. "I don't think I care for that kind of involvement, compassionate or not."

"Any meetings between Miles and me will now be strictly business." She assured him of her resoluteness with a tight hug and kiss before he left. In the driveway he waved to Tilda Kent, who was pulling up to the curb. He'd already given her all the details he could and now she wanted to hear Ariadne's version of Jason's capture.

After Tilda had interviewed her and left to write her newspaper story, Ariadne talked to David on the phone, with Cassandra crouched on the counter top beside her.

"Mom, are you all right?"

His voice helped raise her spirits. "I'm not hurt, David, just shaky and exhausted."

"What the hell was that guy doing there again?"

Ariadne explained the rumor and its origin.

"That sounds way over the top, Mom. They must have been really desperate for money. But don't blame yourself. No way could you have known how the story would grow when you told those students about your stash."

"Yes, I guess so," she said, not yet convinced. "Poor Jason confessed to killing Medina with the poker, but he claims it was self-defense. And he's the prime suspect in Allison's murder since she was his girlfriend."

"Why would he kill her?"

Ariadne sat down on a stool beside the kitchen counter and stroked Cassandra's ruffled fur. "I have no idea if he's guilty or not. It turns out that Allison wasn't pregnant but she thought she was, and if she told him that and they hadn't had sex, he would have been furious. They had taken an abstinence oath at a student retreat last year—"

David snorted. "Horny boyfriends don't care about those dumb promises."

"That's Judith's take on it, too. I don't know. But if they broke the oath, I can't believe he'd kill the mother of his child no matter how angry he might have been."

"Are there other suspects?"

"I think so. But the sheriff wouldn't talk about them just yet. Probably other students and possibly professors as well."

Ariadne glanced at the clock. "Talking to you always cheers me up, David. But I'm behind in my term-paper grading, so I have to go. I'll call you when I hear more."

"Always the professor." David laughed. "But it's good for you to keep your mind occupied with something other than murder. Until later, then. I love you, and please get a home security system put in."

Twenty minutes later the doorbell rang again. When Ariadne opened it, Miles grasped her shoulders, holding her at arm's length, while he studied her face. "You look exhausted, my sweet. Not surprising after what you've been through. Although from what I hear, you've been acting like a heroine with help from your cat and a flying cockroach."

"I can't stand those beastly bugs, but I sure appreciated that one's timing."

Miles hugged her close to him. "I'm Jason's lawyer. He told me most of what happened when he broke into your house. I was angry with him for scaring you with his threats and intimidation with the gun. But he's contrite and feels very bad about frightening you."

"I was frightened all right, but now I feel guilty about having told students that ridiculous story about money in my Shakespeare books, and I sympathize with Jason's need for money. Did Randall Medina intimidate him? And what about Allison's murder? Did he do that, too?"

Miles laid a finger on her lips. "Sorry, Sweetheart, don't ask me questions I can't answer. Lawyer-client privilege, you know."

When he held her close, Ariadne pulled away gently. "Miles, my relationship with Beau has become serious and I—"

Miles's laugh took her by surprise. "I know how things are with you and him, my dear. Everyone knows. You can't keep things like that secret in a small town." He kissed her lightly. "I can't say I'm not disappointed but you know me. A ladies' man. Isn't that what people call me behind my back?" He laughed again. "I prefer 'confirmed bachelor,' if you please. And don't worry, I'll have another love interest before the week is out."

Just as Judith predicted, Ariadne thought, relieved that he was taking the news in typical Miles' fashion.

"And I'll always be here if you need me, Doll! After all, what are friends for?" He hugged her again before striding out the door, calling back over his shoulder, "If it doesn't work out with Beau, give me a call."

Fat chance, she wanted to shout, but of course did not.

26

"One woe doth tread upon another's heel,
So fast they follow ...."
Hamlet

THE NEXT MORNING Ariadne rose early to read her history students' mid-term research papers. She took a quick shower before scrambling into jeans, an old lime-green sweatshirt, and warm fuzzy slippers.

"Meow!" Cassandra howled from the kitchen.

"I'm coming, you impatient puss." Ariadne doled out canned cat turkey, then brewed coffee and microwaved a bowl of oatmeal. Carrying her breakfast on a tray into the study, she settled at her desk.

At mid-morning, after finishing her grading, she went outside to check the curbside mailbox. On the way she stopped to admire the red pyracantha berries just beginning to ripen on the bush. She smiled and waved at her neighbor out raking up pine straw and packing it around his azalea bushes. Elias would be over this afternoon to do her yard work. This time she'd have a check ready for him.

She pulled her mail out of the box, along with a large manila envelope with her name centered on it and "Mary Matthews" in the upper left-hand corner but no postage. Mary must have slipped it into the box sometime in the night or early morning, hoping her essay wouldn't be counted late.

Back in the house Ariadne slid the essay out of the manila envelope and read the title, *The Life and Times of a Nineteenth-Century Northeastern Nebraska Farm Woman as Gleaned from Her Diary and Other Pertinent Sources.*

Ariadne smiled as she remembered advising the students to write titles expressing the content of their papers. Mary had certainly fulfilled that requirement. And was her selection of northeastern Nebraska a fluke? Of course she'd know that I come from that area of the country, Ariadne thought, since I've talked about it often enough in class. From now on, though, she'd be more careful about personal comments in class lectures. Even though Judith and David had tried to assure her that she wasn't responsible for the way the story of cash hidden in her books had escalated over the years, she still felt guilty and sad about having told it.

She settled into her desk chair with Mary's essay and read the first line, "The nineteenth-century seems like ancient history to us in the Age of Technology, but when we read diaries and journals, we enter a world very much like our own, but yet different."

"If you know what I mean," Ariadne added aloud, familiar with Mary's language patterns, and read further. "Take the case of Mrs. Lydia Stuart Torvelson, a northeastern Nebraska farm woman in those days of yore, the nineteenth century." Ariadne smiled but read on without comment because she was always careful to skim a paper for its content and thesis before marking anything in the margins. More often than not, students' imaginative re-creations of history responded to a desire she had fostered in them to connect with the past, even if they were sometimes unsophisticated and awkwardly worded.

Cassandra sauntered into the study and plopped down on the braided rug before the fire, spreading herself out as she sought the most comfortable sleeping position for an overweight cat, front feet poised above her chest, hind legs apart, pointing in opposite directions. Ariadne read on, fascinated by the details of Lydia Torvelson's life that Mary had culled from her diary. The family's pet pig, Squalling Betsy, butchered by her husband and reported unemotionally by Lydia. The births of nine children, first in their "soddy," dug into a prairie hillside and later, as they prospered, in a white frame farmhouse not unlike Ariadne's own childhood home. Lists of Christmas presents: hand-knit shawls, wooden toys, books sent out from relatives back east.

As Ariadne turned another page, several sheets of loose-leaf notebook paper, covered with large sloping handwriting, slipped out and fell to the floor. Probably Mary's notes, she thought, as she gathered them up and started to slide them inside the back cover of the term paper. But she hesitated as she glimpsed a line of large block letters, carefully printed with black marking pen, unfurled like a dark banner across the top of the page.

I HATE HER. I HATE HER. I HATE HER.

The words, the capital letters, and the printing seemed childish. Had Mary copied these words from the Torvelson diary? They seemed much more emotional than anything else she'd quoted so far. The next lines were scrawled in the same large handwriting. "I can't control my thoughts any more or my emotions either. They're spilling out faster than I can write. I hate her. She ruined everything. Before she came into my life I was happy. Then I was devastated." Purple prose, Ariadne thought, not typical of early farm women. She ought to stop reading in case this was Mary's personal outpouring, inadvertently stuck into her term paper. But she was intrigued by the venom in the text, so, against her better judgment, she continued.

"After she arrived I wanted to get as far away from her and her doting mother as I could. Away from my treacherous father, too. He who had loved ME first, then only HER." Again the capitals in thick black ink. Ariadne shifted in her chair, the words beginning to sound familiar. "After I left home I wanted to forget the people I'd left behind, but they haunted me. My best friend Mary Ann wrote to me about the family's happy life together. How Dad and his bitch both doted on their pretty little blonde daughter (who should have been me!). Giving her everything she wanted (things I wanted and would have had if I had been her!). Piano and ballet lessons. Trips to the city for concerts and plays. Birthday parties and holiday celebrations with GIFTS, GIFTS, AND MORE GIFTS. All that money wasted on that brat. I had to scrimp and save and go without to eke out a meager living on my own. I HATED them. Especially HER, who should have been ME. Does that make any sense to you? It does to me."

What hateful and angry writing, Ariadne thought. She read more closely the words she had just skimmed and suddenly it dawned on her. "Diana Macomb," she exclaimed out loud, waking Cassandra. "This is the same story she told me in the gym."

She knew she shouldn't continue to read, but she couldn't stop. After all, Diana *had* confided in her, maybe in an effort to elicit sympathy and compassion. "I hated my father for remarrying and I hated Alice for having that baby. I did all right on my own, but I hated working days and going to school at night. I was so tired. SO TIRED AND SO ANGRY!" The bold black capital letters had become shaky. "I vowed to show them that I was special too. That I could make it in the cold, cruel world without their help. Without their love. The love that was going to HER now instead of to ME."

OH MOTHER, MOTHER, WHY DID YOU LEAVE ME? FATHER, WHY DID YOU BETRAY ME? I HATE YOU! I HATE HER!

The last page was blank except for a few words scrawled across the middle, "To be or not to be, that is the question."

Ariadne sat in stunned silence. This *has* to be Diana, she thought. It's the same story she told me about her mother dying, her father remarrying, her anger at them, how she ran away after the baby's birth. But how on earth did Mary get it?

Startled by the door chimes, Ariadne moved cautiously into the foyer and peered through one of the long windows before pulling the door open. "Am I glad to see you two. I have to tell you about these notes I found."

Judith and Suzanne hugged Ariadne. "Notes? How can you be concerned about research after what you've been through?" Suzanne asked.

"Not notes for an article. I mean notes written by Diana Macomb." She paused. "They're not signed but I'm certain she wrote them. See, I found these loose pages tucked into Mary Matthew's term paper. They tell the same story Diana told me and I'm really worried about Diana. Her notes sound desperate, overflowing with rage and hatred. Please take a look at them and tell me what you think."

"Whoa, slow down," Judith said as she peeled off her sweater and began to talk as fast as Ariadne had. "Did you say the notes were in Mary's term paper? How did they get there? If they were written by Diana, why is she angry? Who does she hate and why?"

"Come in here," Ariadne said, ignoring the questions as she led her friends into the study and handed them the sheaf of papers. "Here, just read this. I'm worried about Diana's state of mind and what she might do to herself."

Judith and Suzanne plopped down on the sofa and read the notes together.

"I see what you mean about the rage. And a lot of frustration, too," Suzanne said, pointing to the capital letters.

Judith pushed her glasses up on her nose and looked at Ariadne. "What makes you believe Diana wrote this?"

"It's the same story she told me one day at the gym. I suggested then that she write down her thoughts, the only therapy I could think of, aside from recommending a counselor," Ariadne said. "Do you agree she might be suicidal?"

"The fact that she quotes Hamlet's 'To be or not to be' soliloquy suggests it, but some critics argue that he's also thinking at the time about killing Claudius."

Impatient with literary criticism, Ariadne snapped, "But what if she is going to kill herself? We should check on her now!"

"Let's try calling her," Suzanne suggested."

The phone rang several times before Diana's voice came on, giving the usual "I-can't-come-to-the-phone-right-now" notification.

Ariadne hung up. "Should I have left a message? How would I ask if she's thinking of suicide?"

The doorbell's insistent ringing interrupted her. At the door Ariadne found Mary Matthews, her black eyes wide and her red hair disheveled.

"Oh, Professor Caulfield, I …I …" Mary stammered.

"Come in Mary. I'd like to talk to you about your research paper." Ariadne ushered her into the foyer as Judith and Suzanne joined them. "I think you left some notes in it."

A bit overwhelmed by being confronted by three professors, Mary backed up against the door. "Did you read them?" she asked, her voice wavering. "I found them at work and was worried about what they said. I, like, wanted you to see them, Professor Caulfield, but I couldn't just show them to you. I mean, I didn't know what to do with them. But I thought you would."

Ariadne tried to calm her down until she could talk more coherently. "Where exactly did you find them?"

"At Mr. Duvall's office, where I work afternoons," Mary said. "I wanted to use the computer and printer there to finish my paper, so I asked Linda, the secretary, and she said I could stay after hours to do that." Mary stopped for a breath.

Judith was less patient than Ariadne. "But how did you find the notes, Mary, and why did you keep them?"

Mary looked down at the blue hall rug, seeming to study its geometric shapes. "This is, like, so embarrassing," she stuttered. "I mean, I found the papers in Ms. Macomb's wastebasket when I was looking for scratch paper. I know I shouldn't have read them but I did. And they scared me. All that hate and anger. You know what I mean?" Mary's eyes filled with tears. "Everything's been so …so …like, not the same since Allison …" She buried her face in her jacket sleeve and began to cry.

Suzanne and Judith backed away as Ariadne led Mary to the foyer bench and sat down beside her. "It's all right,

Mary, that you let me see the notes. We'll see what we can do to help Ms. Macomb."

A soft knock at the door was followed by another, a bit louder. When Judith opened it, Ginger Berline rushed to Mary's side and put her arms around her.

"It's okay, Ginger. We're not angry with Mary." Ariadne said. "She can go with you now."

After the students had left, Ginger guiding Mary with an arm around her, Judith turned to Ariadne. "And just what are we going to do about this?"

Ariadne grabbed her jacket and sneakers from the hall closet. "I know Diana wrote those ominous words and she needs help." She pulled the Coowahchobee phone book from the drawer. "Diana lives at 27 Plover Place. Isn't that on the other side of Town Square?" She started for the door.

Judith retrieved her sweater and put it on. "I don't think we should go there on our own. I'll call 911."

"Are you crazy? We shouldn't go there at all. She could be dangerous," Suzanne said, but seeing that the other two were determined, she shoved her arms into her jacket.

"I'll call Beau," Ariadne said, dialing his cell phone. When she got no response except voice mail, she left a message and then called the sheriff department office, where the sergeant on duty told her the sheriff was out on a call. Ariadne gave him Diana's name and address and asked that Beau meet her there as soon as possible. "Please tell him it's urgent. Someone may be in danger." Then she followed her friends out the door.

27

"The game is up."
Cymbeline

ARIADNE RACED her silver Beetle down the hilly, tree-lined streets and on through the town square, busy with various groups of workers headed for lunch at The Blue Cat Café. At the traffic light on Blue Dasher Drive, she turned left into a modest neighborhood of small houses and trailer homes under tall scraggly pines and then right onto Plover Place, marked by a "no exit" sign.

"Abandon hope, all ye who enter here," Judith quipped.

Number 27 was a small cinder block house set back under a gigantic live oak festooned with Spanish moss. Diana's yellow Dodge Neon hid like an Easter egg beneath a sagging carport. Ariadne maneuvered her Beetle along two dirt tracks serving as a driveway and parked under the tree. Moments later the three women crowded together on a narrow rickety wooden stoop before the front door. Ariadne rang the bell a couple of times and waited, shifting from one foot to the other. "Maybe she's not home," she said.

"Her car's here," Suzanne observed.

Judith stepped off the stoop and threaded her way through several scraggly azalea bushes to a front window and peered in. "Must be her living room and it's a mess. Piles of papers all over the place and a suitcase open on the sofa. Looks like she might be going somewhere."

Ariadne continued to ring the doorbell. "Maybe she's sleeping, though how anyone can sleep through that bell,

I don't know. I can hear it from here. What if something's happened to her? What if she is suicidal and took something?" On impulse she twisted the doorknob and shoved the door open.

The screaming house alarm shocked them. Frozen into a tableau on the stoop, they stared at Diana as she dashed out from a door at the back of the room and punched a code into a small box on the wall. The noise stopped abruptly, leaving them in stunned silence.

Diana, with disheveled hair and dark circles under her eyes, faced them, her hands clenched into fists at her sides. "What the hell are you doing breaking into my house?" Her voice rose and then cracked as she raised her arm, palm toward them in a gesture that warned them not to come any closer.

"We're sorry to frighten you, Diana. We thought something might be wrong ...over here." Ariadne stumbled over her words, uncertain of how to proceed.

Diana glared at them and shook her head. "Nothing's wrong. Get out!"

Ariadne, Judith, and Suzanne backed up but stopped as Diana answered a call from her security people, giving them her password and quickly explaining that her alarm had inadvertently been set off. Judith whispered to Ariadne, "Look over there in the suitcase."

Ariadne started toward the sofa but stopped as Diana turned toward them, haggard and restless, shifting from one foot to the other, her arms crossed over her chest, hands rubbing her elbows. "Are you still here? What do you want?" she asked, her voice wavering. Her bloodshot eyes shuttled between Judith and Suzanne near the door and Ariadne peering into the suitcase.

"Are you going somewhere?" Judith asked, trying to distract her.

"What's in your suitcase?" Suzanne asked, edging toward Ariadne for a closer look.

Diana glared at them as she grabbed the suitcase and slammed the lid closed, hiding its contents. "None of your business. Go away and leave me alone."

Ariadne stepped closer to Diana, speaking softly and slowly. "How are you feeling these days? Better, I hope. And did you ever start that journal I recommended?"

Diana's eyes narrowed. "No, I didn't. Everything's fine in my life now, so I don't need to write about it."

"So you didn't write about hating your stepmother and being angry at your father's betrayal?" Suzanne asked.

Red blotches appeared on Diana's pale cheeks. "What the hell are you talking about?"

"I'm talking about pages from a journal, some of it in capital letters, spelling out someone's hatred, anger, and desire for revenge. For some odd reason Ariadne thinks it's yours."

Diana glared at Ariadne. "What is this about?"

Ariadne kept her voice soft and low. "I found some notes that reminded me of what you told me in the fitness center the day you hurt your leg. Remember? You were upset about the anniversary of your mother's death that day and then you told me how angry you were at your father for remarrying and how much you hated your stepmother. The pages I read echoed your story and so I thought … we thought …that you might be despondent and desperate enough to …hurt yourself."

"Commit suicide!" Suzanne cried out, "We thought you were going to kill yourself!"

Diana's dark eyes flashed anger. "You thought wrong. Completely wrong. I shouldn't have told you anything, Ariadne, and how the hell did you get my notes anyway? By now my life history is probably all over Rutherford's campus. Hell, it's probably all over Coowahchobee."

Ariadne stepped toward her, keeping her voice low and even. "Please calm down, Diana. And don't worry. No one's told your story anywhere. We've kept your secrets, but I think they're haunting you. Maybe making you ill."

"There's nothing wrong with me and you need to get the hell out of my house. Now!" Diana waved her hands toward the door as if pushing the women out.

Ariadne stood her ground, continuing to speak in soft, measured tones. "You told me about the half-sister you hated because she took your place in your father's affections. The soft, sweet baby, the pretty little blonde daughter who got everything she wanted, while you had to scrimp and save and eke out a meager living on your own." She spoke in a rhythmic cadence, trying to make her voice hypnotic. "That baby, that daughter, I think, was Allison."

Diana blanched at the name and clenched her fists at her sides. Ariadne continued slowly. "Allison was the sister you hated, wasn't she? And you killed her in a fit of despair and passion, didn't you?"

Diana stared at Ariadne with wide eyes as she began to harangue her. "You crazy bitch! You have no idea what you're talking about. I never knew my sister and I wouldn't know her today." She waved her arms frantically, screaming, "Get out! Get out now!"

"But you knew her name was McEnvoy, the same as yours before you changed it. And I think you traced her to Rutherford and came here to find her. That's why you were so interested in the students," Ariadne said softly.

Judith's eyes were as wide as Diana's. How did Ariadne figure this out and why hadn't she shared her surmises? But no time to wonder about that now. She gathered her thoughts and, unobserved by Diana, pulled something out of the suitcase and held it out in front of her. "This should prove that you were in Allison's room, Diana. Her pretty pink pillow. The police say it was stolen by the killer."

Long, dark hair flying, Diana leaped at Judith and grabbed the pillow away. Holding it close to her left side, she pulled open the drawer of a side table with her other hand and drew out a small gun. Eyes wide and glassy, she waved it back and forth from one woman to another.

Oh, god, no, Ariadne thought. Threatened by a gun again! With Jason she had acted instinctively, picking up the weapon from the floor, and aiming it at him. Then Ellen had rescued her. Where was she now? And Beau? Didn't he get her message? Out of the corner of her eye she saw Suzanne begin to sidle sideways, very slowly so as not to alarm Diana, while trying to signal Ariadne with raised eyebrows. What was she up to? Trying to get close enough to jump her? Too dangerous.

Ariadne squinted and shook her head. She had to try something else.

She began to sing softly, "Hush, little baby, don't say a word. Momma's gonna buy you a mockingbird."

Judith and Suzanne froze, thinking similar thoughts. What was Ariadne doing? If they didn't want to be shot, they needed to take Diana down. Shit, why hadn't they enrolled in Adam Gooch's self-defense course? By now they'd be a crack defense team instead of helpless weaklings.

As Ariadne continued to sing, Diana's eyes filled with tears. Her mouth dropped open, her lips quivering, as the anger drained from her face.

Ariadne took a step forward. "Give me the gun, Diana, you don't really need it," she crooned in a singsong cadence, and then continued with her lullaby. "And if that diamond ring is brass, Momma's gonna buy you a looking glass."

Judith and Suzanne remained still, staring at Diana as her manner changed from fury to grief. Slowly she lowered the gun.

Ariadne took a few more steps forward. "And if that looking glass gets broke ..."

Diana stared vacantly at Ariadne. "Mother? Mama? Why are you here? What do you want?"

"What's this? Diana thinks Ariadne is her mother?" Judith whispered to Suzanne as they glanced helplessly at each other, not comprehending the scenario but not daring to interfere.

Diana began to sway in tempo with Ariadne's soft crooning. "I would have saved you, Mama, if I could. I couldn't stop the truck from hitting you." Her dark eyes filled with tears. "If I'd been with you, I'd have made you stop the car at the intersection." Her eyes drifted across the ceiling. "Or I would have died with you. Sometimes I think I did."

Ariadne inched closer. "Diana, my child, my daughter. It's over now. Please give me the gun. You don't need it."

Diana's wild eyes tried to focus on the gun. Her left hand dropped down and the pillow slipped to the floor. Slowly she brought the gun up and held it with both hands in front of her, pointing at Ariadne. Judith tensed, wanting to spring out and grab it, but indecision rooted her to the spot. Ariadne blanched but held out her hand. "Come, Precious, give Mama the gun. You don't want to hurt me. Or yourself. Just give it here."

Later Suzanne would swear that they stood in this tableau for minutes, but in reality it was only seconds. Then Diana stepped closer to Ariadne and laid the gun in her hand. Sinking down on the sofa, she picked up the pink pillow and wrapped both arms around it, drawing it to her as she rocked back and forth, sobbing.

Judith grabbed Suzanne's hand and inched toward Ariadne, begging sotto voce, "Let's get out of here."

But Ariadne stood still in front of Diana. "And Allison. What about her?" she asked softly.

As Diana raised her head her expression morphed again, from sadness to anger. Jumping up, she held the pillow out in front of her, then dropped it on the floor and kicked it away. "Allison? Allison? I hate her! And her bitch mother, my father's whore. And my poor dead father. They loved the beautiful Allison. The *sweet* Allison!" Her voice rose almost to a screech and then lowered to a growl. "They doted on her, gave her everything. Everything that should have been mine. I lost everything the day that brat was born. My sister, that's a laugh. She stole everything from me. My father's love, my rightful inheritance, my life." She collapsed again onto the sofa, cradling her head in her arms.

"Give me the gun, Ariadne." Beau's voice from the open door was quiet but firm.

Keeping her eyes on Diana, Ariadne backed up and handed the weapon to him. Ellen moved into the room, gun drawn.

Seeing them, Diana broke into raucous laughter. "The Law arrives, 'the hideous law,'" she sneered. Then she slumped down, hands covering her eyes, "It's over. 'I have been a truant in the law.' And now I am one 'whom the law condemns.'"

Good grief, Judith thought, recognizing the Shakespearean quotations.

Diana looked up again with unfocused eyes as her voice rose. "Yes, I killed her. My little sister. Their precious baby. So beautiful lying there sleeping like she was innocent. But she wasn't. She'd robbed me of everything! Their love. My life. My money. Everything!"

Beau stepped toward her, starting to say something, but Diana waved him back. "Don't come near me. There's blood on my hands. See?" She stretched both hands out before her and began rubbing them together. "'Out, damned spot. Out, I say!'" Her laugh was hoarse as she looked around at them without really focusing. "Charades, anyone? Guess who I am. 'Sweets to the sweet.'" Then she frowned, shaking her head. "No, that's not right. Wrong play, wrong play."

Ariadne spoke firmly, "Diana, you're confused. You need to rest. Please let us help you."

Diana's unfocused gaze swept over the room. "'What's done cannot be undone.' That's what the lady said. 'Give me the daggers.'" She shook her dark hair down over her face. "I didn't have a dagger. Just the pillow and my hands. But they did the trick. The brat was already half dead, sleeping so soundly with her mouth open. It was easy. Easy. Just a gentle push and then another and another. And it was over." She emitted another peal of hysterical laughter. "'To be or not to be.' I answered that question. I'm not the victim, I'm the hero. Not suicide but murder."

As the sheriff slipped handcuffs on her, Diana raised her head and stared blankly at something, or nothing, behind them. "Hell is murky.' And we're all in it."

Ellen read Diana her rights and led her outside to be checked by the paramedics and then put her into the police car. Looking both annoyed and relieved, Beau stood for a minute frowning at Ariadne. Then he hugged her to him and smiled at Judith and Suzanne.

"Why did it take you so long to get here?" Ariadne's voice quavered.

"I'm really sorry about that. We were way over at the county line with the ambulance crew at a bad car accident when I got your message." He held Ariadne away from him as he looked deep into her hazel eyes. "How did you wind up over here? Can't you stay out of trouble? Do you seek it out or does it find you?"

Ariadne clung to him. "Believe me, it's a little of both. Do you want to hear the whole story?"

"Not here but at the precinct. We'll need you to come over there now and fill out reports."

The women nodded and followed him outside.

"Damn, those were some performances!" Suzanne said as Beau headed for his car. "Diana deserves an Oscar."

"She's obviously out of her mind." Feeling shaky, Ariadne sat down on the stoop.

"Probably why she identified with Lady Macbeth," Judith said as she sat beside her friend. "I'm amazed she knew the play that well, better than I do and I've taught it a few times. Maybe she was an actress in another life." She put her arm around Ariadne's shoulders. "And what about your gutsy performance? How did you come to think of playing her mother?"

"In the fitness center she told me I reminded her of her mother, blonde but with blue eyes. Her mention of the resemblance must have been in the back of my mind. Just now, when I began singing that lullaby, one I used to sing to David, it wasn't a conscious decision. It just came to me when I saw her clutching that pillow."

"It was an inspired idea. Better than my impulse to tackle her. And it worked. Pretty risky, though, in retrospect." Judith stood up and joined Suzanne, who asked, "When did you come up with the theory that she killed Allison? And why didn't you tell us?"

"It occurred to me when I was reading about all that hate for her baby sister, but I still thought it was so far-fetched I couldn't mention it to you. Sorry about that."

Judith shrugged. "So your intuition gave you the insight?"

"Yes, just like Ariadne Oliver."

Suzanne raised her eyebrows. "But in real life, in Coowahchobee, Florida."

Ariadne laughed. "Let's go give the officers our report."

"And after that, let's get something to eat. I'm hungry enough to eat a horse," Suzanne said.

"Me, too. Let's go over to Ott's. When I was there with Beau and Ellen, I opted for the salad, but I think I'd like to try the pulled pork."

"Okay." Judith grinned as she wrapped her arms around Ariadne and Suzanne, hugging them both tightly. "I'll bet even horse would be tasty with barbeque sauce."

28

"How many goodly creatures are there here!
How beauteous mankind is! O brave new world
That has such people in't !"
The Tempest

OF THE SEVERAL costumed children who arrived on her veranda at seven o'clock sharp, before the sun had fully set, Ariadne recognized only the Fullers, dressed as the Disney version of the seven dwarfs. The eldest daughter Haley, as Snow White, carried baby Zack in a Dopey costume, one he got by default, being the youngest and unable to talk.

"Trick or treat!" the rest yelled in unison, with Haley admonishing them, "Ya'll say 'please, ma'am.'"

"I see you have an addition to your group this year." Ariadne chucked Zack's chin as she dropped bite-sized candy bars into the children's plastic pumpkins and paper bags.

"Thank you, ma'am," they chorused and backed off the porch as an assortment of ballerinas, ghosts, cowboys, and pirates arrived for their turn at the treats.

Julian and his children were missing tonight and Ariadne knew why from rumors reported to her by Judith and Suzanne—that Elizabeth had left him and taken the children up North to stay with her parents. "No one has seen or heard from Julian," Judith had added. "And rumors are flying around the college that Julian's promotion and tenure committee has heard about his involvement with the murdered student."

If those rumors are true, Ariadne thought, then Julian will have to look elsewhere for another job.

"Bastard!," Susanne had exclaimed. "Surely the college will begin to better enforce our sexual misconduct policies after this"

Ariadne's reflections were interrupted by a short replica of a T-rex who asked her "Are you Glinda, the good witch?"

"Yes, I am," she replied, smiling and handing the dino some candy. "I'm glad you recognized me."

Sometime later, after running back and forth between the door and the party tables set up in her back garden and deck, Ariadne was happy to have Judith and Suzanne arrive to help her. Suzanne was svelte and handsome in a black tuxedo pants and a flaming red ruffled silk shirt. "I'm not in costume," she explained. "I'm no good at pretending to be someone I'm not." She put her arm around Judith, saying, "How do you like her costume? She spent a lot of time getting it together."

"It's beautiful," Ariadne said, circling around Judith for a better look.

"Guess who I am." Judith pirouetted before the hall mirror, showing off her white muslin dress, striped with brown threads, and her white lace parasol, which she opened with a flourish to reveal its pink lining.

"That's easy," Ariadne replied, smiling at her. "Edna Pontellier. You're wearing an exact replica of her beach outfit!"

"Thanks. I was sure you'd recognize her. *The Awakening* isn't popular reading anymore but it was in its day so it fits your "popular culture" theme."

When the doorbell rang again, Ariadne greeted Ellen Nolle and her husband Darrell, who was carrying a large white handkerchief and a trumpet. "Satchmo at your service," he laughed as Ellen introduced him.

"He really can play that thing," she said. "I'm supposed to be Ella Fitzgerald, but don't ask me to sing because I can't carry a tune."

Right behind them came several Rutherford faculty members, including Chris Bannerman, dressed as Superman, with his date, a small woman in a padded-shoulder, short-skirted suit, wearing black-rimmed glasses and a pillbox hat. "Lois Lane," Chris said, "aka Julia Romano, our new department secretary."

"Not as glamorous or as young as his usual conquests. Could the leopard have changed his spots?" Judith whispered to Suzanne as they escorted the new arrivals to the back yard, where Darrell joined a jazz trio hired for the occasion. Before long he was happily jamming with them.

Half an hour later Judith tugged at Ariadne's sleeve and pointed to a figure on the back patio. "Who is that?" she asked, raising her voice to be heard above the music and party chatter.

Ariadne laughed in relief. "It's Beau! He wasn't sure he could make it."

Beau, dressed in a light blue robe decorated with silver stars, and a dark blue beret atop a white wig of long flowing hair and a white beard, crossed over to them and said in a mock serious voice, "I've come to work magic, fair ladies!"

"You're a magus, right?" Ariadne remembered their earlier conversation about white magic.

"Are you Prospero?" Judith asked. "From an enchanted island?"

"Yes, and I'm here to carry this lovely good witch off with me to live happily ever after on it."

Judith laughed and excused herself so as to leave the couple alone.

Putting his arm around Ariadne, Beau led her to a quiet corner under a white flowering crepe myrtle near the patio. "I'm afraid this outfit is a bit cheesy, but Tilda Kent's cousin made it for me, and I couldn't disappoint her by refusing to wear it."

"It's excellent. Very authentic, according to illustrations I've seen in Shakespeare anthologies."

"I'm not sure that Shakespeare's plays are 'popular culture' today though they certainly were in his day. I came as Prospero to announce my decision to retire and live in my island beach house, where I'll have plenty of time to read, fish, go boating, and maybe do some magic."

"That sounds wonderful," Ariadne said, but a bit hesitantly, wondering what this move might mean for their relationship.

Beau pulled off his beret, along with his fake hair and beard, dropping them to the ground as he took her in his arms. "But not alone," he whispered in her ear. "Please marry me. You'll love living on the enchanted island."

Ariadne was stunned, though she had sensed their recent conversations were leading up to this. She kissed him and then drew back a little. "Beau, you know I'm not ready to retire yet. I'm still happy teaching and a commute from the beach to the college every day would be a difficult trek for me." She paused and then, hugging him close, she said, "And I don't think I'm ready for another marriage just yet." Feeling him pull away and seeing his face fall, she quickly added, "But I do love you."

Beau's faint smile barely lightened his crestfallen look, but he rallied, saying, "I love you too and I hope you'll soon change your mind about marrying me. But until then, you'll join me on the island on weekends, won't you?"

"Of course I will," Ariadne said, pulling him to her again.

"Let's dance," Beau said, hearing the jazz trio begin a slow number.

Ariadne raised her eyebrows in surprise. "I didn't know you danced," she said.

"I do now," he responded, drawing her closer for another kiss before expertly guiding her back onto the patio for the last dance of the evening.

About the Author

After retirement from the Florida State University English Department, Bonnie Hoover Braendlin published *Love and Death in Venice* as the first volume in her *Caulfield, Sheridan Mystery* series. *Shakespeare's Secrets* is its sequel. Visit her webpage: www.bonniehooverbraendlin.com.

CPSIA information can be obtained
at www.ICGtesting.com
Printed in the USA
BVHW082107281120
594340BV00003B/133

9 781640 660984